# DEATH ON THE DOORSTEP

## SILVER AND GREY
## BOOK 7

# MARY LANCASTER

## ARE YOU SIGNED UP FOR DRAGONBLADE'S BLOG?

You'll get the latest news and information on exclusive giveaways, exclusive excerpts, coming releases, sales, free books, cover reveals and more.

Check out our complete list of authors, too!

No spam, no junk. That's a promise!

### Sign Up Here

www.dragonbladepublishing.com

*Dearest Reader;*

*Thank you for your support of a small press. At Dragonblade Publishing, we strive to bring you the highest quality Historical Romance from some of the best authors in the business. Without your support, there is no 'us', so we sincerely hope you adore these stories and find some new favorite authors along the way.*

*Happy Reading!*

*CEO, Dragonblade Publishing*

# Additional Dragonblade Books by Author Mary Lancaster

**Silver and Grey Series**
Murder in Moonlight (Book 1)
Evidence of Evil (Book 2)
Ghost in the Garden (Book 3)
The Trick of the Treasure (Book 4)
Word of the Wicked (Book 5)
Vengeance in Venice (Book 6)
Death on the Doorstep (Book 7)

**One Night in Blackhaven Series**
The Captain's Old Love (Book 1)
The Earl's Promised Bride (Book 2)
The Soldier's Impossible Love (Book 3)
The Gambler's Last Chance (Book 4)
The Poet's Stern Critic (Book 5)
The Rake's Mistake (Book 6)
The Spinster's Last Dance (Book 7)

**The Duel Series**
Entangled (Book 1)
Captured (Book 2)
Deserted (Book 3)
Beloved (Book 4)
Haunted (Novella)

**Last Flame of Alba Series**
Rebellion's Fire (Book 1)
A Constant Blaze (Book 2)
Burning Embers (Book 3)

**Gentlemen of Pleasure Series**
The Devil and the Viscount (Book 1)
Temptation and the Artist (Book 2)
Sin and the Soldier (Book 3)
Debauchery and the Earl (Book 4)
Blue Skies (Novella)

**Pleasure Garden Series**
Unmasking the Hero (Book 1)
Unmasking Deception (Book 2)
Unmasking Sin (Book 3)
Unmasking the Duke (Book 4)
Unmasking the Thief (Book 5)

**Crime & Passion Series**
Mysterious Lover (Book 1)
Letters to a Lover (Book 2)
Dangerous Lover (Book 3)
Lost Lover (Book 4)
Merry Lover (Novella)
Ghostly Lover (Novella)

**The Husband Dilemma Series**
How to Fool a Duke (Book 1)

**Season of Scandal Series**
Pursued by the Rake (Book 1)
Abandoned to the Prodigal (Book 2)
Married to the Rogue (Book 3)
Unmasked by her Lover (Book 4)
Her Star from the East (Novella)

**Imperial Season Series**
Vienna Waltz (Book 1)
Vienna Woods (Book 2)
Vienna Dawn (Book 3)

**Blackhaven Brides Series**
The Wicked Baron (Book 1)

The Wicked Lady (Book 2)
The Wicked Rebel (Book 3)
The Wicked Husband (Book 4)
The Wicked Marquis (Book 5)
The Wicked Governess (Book 6)
The Wicked Spy (Book 7)
The Wicked Gypsy (Book 8)
The Wicked Wife (Book 9)
Wicked Christmas (Book 10)
The Wicked Waif (Book 11)
The Wicked Heir (Book 12)
The Wicked Captain (Book 13)
The Wicked Sister (Book 14)

**Unmarriageable Series**
The Deserted Heart (Book 1)
The Sinister Heart (Book 2)
The Vulgar Heart (Book 3)
The Broken Heart (Book 4)
The Weary Heart (Book 5)
The Secret Heart (Book 6)
Christmas Heart (Novella)

**The Lyon's Den Series**
Fed to the Lyon

**De Wolfe Pack: The Series**
The Wicked Wolfe
Vienna Wolfe

**Also from Mary Lancaster**
Madeleine (Novella)
The Others of Ochil (Novella)

# CHAPTER ONE

CONSTANCE STRODE THROUGH the gracious streets of Mayfair just as servants were beginning to open doors and shutters to greet the first, early sunshine. It was a glorious morning, alive with the promise of summer. Ecstatic birdsong mingled with the clatter of horses' hooves and the lively chatter of carters and delivery boys, milkmaids and servants.

It all filled Constance with a happy sense of familiarity, and yet she appreciated it anew. So different somehow from the sounds and smells of Venice, which had been home for two whole, wonderful months. She missed it already, and yet her heart sang to be home, beating fast with anticipation to greet her old friends and catch up with their news. In the midst of her happiness, she had missed them.

She turned into Grosvenor Square and then on to the discreet, crescent-shaped cul-de-sac leading off it, and there was her establishment, her achievement, basking in its disreputable success, here among the supremely respectable houses of the wealthy, the aristocratic, and the equally successful.

No shutters were open yet on her house—its occupants kept late hours and only a few would be awake, most of them in the kitchen. Even the porter at the front door should have gone to bed now, since all visitors should have departed by dawn.

Extracting the keys from her reticule, she descended the area steps, where a milk churn already awaited collection. She was about to insert her key when she heard the voices at the back of the house, where another door led from the kitchen into the backyard and the little garden where herbs and flowers grew.

She let her hand fall to her side. She knew the voices, of course. Jeremy, who looked after the outside of the house and the grounds, and Bibby, recently promoted to assistant cook. But something about the pitch of those familiar voices was unnatural, wrong.

Constance turned and hurried along the narrow path that led around the side of the house to the garden, inexplicably worried by what was surely only a minor quarrel. She was used to sorting out dozens of those a day, often all at the same time.

But Bibby and Jeremy did not appear to be quarrelling. The tiny, skinny girl and the large, burly man were actually clinging to each other and staring at the kitchen door.

"Not here," Bibby was saying, shaking her head furiously. "Oh, not here, not here…"

"Maybe they're asleep," Jeremy rumbled.

And then Constance saw them.

Just in front of the half-open door, sitting on the step, were two men, leaning against the stone wall on either side of the doorframe, almost like bookends. One wore the evening dress of a gentleman. A tall silk hat even sat on his knees. The other was in dirty, ragged raiment, his battered cloth hat squashed between the back of his head and the wall. Their eyes were open and staring sightlessly.

*Not here, not here…* Constance heartily concurred. It added a new horror to what was becoming an all-too-familiar situation.

Some sort of exclamation must have escaped her lips, for both Bibby and Jeremy whipped around to her, their mouths agape with fright and guilt.

"Oh, it's you, ma'am!" Bibby ran to her, almost like a child seeking her mother's protection. "Thank God you're home! What on earth are we to do? It wasn't us, honest, ma'am, it wasn't!"

"Of course it was not," Constance agreed, patting the girl's shoulder and pushing her gently aside. "Are they both dead?"

"Never seen anyone look less alive," Jeremy said. "We just found them, though…"

Constance stripped off her gloves and walked up to the still figures on her back doorstep, trying to give the impression of brisk confidence. But her fingers shook as she laid them on the well-dressed gentleman's neck. It was cold to the touch and she could find no sign of a pulse, or any warmth at all, even when she felt inside his collar. When she tried to lift his hand from his hat, it was stiff as a board.

Rigor mortis had set in. The man must have been dead for hours. His companion appeared to be in the same state.

"Do you recognize either of them?" Constance asked. "Have you ever seen them before?"

They both shook their heads, though Bibby was frowning. "Not sure about the poor one. I might have seen him somewhere."

"Begging, maybe," Jeremy said.

"Maybe," said Bibby doubtfully.

Constance straightened and drew in a breath. "Jeremy, run and find a constable and bring him here at once. Bibby, go inside and make some strong tea. Close and lock the door behind you. No one is to use this door again until the police have been here."

Jeremy took off down the garden toward the mews like a bullet, clearly relieved to have a reason to leave. Bibby whimpered as she edged between the bodies, although she seemed to have swung blithely past them on the way out without noticing.

"They're dead, Bibby," Constance said. "They can't hurt you."

"Ain't true, ma'am. They can hurt all of us now, but mostly me and Jeremy."

"Finding a dead person is not a crime," Constance said mildly. "In you go. I'll come in the front in a moment."

The door closed quietly and the lock clicked home.

Dead bodies outdoors were not common in Mayfair, particularly not in the warmer months. Discovering two at a time was,

Constance thought, unprecedented. She could see no blood, no obvious signs of attack. But the likelihood of two people dying of natural causes side by side on the same night was not high.

There was something…grotesque about these two. Standing back, she examined them.

The door that formed the background to their rest was somewhat ornate, for before the rest of the crescent had been built, this house had faced the other way. Only later had it been altered to match the newer homes on either side. The well-dressed man looked almost at home there, like some gentleman out on the tiles all night and waiting to be let in to his own home. The poor man, however, was decidedly out of place.

There was a clear space between them on the step, and at first sight, they appeared to be resting comfortably. But to Constance, they looked curiously…twisted. Their hips and legs faced straight ahead, their upper torsos leaning to the side in positions that could not have been comfortable.

Almost as if they had not died here but had been placed.

Glancing around, she found no obvious scuff marks on the paths, and the earth and plants of the garden appeared undisturbed. She would look more closely later, but for now…

She should not touch anything until the police had been, though she would have no opportunity once they had removed the bodies. With inevitable pity, she wondered who the devil these men were, the gentleman and the vagrant. Or at least that was what the second man looked—and smelled—like, his face and hands weathered and lined, his person thin to the point of scrawny beneath his worn, ragged clothes. The fingers of one hand were curled, speckled with ingrained dirt, his matted hair receding, his cheeks thin and pale and deeply lined.

She moved nearer the bodies again and crouched down. Another smell that she could not immediately place hit her. Warily, she inserted her hand into the tramp's coat pocket. It felt greasy, full of crumbs and fluff, until her fingers closed around something clean and distinctive. She drew it out.

A fine, soft leather notecase. Inside were a few banknotes and several visiting cards in the name of Terrence St. John, with an address in Grosvenor Square.

*I don't think so.* She returned the notecase to the disgusting pocket and regarded the other man. The notecase could well be his and the vagrant had stolen it. Or the vagrant could have stolen it from someone else, at any time in the past. She felt inside the gentleman's pockets, finding a few coins and a monogramed handkerchief—*TSJ.* So the wallet and the vising cards *were* likely his. Certainly, he carried no other notecase, because there was only a pair of gloves in his other pocket.

What on earth had happened here? A robbery? After which the pair had sat down together to die? And why had it all taken place in her garden, right on her doorstep?

She replaced the gloves, coins, and handkerchief where she had found them and sat back on her heels. If the gentleman was a neighbor, she did not know him. He was not a client of her establishment. Sarah, her capable lieutenant, had been under instructions to admit no new members while Constance was away, unless she was very, very sure and had written guarantees in triplicate.

He was not a young man, perhaps in his forties, but was handsome and fit, without much middle-aged thickening around his middle. From his dress, his hands, and the quality of the silk hat, he was rich.

The gate at the foot of the garden crashed open and a breathless Jeremy dashed in with a middle-aged constable panting behind him.

Constance rose to her feet. "Constable."

"Madam. Dear me. Are you sure they're—"

"Quite sure," she said, making way for him. "But by all means look."

"And you are...?"

"Mrs. Grey," she said, before she remembered that she had intended to continue calling herself Mrs. Silver at the establishment. Oh well, a little respectability worked better with the police. "This is my house. My people found these men just a few minutes ago, just as you see them now."

"Any idea who are they are?" the constable asked, moving closer.

"None at all," Constance said, keeping to herself the name on the visiting cards. The police would discover those soon enough.

"He's not a neighbor, then?" he asked, bending down to the gentleman.

"He could be, but he is not known to me."

The constable took the dead gentleman's shoulder in his large hand and shook him with unexpected vigor. The stiff body did not bend, but the head was bumped against the wall and the whole corpse suddenly rocked and fell to the side until it was actually leaning against the back door in an even less natural position.

It revealed the dead man's back for the first time, and the mother-of-pearl-handled pocketknife sticking out between his shoulder blades.

The constable gasped, and Jeremy bolted around the side of the house.

"Well," Constance said shakily, "that explains *him*. What about the other one?"

"I need to send for my superiors," the constable said, stepping hastily backward and almost falling over his own feet. He took the whistle from his pocket. "What is this address?"

When Constance told him, his jaw dropped and he blushed like a girl.

"Please go inside, ma'am. No one is to leave the house until the detectives say so." He jammed the whistle into his mouth and blew several ear-splitting summonses. Obediently, Constance fled around the house to the area door and let herself in.

Everyone who was awake was in the kitchen while Bibby and Jeremy retold their story.

"Well," Constance interrupted, "this was not quite the homecoming I had planned. What on earth have you been up to?"

At the kitchen table, heads snapped up. There was a surge of movement toward her, a clatter of chairs, cries of delight. She was seized and dragged to the table, enthroned in the most comfortable chair and asked so many questions all at once that she laughed and forgot for a moment that there were two dead men on her doorstep.

"When did you get back?"

"How is it being married?"

"What is Italy like? Are the women beautiful? Are the men?"

"Is that gorgeous gown from Italy?"

"Where is the husband?"

"Did you ever leave the bedroom?"

"Fall over any mysteries?"

The last came from Janey, of course, who had been minding the Silver and Grey Inquiries office, and it was this question Constance chose to answer.

"Funnily enough, we did. A story for another time. Did you?"

"Fall over mysteries? They're falling over me! There's a mountain of inquiries in the office. I made a start on a few and solved two myself—with Lenny Knox's help."

"Good for you," Constance said warmly. "You can tell me all about them as soon as we are allowed to leave the house. Now, what has been happening?"

While they told her all the establishment news, the footmen took it in turns to watch out of the back window and report any happenings. Several constables and a sergeant turned up, then most of them left again.

"Now we have men without uniforms. Two of 'em," Max said.

"They'll be the detectives," Constance said calmly. "They're going to want to speak to all of us."

Janey swore long and fluently, as though she had been saving up the words for just such a situation. Constance raised an eyebrow at her, and she actually blushed. "Bad situation, ain't it?"

she said aggressively. "Bloody coppers swarming all over the house, trying to arrest us all and shut us down. I been there before."

"Oh, no, they can't!" Bibby exclaimed, staring at Constance in distress. "Can they, ma'am?"

Constance glanced around at the suddenly frightened faces of the women who had become her friends and the men who helped protect them all. For some, this was the first safety they had known, the first certainty of food and shelter. For all of them, it was home, whether temporarily or not.

Plus, the police in general were the longstanding enemies of most of them.

"No, they can't," Constance said. "The house is mine. Everyone lives here as my friends, guests, and servants."

"They don't pay any attention to stuff like that," Max said in disbelief.

"They will here," Constance said. "We are well protected." And they were, although she rather wished there was a way of getting a message to Solomon... "Besides, they are investigating the bodies. All you need to do is tell the truth, without hostility, about where you were during the night. You need not say whom you were with unless you're pressed—it is not a crime to have a lover, and the importance of our guests will almost certainly stave off further investigations. I won't leave you to be questioned without me, unless you wish it. Now, I suggest we all get on with our work of the day." She rose from the table. "I shall be in the reception room—bring the police to me there."

Her calmness seemed to reassure most of them, as they scattered about on their usual business. She lingered only to see the still-distraught Bibby set to work on breakfast with Mrs. Cate, the experienced cook, before, satisfied, she turned toward the stairs. She was only halfway up before the bell at the area door rang.

Constance paused to lean over the banister. She nodded at the frozen Jeremy and Max, to remind them of her instructions, then whisked herself the rest of the way upstairs to the entrance hall.

Tony the footman was skulking just on the other side of the baize door, scowling. Constance jerked her head toward the stairs. "Fetch me if there is any trouble," she murmured. "Otherwise, treat them as any other guest."

The hall and the reception room were just as gleamingly clean as they should be. Glad standards had not dropped during her absence, she picked up a fashion magazine from the table and sat down in one of her favorite armchairs to flick through it. She barely saw the images before her. Most of her mind seemed to be clinging to the dead faces on the back doorstep. The rest was worrying about her staff and hoping that the detective assigned would be Inspector Harris, whom she and Solomon had helped before. That would be the best situation for everyone.

She did not have long to wait.

Tony entered the open door. "The police, madam," he said woodenly.

He was almost barged out of the way, which should have given her some warning.

The only-too-familiar figure of Detective Constable Napier strode into the room.

"Well," he gloated, "it really *is* you."

Not the best but the worst of all possible situations.

SOLOMON GREY LET himself into the offices of Silver and Grey with a quiet sense of satisfaction.

It felt almost like the first, exciting day they had opened, both he and Constance abuzz with the anticipation of their new venture into the private inquiry business. If he was honest, most of his excitement had been to do with Constance herself and the heady opportunity of seeing her every day as they worked together. He had known then it would either cure him of his obsession or confirm it. Foolishly, he had even hoped it would distract her completely from her other business, her "establishment." It hadn't, of course, but he had more understanding now, and more tolerance.

The establishment was so much more than a high-class brothel. And Constance herself was so much more than he had begun to guess even then. More than simply his friend, or his secret infatuation.

She was his wife, and she had taught him joy.

His skin prickled with memory and expectation as he hung his hat on the stand in the hall. He didn't even mind that the establishment was her first concern on their return to London. She would join him here later.

"Janey?" he called, extracting a couple of letters from the box in the front door. He was looking forward to seeing her again, all bright, intelligent eyes and wayward tongue—quite aside from his need to learn what had been happening with the business. They had taken a chance leaving it in Janey's hands, perhaps, but she had proven trustworthy, sensible, organized, and even surprisingly good at the inquiring.

But, of course, it was too early. She would probably be late today because she still lived at the establishment and Constance would be there. Strolling along to Janey's little office, he found it empty. Her desk was neat, the closed appointment diary in the center.

He glanced through it and discovered no new appointments before next week. Walking through to the little kitchen, he lit the stove to make tea, then wandered off to his office. A large pile of letters had been left on his desk—all had *Answered* scrawled across the top, together with a date. On the other side were short reports, some with letters attached, of cases she and Lenny Knox had managed to deal with.

Solomon smiled, impressed, as he read them through. He and Constance had talked about taking on another girl to do the reception work, freeing Janey for more actual investigating. Before the wedding, the amount of work had certainly justified it.

When he had made his tea, he took the cup and saucer back to his desk and began to plow his way through the waiting correspondence. It was only when the knocker sounded that he thought to glance at his watch. It was after nine o'clock.

Had Janey forgotten her key? Rising, he went to the front door, and discovered Lenny on the doorstep.

Lenny's thin, sad face lapsed into a sudden smile. "Hullo, Mr. Grey! Good to see you home!"

"Thank you." Solomon stood aside to let the man in.

"Janey not here yet?" Lenny said. "I was going to help her with a lost property case."

"I suspect she's with my wife." Solomon still liked saying that. He thought he always would. "Cup of tea?"

"Go on, then. How is your wife?"

Although Lenny asked quite naturally, Solomon immediately thought of the man's own wife, who had died so tragically along with their child less than a year ago, in the collapse of a slum building. He had come a long way in these months, returning gradually to life and picking up what carpentry work he could, along with helping Silver and Grey out on a casual basis.

"She is very well," Solomon replied. "And we both want to compliment you on the work you did in the house while we were away. We're very happy with it."

Lenny nodded. "I was pleased with it—glad you approve."

"Come through to the office and tell me the news. I expect you're more concise than Janey."

"She makes her points," Lenny said mildly, and yet it was somehow defensive of Janey.

*Interesting.*

They had drunk their tea and briefly discussed the solved cases and the current one when Lenny shifted restlessly and looked at his battered old watch.

"She should be here by now, or at least have sent a boy with a message. It's not like her."

Solomon frowned. "You're right. It isn't." A vague but ominous alarm was seeping into his bones. "Something must be wrong."

Lenny jumped up. "I'll go, if you tell me where she lives."

Solomon blinked. If Lenny knew of the establishment's existence, he clearly did not know where it was, or even perhaps that Janey lived there. According to Constance, Janey was at least half in love with Lenny and had not yet told him about her disreputable past. Well, that was up to Janey.

Solomon stood, too. "No, I'll go. If you would oblige me by remaining here to take any messages?"

"Of course."

Was the man disappointed? Solomon, with an increasing sense of urgency, did not linger to find out. Something had happened that must be affecting both Janey and Constance.

# CHAPTER TWO

"UNDOUBTEDLY IT IS I," Constance drawled. "Constable Napier, is it not? We meet again in unfortunate circumstances."

Napier glanced around the tasteful, elegant room, aiming for contempt, though he ended by looking more surprised. Perhaps he had been expecting cheap red velvet and chipped gilt, and blowsy half-dressed women sprawling on the furniture. "Your circumstances don't look so unfortunate to me."

"I was referring to those of the dead men on my doorstep," Constance said. She met the gaze of the second man, who was slightly older and in uniform and wore an expression of appalled bewilderment. "Sergeant, I am Mrs. Grey. Do sit down."

"Sergeant Bilston, ma'am, from Bow Street," the older man said with an awkward bow. He sat opposite her, and so did Napier, perched rigidly on the edge of the seat. "You are not, then, the owner of these premises?"

"Yes, I am. I am recently married and so I am no longer Mrs. Silver."

"Grey?" Napier pounced, staring. "You married him? Fitting!"

"Was that your good wishes, constable?" Constance said affably. "Thank you. Sergeant Bilston, do you have any idea who the dead men are or how they came to be on my doorstep?"

"We are looking into that, ma'am. The gentleman certainly appears to have died by violence, but that is really all we know so far. Tell me, are you acquainted with your neighbor in Grosvenor

Square, Mr. St. John?"

"No, I don't know the name. Or the face."

"Then he isn't one of your…clients?" Napier sneered.

"I believe I said I did not know him."

"Of course, ma'am," the sergeant said nervously. "Was it you who found the bodies, ma'am?"

"No, it was my gardener and my assistant cook—they had just come out of the back door and discovered them when I arrived."

"Arrived from where?" Napier interrupted.

"From my home."

They both looked confused now.

"I thought this *was* your home?" Bilston said.

"It was, before my marriage." She opened her reticule and fished out one of the new cards inscribed *Mr. and Mrs. Solomon Grey*, with the address in smaller print beneath.

"Then this is just your place of…business?" Napier said.

"Sort of, I suppose," Constance replied. "My friends continue to live here. They pay rent, of course, and help me run the club and the charity."

Napier laughed. "Is that what you call it?"

"Yes," Constance said.

Napier's lips curled with contempt. "I think we all know what this—"

"Constable!" Sergeant Bilston cut him off, almost with desperation.

Constance suspected that the sergeant was well aware of her establishment, which no one ever looked too closely at because there was never any trouble, let alone complaints. He would not disturb the status quo, but Napier was a loose cannon and would like nothing better than to pin a murder on someone associated with this house, preferably Solomon himself. Especially without Inspector Omand, his superior, to keep him in line.

"What time did you arrive here this morning, Mrs. Grey?" Bilston asked civilly.

"Before seven, perhaps a quarter to the hour or thereabouts. I heard voices in the garden at the back and they sounded alarmed, so I went straight round."

"And that was the first time you saw the bodies?"

"Indeed."

"Who else was there?" Napier asked. "You said the cook and the gardener."

"My assistant cook, Bibby Barton. And Jeremy Carter, who looks after the garden and the outside of the house."

"No one else from the household?"

"No. Jeremy had swept the front steps and the area and the path to the back garden. Bibby had just come out the back door to speak to him when they saw the bodies."

"How did she get out the back door with the body leaning against it?" Napier demanded.

"It was leaning against the wall then. The first constable who came tried to wake him up and the body toppled into the position you see him in now."

"We'll need to speak to these two first," Napier said. "Send for them. Then we'll see the rest. You can go for now."

Constance regarded him in silence. The sergeant looked nervous, no doubt because of the blatant incivility, but criminal investigations of this sort were clearly outside his experience.

"Constable, I am prepared to accompany you downstairs to the cook's sitting room, where you may interview my people in my presence."

"Oh, no," Napier said rudely. His back was to the door, so he did not see Solomon come quietly into the room. Constance's heart lifted immeasurably. "I want the truth and I won't get it with your threatening them behind my back."

"Good morning," Solomon said, strolling across to Constance.

Bilston sprang to his feet and so did Napier, though with surprise rather than respect.

"Solomon," Constance said, throwing out her hand to him.

"I'm so glad you're here. Something dreadful has happened."

"I know," he said, taking her hand, although his eyes were hard and cold as slate as they focused on Napier. "Max told me. Constable, my wife will have your written apology by tomorrow morning. As it is, you will treat everyone in this house with respect or I will demand a different investigator. And we'll get one."

Napier flushed with anger. He must have known he was in the wrong, understood Solomon would get his way, and this infuriated him. He regarded Solomon as somehow inferior simply because of the color of his skin, regardless of his education, his wealth, and his worldly success. It seemed to madden him that important men, including his superiors, treated this "foreigner" with respect. But then, Napier's world was very black and white in every way.

"I am investigating murder!" he snapped. "And no one will stand in my way. Your obstruction smacks of guilt."

"Constable!" wailed the sergeant.

"On the contrary," Solomon said. "It smacks of common decency."

"Decency!" Napier exploded. "In *this* place?"

"Precisely," Solomon said coolly. "Need I have you escorted from the house?"

"Wind your neck in, constable," Bilston growled. "I'm Sergeant Bilston, sir, from Bow Street. We would be grateful for the co-operation of yourself and Mrs. Grey."

"Then, as my wife suggested some time ago, we shall accompany you downstairs and borrow Cook's sitting room, if she is willing." Solomon offered his arm to Constance.

Seething, Napier had no choice but to follow them, especially when the sergeant did.

Below stairs was unnaturally subdued, despite the delicious smells of breakfast, cooked largely by Bibby.

"Mrs. Cate, do you mind if we use your sitting room for a while?" Constance asked. She wondered if the courtesy would rub off on Napier but doubted it.

"Whatever you wish, ma'am," Cook said cheerfully. "Shout when you want to eat."

"Thank you. Bibby? Come and talk to the sergeant. Would one of you find Jeremy?"

Bibby, looking terrified, had to be led into the room. Constance sat her by the unlit fireplace and then took the chair beside her. Solomon set two chairs opposite and perched his hip on the table under the window.

"Your full name?" Napier barked, getting out his notebook and pencil.

"Elizabeth Barton, sir, but everyone calls me Bibby."

"And your position in this house?"

"Assistant cook, sir."

Small-mindedly, Constance wanted her to stop calling Napier "sir" all the time.

Napier fixed her with his harsh gaze. "Is that your only position?"

Tears sprang into Bibby's eyes, for in truth she hadn't been respectable for very long, and the idea that she was now meant everything to her. Constance had to bite her lip to stop herself from interfering.

"Yes, sir, I'm a good girl."

"Of course you are, dear," Bilston said in a soothing, fatherly kind of way. "So when did you get out of bed this morning?"

"Six o'clock, sir, like always. The boy lights the fire, but I make the tea and do the preparations for first breakfast."

"First breakfast? For the servants, you mean?"

"And anyone else who's up." She blushed crimson. "Some of the g…household rise late, so we do a second breakfast, too."

Napier's sneer showed that he understood perfectly. So did Bilston, for he moved on hastily. "What time was it when you went outside?"

"After half six…maybe twenty to? I saw Jemmy's shadow outside and went to see if he wanted a cup of tea. It was a lovely morning, until…" She swallowed hard.

"You went outside," Napier repeated. "Down the step?"

"Yes, sir. I called to Jemmy—that is Jeremy, the gardener—and he turned round toward me and his mouth fell open. He made a funny noise in his throat and I turned to look where he was looking, and there they were."

"Did you know them?"

"No, sir."

"Then neither of them had ever been in this house?"

Bibby shook her head. "Not that I ever saw, sir, though I'm mostly downstairs."

"Where were you last night?" Napier asked. "Say, from midnight."

"In bed, sir. I got the little room in the attic next to Mrs. Cate's, and it's all my own."

"Was anyone with you?"

"No, sir!" she gasped.

Constance patted her hand, glaring at Napier. "He means did anyone wake you during the night? One of the others going to bed later, perhaps?"

"Lord no, I was out like a light and slept like the dead till six. Oh!" Clearly remembering the dead outside, Bibby slapped her free hand across her mouth and clung to Constance.

"Then you didn't hear anything unusual outside?" Napier prompted her. "No voices? No commotion?"

Bibby shook her head.

"Her room's at the front of the house," Constance said.

Napier actually wrote that down too. He seemed much more competent when he was recording details than when he was distracted by his own prejudices. "Very well, that will be all just now. Send in the gardener."

"Well done," Constance murmured. "Back to work!"

Bibby fled and Jeremy walked in, scowling, his cap in his hand.

For Constance, this was a slightly trickier interview. She

could hardly pat Jeremy's hand for comfort without causing speculation, and yet he was liable to need it more than Bibby. He did not do well indoors, discovering the bodies had given him a fright, and he was likely to lose his temper if he perceived any threat to Constance.

He sat in the chair next to her only when she told him to, but when asked by the policemen, he recited his name and occupation clearly enough. "I look after the outside of the house and the garden. And the horses when I'm needed."

He told the same story as Bibby about discovering the bodies, having only noticed them when he turned toward the house in response to Bibby's call.

When asked where he had been during the night, he said, "Stables. I sleep there."

"In the mews," Constance explained. "Jeremy and a couple of the grooms have quarters above the stables."

"All in the one room?" Napier pounced. "Did any of you go out?"

"No, they're up early with the horses, and I've got the area to clean and the paths to sweep afore anyone's up," Jeremy replied.

"What time is that, then?"

He shrugged. "When it's light."

"And were all the grooms there when you got up?"

Jeremy thought about it. "Yes."

"Did you hear any unusual commotion during the night, happen to see anyone going into the back garden from the mews?"

Jeremy shook his head. "Sleeping."

Napier changed tack. "How did you get from the mews to the garden without seeing the bodies?"

Jeremy twitched, which was not a good sign. "Went round the roadway."

"Why?" Napier demanded.

"Always do. I like it. Wakes me up. No one around. I start at the front steps, then clean the area and sweep the path round to the back. When I've swept all the paths, it's breakfast."

"I see," Napier said, staring at him.

Jeremy relaxed.

"How long have you worked here?"

He frowned. "Dunno. Two summers before this."

"Where did you work before?" Napier asked.

Jeremy's twitch was more agitated this time.

"I don't think that's relevant, is it, constable?" Constance intervened. "Thanks, Jeremy, you can go back to the garden now."

Jeremy sprang up. So did Napier, his angry mouth already open to object. If Jeremy noticed, he didn't let it stop him, and when Napier bolted after him, Solomon stood in his way. And yet she didn't think she'd ever told Solomon Jeremy's story. He had just gathered what to do from watching her—or perhaps Jeremy himself.

"You are obstructing me!" Napier said furiously, trying to swat Solomon aside.

Jeremy swung around, his face grim, ready to step in.

Constance said quickly, "It's fine, Jeremy. Mr. Grey is here with me. You carry on."

Jeremy glared hard from Napier to Solomon, to the worried-looking sergeant, then back to Constance. He nodded once and left, closing the door behind him.

"Let me explain, constable," Constance said quickly, before Napier exploded. "Jeremy does not do well indoors. He was ill treated, kept in chains in conditions you would not leave a dog, and forced to fight for sport. It's not good to remind him. He's not an aggressive man, but he is protective of those who got him out of that place."

"*You?*" Napier said in disbelief.

Solomon stepped back. "Most of the people here have been rescued from one form of abuse or another."

Napier, however, was nothing if not single-minded. "Then he's dangerous?"

*Another pitfall.* "Not if you don't shout at me," Constance said, "and even then he would do no more than necessary to throw you out. He is gentle by nature."

For the first time that she had ever seen, Napier looked confounded, but he continued to stare at her, as though daring her to admit something else. Until the door opened quietly and Inspector Harris walked in.

At this point, Constance regarded him as an old friend and smiled at him. He paused, blinking.

"Ah, Napier. Inspector Omand was looking for you." He inclined his head to the rest of the room. "Mrs. Silver. Mr. Grey. Sergeant, my thanks for holding the fort, as it were. I believe we needn't keep you any longer. You can finally get off to your bed."

"Thank you, sir," Bilston said with considerable relief. He rose and effaced himself, muttering, "Ma'am, sir," in the general direction of Constance and Solomon.

"Well," Inspector Harris said, "corpses a little closer to home, this time. Why did I have to be landed with you? I'm not going to find the Tizsas in the drawing room, am I?"

The Tizsas were a pair of well-born amateur sleuths—an English duke's daughter and a Hungarian revolutionary refugee of noble birth—who had first introduced Constance and Solomon.

"Not today," Constance said. "How are you, inspector?"

"I was well until I got to the office."

"And Sergeant Flynn?"

"You may ask him yourself. He has gone to the house of this Terrence St. John to see if he is indeed our corpse."

Napier appeared deflated that Harris already seemed to be au fait with the case. "Do I have to go back to Scotland Yard, sir?"

Harris regarded him. "Well, you are commended for the initiative of being here so quickly. And Mr. Omand is up to his neck in reports. He is willing to lend you to me as long as I need you. Considering this case would appear to involve several important people, I'll need all the help I can get to solve this quickly and discreetly." He smiled a little wolfishly. "But be warned—I'm not as tolerant as Mr. Omand. Neither is Sergeant Flynn. Now, then, where are we with witnesses?"

A short rap at the door heralded Janey, marching in with purpose. "If you please, ma'am," she said, glaring around the room, "if I'm wanted, can I be questioned now? I need to get to work."

"Work?" Napier said with loathing.

Janey looked down her nose at him. "I'm Mr. and Mrs. Grey's assistant at Silver and Grey Inquiries."

"Are you, indeed?" Harris said with interest. "Then by all means, let's have you in…"

By the time Sergeant Flynn appeared, grinning amiably at Constance and Solomon, most of the domestic staff had been interviewed and revealed nothing, and the other girls, wakened by all the fuss, had begun to trickle downstairs looking for their second breakfast.

"Well?" Harris demanded of Flynn, having released Max from his questioning.

"Looks like St. John is our gentleman," Flynn said. "He's not at home, though they searched the house for him and sent servants flying to all likely places in search of him. Mrs. St. John has agreed to come down to the mortuary to identify him. I said afternoon would do."

Harris sighed. "When was he last seen?"

"By his family, at dinner last night. He went out for the evening alone, and came home about eleven o'clock. His valet waited on him but was sent away. Mr. St. John said he was going to bed. The rest of the household had already retired. The doors were all locked this morning when the servants got up, the back doors bolted from the inside. None of the household reported Mr. St.

John appearing upset or worried or behaving any differently over the previous few days. And he was, apparently, in perfect health."

"Is there any connection between him and the vagrant?" Solomon asked.

"Not that we've discovered so far. Except that Mr. St. John was something of a philanthropist."

"He is," Solomon said. "He is on the committee of St. Peter's Hospital in—"

"Couldn't you have told us that before?" Napier exploded.

Solomon raised his brows. "No one asked. I came late to the proceedings, if you recall, and I never saw the bodies. But if you're interested, I have not seen Mr. St. John in several months, and we were only ever on nodding terms."

"I don't suppose you moved in the same circles," Napier said, his sneer returning.

"Never suppose without proof," Harris said curtly. "So who is this St. John? What does he do? Is he well thought of?"

"Of landed family, I believe," Solomon said, "though his fortune comes mainly from stocks and investments. He certainly gives generously to charities. Or did."

"Charities for the homeless, perhaps?" Harris asked hopefully. "Could that be how he knew the vagrant?"

Flynn stirred. "Not many gentlemen—er…get their hands dirty in their charitable giving."

"In this case, I could not say," Solomon replied.

"Would anyone like breakfast?" Constance asked. "I'm starving."

ALL THE GIRLS had been interviewed, Flynn was escorting Mrs. St. John to the police mortuary, and Napier was dispatched back to Scotland Yard before Solomon and Constance had the chance to speak alone to Harris.

"How did they die?" Constance asked him bluntly.

"I imagine you know as much as I do by this stage. As far as the gentleman is concerned, the knife in his back would appear to be the cause."

"But there was no blood," Constance said.

Harris's gaze rose swiftly to hers. "You noticed that, did you? I'm afraid we need the doctor to explain it."

"And the vagrant?" Solomon asked.

Harris shrugged. "No obvious marks on him. It's as if he just died. Not unusual with those who live on the streets. They get lung infections, or poison themselves with bad food, and die. However it happens, they tend not to live long and healthy lives."

"No," Constance agreed. Girls working on the streets had many of the same problems. She hesitated, then said, "The bodies were in odd positions when I saw them. Their legs faced front, but their upper bodies didn't."

"You think they were moved?" Solomon said.

"The gentleman certainly was. Either that or he moved himself after he was stabbed and put his back against the wall—while leaving his legs and feet pointing straight ahead. Like the tramp."

"Either way, you have another problem," Harris said.

*Napier,* Solomon thought wryly.

"If they died on your doorstep," Harris said, "why were they there? And if they died somewhere else and were somewhat inexpertly posed on your doorstep, why? Why *your* door?"

# CHAPTER THREE

WHEN THEY FINALLY stepped into the carriage outside the Silver and Grey offices, it was the end of the day and they had barely had time to look at the new cases coming up next week. Constance fell back against the comfortable cushions beside Solomon and took his hand.

"I feel as if we've been home for two months and I haven't slept for any of them. Do I really have to entertain my mother tonight?"

"You invited her," Solomon pointed out. "And my brother."

"So I did. And I will be glad to see them, really. I would just rather go to bed."

"Well," Solomon said, "I'm sure that can be arranged, too."

She opened her eyes with that lazy smile that made his pulse race. She didn't blush so often now when he said such things, but it was an endearing trait in a woman of her profession.

When she didn't reply, merely caressed his fingers, he said, "Why did you never tell me about Jeremy's past?"

"I suppose it never came up."

"Then you weren't shielding me from the similarity with David's past?"

She thought about that. "Because they were both imprisoned, you mean? I suppose Jeremy was young too, though not as young as David. I never thought of it as similar... Everyone's story is different. I tend not to compare them."

He suspected there was more than that. Though she would

not hide things from him now, loyalty to her girls, and to the rest of the household, most of them waifs and strays of one order or another, compelled her discretion. She had known most of them longer than she had known him.

"He likes you," Constance said. "Jeremy. He was happy enough to leave you to protect me."

"I don't think I've ever spoken to him!"

"You probably said thank you, or he noticed the way you pat your horses. He notices a lot, does Jeremy. He's a very good judge of character."

Which was no doubt why he reacted badly to the bully in Napier.

Constance snuggled closer, resting her head against Solomon's shoulder, and gave a contented little wriggle. "Actually, this is quite exciting. It's our first night coming home after a day's work."

"And our first dinner party."

"Dinner party?" she repeated, a ripple of amusement passing through her. "It sounds a little too civilized for a feeding of my mother!"

JULIET SILVER WAS an eccentric, larger-than-life character in most people's opinions. She bustled in behind Lottie the parlor maid, wearing a massive, tentlike garment that defied fashion rather than ignoring it. It appeared to be a cross between a loose tea-gown and a sack, yet with her improbably bright gold hair and the long ropes of pearls, it somehow looked right on her.

She was beaming as she entered the room. "Good house, Connie, though a bit modest for you, isn't it? Not as grand as the other place. Evening, son. My, don't the pair of you look well and smug, just as you should. How was Italy?"

"We brought you a gift from Venice," Solomon said, presenting her with the box. "Which somehow survived the journey home. Sherry? Brandy?"

"I'll have a sherry, love, since we're celebrating. But you didn't need to bring me gifts."

"That's the whole point of them, isn't it?" Constance said.

She was always a little prickly around her mother, although she seemed to have abandoned the downright rudeness that had shocked Solomon when he first saw them together. They had reached a better understanding of each other based on the fact that beneath their various failings, abandonments, and insults, they both cared a great deal.

Even now, as he set a glass in front of each of them, Constance had her eyes on her mother, almost anxious about her reaction.

Juliet lifted out the unique, bowl-shaped vase. It was made of fine Venetian glass and shot through with flashes of color, almost like reflections on the sea. Her pudgy little hands held the vase up to the light and somehow, in the delicacy of their touch, seemed elegant themselves.

"It's for the flat, not the shop," Constance said.

With Solomon's help, Juliet had recently opened a shop of antiques and curios in Covent Garden. It had a pleasant flat above that she was inordinately proud of.

"Oh, I know that," she said, her voice gratifyingly awed. "I could never bring myself to sell *this*… It's the most beautiful glass I've ever seen."

"Glad you like it," Constance said gruffly. "Solomon chose it."

Which was a lie. Solomon refused to allow it. "*You* did. I was merely there to approve. We're glad you like it, Juliet. How is the shop?"

"Doing really well," Juliet replied, her attention still focused on the vase. "I might need to take on another assistant soon… Maybe one of your girls, Connie?"

She could not have said anything more guaranteed to please

her daughter. The "establishment," so much more than a brothel, was a safe haven for the girls Constance rescued from the streets or from particularly brutal houses of ill repute. The girls were fed and clothed and given the offer of training in some occupation. Those who preferred to stick with prostitution were given a safe place to do so with clients vetted by Constance herself, who came as much for the social gatherings as for the more private entertainments. It was run as a co-operative. Everyone contributed and everyone shared the proceeds. Many of Constance's girls were now in domestic service, or working in shops, offices, or factories; some were even teachers and bookkeepers.

"Let me know," Constance said, "and I'll see whom I can find."

Juliet glanced at her and lowered the vase into her lap. "Decent wages. I can afford it."

A smile flickered on Constance's lips. "Good." She turned to Solomon. "Do you suppose David is coming?"

Solomon was beginning to wonder the same thing himself. His brother was a troubled soul, currently living in Solomon's former home behind the Strand. A couple of letters from him had reached Solomon in Venice, but there had been no time today to visit him in person.

"Can we give him another five minutes?"

"Of course," Constance said.

In fact, he arrived in four, wearing one of the suits Solomon had given him, though he spoiled the effect by tugging frequently at the collar. A wave of unease hit Solomon as soon as his brother entered. Their first meeting after his ten-week absence should have been less formal and probably in private, but it was too late now.

Fortunately, Constance and her mother were both skilled in covering awkward social moments. The sherry Solomon gave him was gone in two mouthfuls. While Constance placed the wrapped present in his lap, Solomon quietly refilled his glass and Juliet told an amusing tale of blocked traffic in Covent Garden behind a cart that had shed its load all over the street. The subsequent quarrels, retrieval, and disentangling of horses and vehicles—including a full omnibus—had led to fantastically brisk business in her shop.

Solomon listened with half an ear and smiled. Most of his attention was on David as he unwrapped the oil painting by the Venetian artist Domenico Rossi. His heart lifted at the expression of awe and delight that filled David's face—only to vanish into a sort of desperate misery quickly hidden in a smile.

"This is wonderful," David said, placing it carefully face down in its wrappings. "Now I long to go there myself."

Lottie appeared at the door. "Dinner is served, ma'am."

"So tell us all about Venice," Juliet said cozily as they sat down to a delicious-smelling clear soup. "Didn't you find it wonderful just to leave off snooping for a while?"

Solomon and Constance exchanged glances.

Juliet laid down her spoon. "Oh, no! Not on your honeymoon! What is the matter with you two?"

Surprisingly, Constance laughed. "Pax, Juliet, we didn't really have a choice. Not after I was kidnapped and poisoned and we were both suspected of murder." She broke off at the genuine expression of anguish that briefly flooded Juliet's face and vanished. "It was fine in the end, and never as bad as I've made up to entertain you."

Between them, she and Solomon told an edited version of their Venice adventures, which eventually included the name of the mysterious British diplomat Sebastian Kellar.

Juliet did not quite drop her spoon, but her fingers tightened on it and her gaze was fixed unblinkingly on her soup.

"Oh, he asked to be remembered to you, Mother," Constance said carelessly. "Apparently he knew you in your youth."

"Did he?" Juliet said. "I knew so many people then."

Constance did not push further but continued to the end of the tale, leaving out her own danger, though mentioning Kellar's timely arrival and the bravery of the servants.

She turned to David. "Have you been painting?"

He shrugged. "Off and on. I've spent some time at galleries and exhibitions of various schools and styles. I'm not sure it's for me."

"Liking London, love?" Juliet asked cheerfully.

"Of course. One is never bored here."

It was too pat, too rehearsed. And yet Solomon's brother looked well, better nourished, fit and healthy. After the first course, there wasn't even any awkwardness in his table manners, as if he were recalling childhood in Jamaica. He had probably enjoyed no formal meals since then. Even now that he had a little money, Solomon suspected that if David ate out, he did so at pubs and cheap eating houses.

"Well, Mother," Constance said at the end of the meal, "shall we pretend to be civilized and leave the gentlemen to their port?"

"Only if you've got some in your drawing room," Juliet said, dropping her napkin on the table and rising to her feet. "Take me there."

After the ladies departed, Solomon fetched the decanters and the glasses and sat back down. "You'll forgive us playing at houses," he said deprecatingly.

"I like it," David said unexpectedly. "It's part of your life now, yours and hers. I'm glad to see you so...*comfortable* together."

Sipping their port, they lapsed into silence. Then David said abruptly, "I thought I might go back to sea."

Immediately, as though a switch had been thrown, Solomon felt the stab of loss. But he had almost expected it. David, clearly, had itchy feet. He wasn't used to staying in one place.

"We'll miss you," Solomon said. Then, recognizing that for the evasion it was, he added in a rush, "*I* will miss you. You won't vanish again, will you?"

A smile flickered. "No. No, I won't do that."

"When will you go?" It felt as if David were already on his way out the door.

"Oh, I don't know. I was just thinking about it."

"Do you ever think about going back to Jamaica?"

"No," David said. "Do you?"

"It crosses my mind. Less so recently. I suppose I have roots here now."

David met his gaze. "They are good roots," he said earnestly.

The trouble was, they weren't David's.

⟫⟫⟩⟨⟨⟨

IN THE DRAWING room, Juliet stretched her legs out comfortably, and Constance pushed a footstool beneath her feet.

"You're a good girl, Connie," her mother said. "And that was a dashed fine meal. Note my moderate language."

"I do, and it was. In just a little, I want Bibby to come and assist our cook here, to learn more from her. Frees up another place at the establishment."

Juliet eyed her. "I told himself once you would leave the establishment to be with him. But you won't, will you?"

"He doesn't even want me to anymore. He is trying a differ-ent tack—trying to make me and the establishment respectable. We get very generous charitable donations now, you know."

"Clever," Juliet drawled, "but they'll throw away the key if they sniff one hint of embezzlement."

"There is none. I'm very careful to keep the donations very separate."

"From the immoral earnings? Can't you give up that part altogether? It'll never be respectable, Constance, and he deserves that."

"I know what he deserves," Constance said, turning away, "and it isn't me. However, it's me he wants and has to live with."

"You've given lots of people a chance, Connie, a good chance. It's time to step away. Be his wife, not a madam or an investigator."

"I intend to be all three. And really, Juliet, are you in any position to lecture me?"

"No. I suppose I forfeited that a long time ago. But I'm pulling myself back up, Con, and I don't want you to lose the chances you've won."

Constance hadn't been going to bring it up, but she did, partly in retaliation, partly because she was curious to know the sides of her mother that Juliet had always kept hidden. "You fell a long way, didn't you?"

Juliet was silent. Then, "I never wanted that life for you."

Constance waved her arm, encompassing the whole house. "And I don't have it, so you were successful. I earned all this—but it's what you fell from, isn't it?"

"Don't be daft." Juliet's Cockney accent was more pronounced now.

"You could read and write."

"Went to a ragged school, didn't I? So did you, when I took you there myself, only you wouldn't stay put."

"I could already read and write because you taught me. You were a lady's companion."

Her lip curled. "Seb Kellar tell you that? He was always a fantasist. What's he doing in Italy, anyway?"

"He's a diplomat of some kind."

Juliet sniffed. "What ails the twin?"

Constance thought about pursuing the matter—there was a lot more she wanted to know. But it was Juliet's life and she owed her acceptance. So she allowed the change of subject. "Nothing. He just isn't used to family. You know they were separated for twenty years."

"And here they are."

Whatever had been discussed in the dining room, David seemed to have mellowed, and became much more part of the conversation. It turned out to be a surprisingly pleasant evening, and for Constance, it was followed by a particularly delicious night and morning with Solomon.

It was only when she rose to dress for the day that Constance again remembered the bodies on her doorstep.

"Harris is right," she said abruptly. "Why *my* doorstep?"

"Bad luck, probably," Solomon said, kissing the back of her neck in passing.

"Not someone playing a cruel trick on the immoral women of my establishment?"

"It's possible, of course, but murdering someone, let alone murdering *two* people, is going rather beyond a trick on an unwanted neighbor."

"Whoever put them there needn't have murdered them," Constance argued. "Just found the bodies and moved them to my property."

"And stuck a knife in one of them," Solomon reminded her. "Then it's hard work moving bodies. Besides, if there's one thing more likely than a discreet brothel to lower the tone of the neighborhood, it's murder, dead bodies, and the swarming of police with awkward questions."

"Fair points," Constance allowed. "I shall call in at the establishment first, in the hope of finding Inspector Harris there, and hope nothing else has happened. I'll join you at Silver and Grey afterward."

Much to her relief, she discovered the much more usual good-natured organized chaos reigning in the establishment. Janey had already left for work and the domestic staff were clearing up after last night's soiree. Apparently it had been a pleasant and successful night and Sarah was counting the takings.

"Peeler in the kitchen, though," Max told her from his precarious perch on the ladder from where he was cleaning the hall chandelier. "Hoping to speak to you, I believe."

"Which peeler?" Constance asked warily.

"Peeler-in-chief—Harris?"

"Well, that's fine." Constance decided to go down to the kitchen instead of summoning him, and discovered the inspector on the point of departure.

"I'd given up on you," he said mildly.

"Let's talk in the garden," Constance suggested. "Bibby will bring us a cup of tea."

"So I will, ma'am!" Bibby said cheerfully, and Constance led the policeman outside to the bench where she occasionally sat to take the air and appreciate what she had.

"So what have you learned?" she asked him, sitting down on the bench by the small lawn and gesturing for him to sit beside her.

Harris sat, turning his face up to the sunshine. "Our corpses have names. Terrence St. John, as we suspected—his wife identified him yesterday afternoon—and a vagrant known as Nevvy, real name apparently Gareth Neville, according to St. Peter's Hospital."

"St. Peter's?" Constance pounced. "Isn't that one of St. John's charities? Did they meet there, then?"

"We don't know that, though Nevvy was, apparently, a patient there. He was in the final stages of consumption. No one is surprised he expired."

"And St. John?" Constance asked.

"Ah, well, that is more interesting. There was a quantity of opium in his stomach. Enough to kill him."

"Was there indeed?" she murmured. Her voice, her whole person, felt suddenly shaky. She had considerable sympathy for anyone facing the misery of poisoning, let alone dying of it. In her mind, everything sped closer, became more personal. "How very… Why stab him, then?"

Harris scowled. "Presumably in the hope that no autopsy would then be considered necessary. But I pressed for one anyway. You were right—he was already dead when he was stabbed. He died of the opium poisoning."

"He ate at home," Constance pointed out.

"And no one else was ill in his household. They all ate the same things."

"Who served them?"

Harris's lips twitched. "The family served themselves from the same serving dishes. There's certainly a bottle of laudanum in the St. Johns' stillroom, but I don't see how it could have got into only Mr. St. John's dinner."

"Did they all drink the wine?" she asked.

"The family all did, and even the butler quaffed the dregs before bed. None of them noticed a peculiar taste to it. Are you afraid I didn't ask the right questions?"

Constance smiled. "Sorry. I'm thinking aloud. I suppose we can't know how St. John's notecase got into Nevvy's pocket?"

"I guess a charitable man might have given it to pay for his hospital treatment."

"Why give him the wallet as well as the money?" She shook her head. "Whoever did this does not think highly of the police. You're meant to think that Nevvy stabbed St. John to rob him, and not realize he was poisoned. But even that's too simple, isn't it?"

Harris's face remained expressionless. "Why do you say that?"

"Because I have seen people die of consumption. I don't see how he could have got here from wherever he sheltered, let alone had the energy to stab anyone."

He was not remotely surprised. "How well do you know your neighbors, Mrs. Grey?"

"We keep ourselves to ourselves, inspector," she said dryly. "The ladies don't leave cards here."

"Your people tell me there has been no trouble, no threats or quarrels with your neighbors."

So he too wondered if the placement of the bodies was a malicious trick. "There never has been. Our existence here has always been discreet, a presence no one acknowledges. But you know that."

"Then your own people would not conceal a recent quarrel

from you? If there was trouble during your absence?"

"No," she said firmly. And yet it was something she hadn't thought of. In the warmth of the morning sun, she suddenly felt cold.

# CHAPTER FOUR

H AVING SENT JANEY and Lenny out to investigate a case of theft from a wealthy home, Solomon was alone in the Silver and Grey offices. He was trying to follow the rambling letter that introduced next week's first new case when the knocker at the front door sounded.

Hoping it was Constance having forgotten her key, he rose and opened it to discover Sergeant Flynn smiling amiably at him.

"Come in," Solomon said at once, standing back.

Flynn entered, looking about him with interest. "Sorry to disturb you." At Solomon's invitation, he walked into the comfortable office and his eyebrows flew up. "Wouldn't mind an office like this one. I'm working for the wrong firm."

"To be fair, the office was not furnished with the profits from this business. We fulfil a different function to the police. As you know. What can I do for you, sergeant?"

"Oh, I only came by to keep you informed," Flynn said, just a little too easily. "Mrs. St. John identified her husband's body, which was stabbed *after* death. He died of opium poisoning. The other body was a vagrant known as Nevvy—Gareth Neville. You may have seen him around here. He tramped mostly about the City. Some of our fellows recognized him."

"Did he die of opium poisoning too?" Solomon waved him to a chair.

"Consumption. He seems to have just died. Who knows where? Inspector Harris suspects the bodies were placed on your doorstep after death, no doubt from different locations."

"A lot of effort to go to," Solomon remarked.

"Which could imply a lot of anger against—er...the occupants of that house."

"I would not have thought the neighbors to be the kind of people to indulge in such tricks."

Flynn shrugged. "Young men, you know, especially in their cups, will go to extraordinary lengths for a perceived joke. They could have been refused entry to the house and borne a grudge. Or it could have been outraged servants or others of lower orders from almost anywhere. The thing is, you and your wife have been away, and the household is not of the type to confide in the police."

Solomon eyed him. "You are asking me if we know something you do not?"

"It is possible."

It was. Solomon barely knew the inhabitants of Constance's establishment, though she trusted them implicitly. "They would have told her."

"Probably. But perhaps she could make sure."

"Did you really come here just to ask me that?"

"Not just that. I want to know anything you can tell me about Terrence St. John."

"I think I already have. We were mere acquaintances."

"Did you like him? Did other people?"

"Yes, they seemed to. I found him very affable. Surprisingly practical about hospital business."

Flynn pounced. "In what way?"

"He was more concerned for the physical wellbeing of the patients than their moral deserts."

"Did you agree with him?"

"Yes. It's a hospital, not a church."

"Did the other committee members agree?"

Solomon shrugged. "Some of them. There were a few minor disagreements that were resolved with compromise. There were no quarrels that I ever witnessed that were likely to lead to killing."

"But St. Peter's was not his only charity, was it?"

"I honestly don't know. It's the only one we have in common, so far as I know."

"Did you ever run into him in Grosvenor Square?" Flynn asked.

"If you mean at Constance's house, then no. Would a man visit such an establishment quite so close to home?"

"He might if he used the back door."

Solomon's lip twitched. "I see your point, but all guests enter at the front. Safety is the house's main concern."

"It may be your wife's main concern, but would her people not make exceptions? Especially if she was away for several weeks."

"I would seriously doubt it. These people are too glad to have left such risks behind them."

Flynn regarded him curiously. Solomon could see the questions in his eyes, but he did not ask them.

"I will look into it," Solomon said mildly. "Do you have any ideas how he was poisoned?"

"Not yet. We can't find anything he ate or drank at home that was not shared with his family. We're trying to trace his movements during the later part of the evening, though we don't stand much chance of witnesses at four or five in the morning."

"Is that when he died?" Solomon asked.

Flynn sighed. "According to the doctor, he must have been dead a couple of hours before the knife went in—too little blood. But he stiffened in the position with his back against the wall. So he was probably stabbed by four o'clock at the latest, and was dead already by two, or shortly after."

"And Nevvy?"

Flynn raised his shoulders. "Your guess is as good as mine. He could have died at any point during the night, most likely where he usually sheltered in the City. Napier's looking into that now."

He rose to his feet. "I have to look into St. John's clubs and friends. Apparently, he had no formal engagements that evening."

"Did he have money troubles?" Solomon asked, thinking it might have made him vulnerable to the wrong kind of company. Or that the wrong kind of company might have played havoc with his finances.

"Not that we know of." Flynn looked almost regretful. "Though since he was paying for his daughter's elaborate wedding next month, I imagine his expenses were unusually high. I suspect you know more than I do. The inquest is this afternoon."

※》》≪≪

CONSTANCE ARRIVED ABOUT an hour later, sweeping into Solomon's office with a book held to her chest and impetuous words on her lips. "I had a talk with Inspector Harris."

"I had one with Sergeant Flynn."

She threw herself onto the visitor's chair on the other side of his desk. "Did you indeed? Did you get the impression they suspect us of knowing more than we're telling?"

"Perhaps not you or I personally, but yes, the possibility has crossed their minds. Like us, they suspect the bodies were moved to where they were found, and they are looking for the reason. *Would* the staff have allowed someone in through the back door?"

"Not a stranger, and not without protection. In the evenings, the footmen are all upstairs. They can't watch the back door or the area door as well, so they are always kept locked. Besides, St. John *wasn't* let in, was he? He was on the doorstep, where he seems to have been put after death. He was certainly moved." She frowned. "I suppose he might have been *trying* to come in and, considering the closeness of home, thought the back entrance might be more discreet."

"Perhaps he saw the vagrant there, obviously ill, and sat

down to help?" Solomon suggested.

"It's a possibility. But we don't really know anything about St. John. *Would* he have come to the establishment?"

Solomon shrugged. "He might have wished to make a donation."

"And still not wanted to be seen there...? The trouble is, I'm not sure how known the establishment is to our more innocent neighbors." She drew in a breath and smiled at him. Even after being so constantly in her company since their wedding, that smile still turned him inside out. "One of us needs to make a condolence call upon the St. Johns and try to discover the kind of man he was. In the circumstances, it cannot be me."

"Then it had better be me. What will you do while I'm gone?"

She set the book she had been carrying on the desk and patted it. "Learn what I can about opium poisoning. I've no idea how long it takes to work, or what symptoms there would be. We should probably know, since we appear to be investigating these deaths."

Solomon opened his mouth in instinctive objection, then closed it again. He didn't want to think about poisons, largely because of what had happened to Constance in Italy. But she was right. And if she could face it, so could he.

"Come. I'll take you for luncheon first, in case the reading matter puts you off."

THE ST. JOHNS' house in Grosvenor Square appeared to be well maintained, outside and in. The family was not obviously short of money. A well-trained footman wearing a black armband showed Solomon into a fresh morning room with flowers on the table, while he took his card to Mrs. St. John.

The footman did not leave him kicking his heels for long and soon led him along the polished parquet floor to the staircase. His feet made virtually no noise. The silence of the house was oppressive.

"Mr. Grey," the footman announced, and closed the door behind Solomon.

He faced four people, all dressed in mourning black. The oldest of them was, presumably, the widow, a slightly bony woman whose face looked understandably pinched, although it still bore the remnants of beauty. She rose to greet him, extending her hand with some curiosity. "Mr. Grey? I don't believe we have previously met."

"My misfortune, ma'am," Solomon said, bowing over her hand. "I called to offer my condolences on your terrible loss."

"You are very kind," she replied. Was the faint spark in her bewildered eyes to do with mere curiosity or something altogether more calculating? "I wasn't aware you were a friend of my husband's."

"We had a charity in common—we both sat on the board of St. Peter's Hospital, which will also feel his loss dreadfully."

"Indeed," she said, and it struck him that she was not actually aware of her husband's connection to the hospital. She turned to the others, who had also risen politely at Solomon's entrance. "My son, Anthony, and my daughter, Bella."

Anthony, a serious-looking youth of perhaps sixteen, bowed a little stiffly. He seemed afraid to speak or smile, as if he didn't yet know what to do with his grief. Bella curtseyed, her eyes tragic and full, as though from recent weeping.

Mrs. St. John turned toward the final occupant of the room, a handsome man perhaps a couple of years younger than Solomon. "Bella's betrothed, Mr. Hanibal Cordell, who is a great help and comfort to us at this terrible time."

"How do you do?" Cordell said, as though bestowing an honor.

"There has had to be an inquest, you know, because he did not die at home," Mrs. St. John said with a nervous flutter. "So unnecessarily brutal. Mr. Cordell attended on our behalf, which was so kind… Do sit down, Mr. Grey."

"What did the inquest establish?" Solomon asked, as the servants brought tea and dainty cakes and sandwiches.

"It was adjourned for further investigation," Cordell said smoothly. "Which is hardly what his family needs."

"Nor the poor people whose doorstep he was apparently sitting on when he died," Mrs. St. John said with unexpected sympathy. "Nothing was ever straightforward with Terrence, but he can't have meant to bring such trouble to them."

Solomon accepted a cup of tea from his hostess and helped himself from the proffered plate of sandwiches. Relieved if somewhat surprised by the widow's attitude to Constance's establishment, he risked saying, "Perhaps he had friends in the house he meant to call upon."

"No, he did not," Cordell said at once.

"At any rate," Solomon said, "it must be of some comfort to you that his last act was one of kindness."

They all regarded him with obvious bafflement.

"To the poor vagrant," Solomon said mildly, "whom he must have stopped to help."

"Oh, no," Bella said. "You have that quite wrong. The beast attacked my father and robbed him." Fresh tears made her eyes swim. Her mother's cup rattled on the saucer as though her hands shook.

"I beg your pardon," Solomon said. "I did not mean to upset you further."

"You haven't," the boy, Anthony, said quickly. "It is just an upsetting time, and policemen asking interminable questions don't make things easier for my mother and sister."

"Of course not," Solomon said. There was considerable strain in the boy's face, and in the nerves of his womenfolk, as if they had no time to grieve because of everything else that was going on around them. In the circumstance, asking more questions seemed both cruel and likely to lead to his dismissal should he wish to call again.

So while he drank his tea, he made sympathetic noises and begged them to let him know if he could be of any assistance at all.

It was Cordell who rose first. "I must go. But I shall call again tomorrow morning. And, of course, you must send for me if you need me before then." He kissed his betrothed's hand and her pale cheek. She clung to him a little, but he detached himself with gentle firmness before bowing more formally to Mrs. St. John.

"I shall take my leave also," Solomon said. "My most sincere sympathies to you all."

In truth, he was glad to leave the strange, nerve-jangling atmosphere of the grieving family, but he also hoped to speak more openly to Cordell. The footman handed them their hats and they left together in silence.

"I'm afraid I have been clumsy and said the wrong thing," Solomon said, adeptly choosing the same direction as his companion. "Did the inquest really decide that that the vagrant attacked and robbed Mr. St. John?"

"Well, not exactly. A policeman asked for it to be adjourned, but in lining up the evidence they did have, it came out that Mr. St. John's notecase was found in the vagrant's pocket, and that the vagrant's knife was in Mr. John's back. I don't think it takes a great deal of intelligence to deduce what happened."

"The vagrant's knife?" Solomon repeated, startled. This was news to him.

"So it was said. Another vagrant claimed to have seen it in his possession many times. But talking of saying the wrong thing..." Cordell met Solomon's gaze. "This is difficult enough for the family. They know St. John was found on a neighbor's back doorstep, but we have carefully kept from them *which* neighbor. I expect you are aware."

"I am."

"Then you will understand the need not to inflict further hurt on the poor ladies."

"Oh, quite. But—forgive me—your attitude implies that you believe St. John was a client there. I understand this was not the case."

Cordell's eyebrows flew up. "How can you possibly know that?" Too late, he realized the likeliest means, and blushed. His nostrils flared. "You are a frequent visitor yourself, sir? I suppose we are both men of the world."

"Not in the way you mean. You might say the house is mine, through my marriage to Mrs. Silver."

Various expressions chased each other across Cordell's face—outrage, consternation, indecision.

Solomon smiled slightly. "Before you denounce me and forbid me the society of your betrothed and her family, allow me to say that both my wife and her establishment are rather more than you may imagine."

Cordell closed his mouth, then shrugged impatiently. "I've heard Rawleigh and others say such things recently. I do not set myself up as a judge, but I still don't want my wife-to-be or her mother to know that's where St. John spent his last moments. It would add insult to injury, don't you think?"

"I could not speak for the ladies," Solomon said tactfully. "There would appear to be several possibilities as to how he came to be where he was found. Was Mr. St. John in the habit of frequenting such establishments?"

Cordell shook his head. "I can't imagine it. He was a fastidious sort of fellow. On the other hand, I believe he did have a long-term mistress." He shot another glance at Solomon.

"Another conversation not to have with Mrs. St. John," Solomon agreed. "But to be honest with you, Mr. Cordell, I am seeking the truth for my wife's sake. I would appreciate the name and direction of this mistress."

"I didn't learn this from St. John," Cordell said quickly. "It's only rumor and gossip. But I have seen him in this woman's company. He even introduced me to her openly as his 'old friend,' Miss Zenobia Paul. Are you thinking he might have been on his way to or from her house when he was killed?"

"It's a possibility. Unless you know otherwise?"

"I dined with the family that evening, after which Mr. St. John went out—to his club, I think. I believe his valet saw him return about eleven, but he obviously went out again. That is all I know."

"Thank you," Solomon said. "It seemed criminally bad manners to question the family, but I do need to know the truth."

"I suppose the police hold your household in suspicion also," Cordell said. "I must admit, I did not bargain for such unpleasantness when I proposed to Miss St. John."

Solomon cocked an eyebrow. "Regretting it?"

"Good Lord, no," Cordell said easily. "Always prepared for the 'better or worse'—I just didn't expect the 'worse' quite so soon!"

"When is it you plan to marry? Will you have to postpone it?"

"At the end of June." Cordell tugged at his left ear. "I don't want to postpone, but I shall leave it up to Bella."

"Most understanding of you. Did you spend the rest of St. John's final evening with your betrothed's family?"

"I did. You sound like the policeman."

"I beg your pardon. What time did you leave the St. John house?"

Cordell blinked.

"Sorry," Solomon said. "I don't mean to interrogate you. I am only trying to establish where Mr. St. John was at what time. Did you see any sign of him, or anyone that might have been him, on your way home?"

Cordell looked thoughtful but shook his head. "I left just after eleven and walked home, but I don't recall seeing anyone. A few passing carriages, perhaps."

"Where is home?"

"Brook Street."

"Not so far, then. Did you remain there, or go out again?"

Cordell cast him an amused sideways glance. "Now you *do*

sound like the policeman. I met friends at my club, which I'm sure the police have already ascertained. I had no reason to kill my prospective father-in-law. I liked him, and he was happily in favor of my marriage to his daughter, of whom he was inordinately fond. I am, you know, an eligible bachelor, of good family, and financially sound. And he knew I was devoted to Bella."

"I never doubted it," Solomon said smoothly. "Forgive me for what must seem unpardonable curiosity. My wife and I run a private investigation business, so asking questions to clarify all aspects of a situation has become second nature to both of us."

"Good Lord," Cordell said, fascination in his gaze. "I've never heard of such a thing. What sort of things do you investigate—er…privately?"

"Oh, various matters, from ghostly sightings to lost and stolen property and missing persons. Some such have involved murder. And then there are the people who wish their prospective employees to be investigated."

Cordell's lip curled. "And wives their straying husbands? Or vice versa."

"We do receive such requests," Solomon admitted, "but we never accept them."

"On the grounds of vulgarity?" Cordell asked, clearly amused.

"On the grounds that we cannot solve private issues of trust."

Cordell tilted his head. "You are a very odd sort of fellow. From all I ever heard of the mysterious Solomon Grey, I thought you were this hideously wealthy semi-recluse from the West Indies, who only emerged into public to secure deals that made you even more money. Now I discover you to be a smart English gentleman married to London's most famous courtesan and employed for purposes I can only call prying."

"Well it is all true to some degree," Solomon said. "Do you not have many facets?"

For an instant, something very like discontent flickered across Cordell's face. "No. I am my father's heir, a good son and a jolly good fellow all round. Ask anyone."

"And if I were to ask you?"

"You already did."

"Then allow me to be more specific. What exactly are you heir to? Land?"

"Yes."

"Private wealth?"

"Yes. I am a gentleman of leisure who employs business managers to look after his interests. No trade tarnishes my blue-blooded hands. Nor profession."

"Do you want one?"

He shrugged. "I have no interests and less aptitude, so no."

Solomon smiled faintly. "I believe that is the first lie you have told me."

Cordell reared back in outrage, his eyes hardening. Then an unexpected bark of laughter broke from him. "You are quite good at this, aren't you? Yes, it was a lie, about the interest, at least, if not the aptitude. I remain untested. My father is very averse to risk—financially, socially, and every other way you can think of. Failure, you might say, can never be contemplated."

"Failure in what?"

Cordell hesitated, betraying uncertainty for the first time since Solomon had met him. He shrugged. "In my case…occasionally, when I'm bored or discontented, I consider going into politics. Amusing, is it not?"

"Not so far. What are you discontented with?"

"The way things are run in this country, and in others. With the poverty that is all around us, only a few hundred yards from where we walk now. With crime and violence. With a foreign policy so out of date that we could easily go to war over something that is not our business and would be better negotiated by all parties concerned."

"Meaning that what kept the peace in Europe after 1815 no longer works in 1853?"

"Exactly." Cordell smiled ruefully. "My father tells me I don't know what I'm talking about. And he is right to some degree. I would like to know more."

"And you have the leisure to learn."

"But no possibility of using that knowledge." Cordell waved a hand. "But we have strayed from the point somewhat. My ambitions, or lack of them, don't really help with the murder of my almost-father-in-law."

"Did he have enemies?"

"Not that I ever heard. Everyone liked him. Amiable man, happy to talk about anything. He even listened to my political ramblings when I'd had one too many glasses of port. He seemed to take me seriously."

Which implied that other people, including Cordell's father, did not.

"Was he involved with politics?" Solomon asked.

"No, but he was interested in many things. A good man to converse with, whether on serious matters or amusing ones."

"Good company," Solomon said.

"Exactly." Cordell grimaced. "I shall miss him. Quite aside from Bella's grief and the possible postponement of our marriage."

Solomon's impression of the dead man was growing but still elusive. "You mentioned a mistress. Did Mrs. St. John know about her?"

"If she did, she was a good wife and pretended not to." Cordell's eyes widened. "You cannot suspect Jacintha St. John of murder!"

"It often is the spouse, you know," Solomon said mildly, "and there is a view that poison is a woman's weapon. But no, I have no real reason to suspect Mrs. St. John. Did you notice him behaving differently in the previous few days or weeks? Did he seem worried or unhappy?"

Cordell half shook his head, then interrupted the action, frowning. "Actually, I did catch him looking intensely unhappy once. He didn't hear me come into his study, and just for a moment, his expression shook me. Then he smiled at me and made some joke, and I saw that I'd been mistaken. Some people do look overly serious in repose when in reality they are thinking of nothing at all."

"So he did not confide in you?"

"My feeling was, he had nothing to confide. His life was an open book, you might say."

"Apart from the mistress."

Cordell's glance was curious. "I expected you of all men to be more tolerant of such peccadillos."

Solomon did not smile. "Facets, Mr. Cordell. My wife is a virtuous woman. A man of your interests could do worse than call at her establishment one evening. Your own virtue need be in no danger, and if you chose, it could certainly add to your understanding of the realities of poverty."

# CHAPTER FIVE

Miss Zenobia Paul had rooms in a respectable street in Bloomsbury, and she surprised Solomon from the outset. Constance had taught him that women of ill repute came in as many shapes and characters as the rest of humanity, so he had never been crass enough to expect either the grasping whore or the empty-headed but amiable antidote to a nagging wife. But Zenobia Paul, he suspected, would always be a surprise.

Her landlady, a respectable widow by her appearance, consulted personally with Miss Paul before showing him up her neatly kept staircase to a suite of rooms on the first floor. He entered a pleasantly cluttered sitting room full of oddities and curios from across the globe, many of them extremely beautiful. Juliet Silver would have loved it. The walls were decorated with exotic landscapes and a few unusual portraits. Between them hung embroidered cloth and colorful beads. There were two jam-packed bookcases, each topped with beautifully carved and painted bookends from India. Small wool and silk rugs adorned the floor and furniture, turning shabby tables and old upholstered chairs into curiously charming pieces.

Miss Paul herself came to meet him from the midst of this treasure trove. She was tall and slender, almost wand-like, with a natural elegance that made one think immediately of beauty. And yet, from her untidily piled hair to her bright clothes festooned with unmatching jewelry, she gave the distinct impression of carelessness. She was older than he had expected, too, perhaps in her early forties, with shrewd, veiled eyes and a rather stubborn chin.

"Mr. Grey," she said, holding out her hand. "You do not look like a policeman."

Her voice was a surprise, too—low, educated, with the clipped vowels of the upper classes.

"I'm not." Solomon bowed over her hand, which was slender and beringed.

He had sent up the Silver and Grey card, but she seemed only to have read his name and "Inquiries." She glanced at it again—she held it still in her left hand—and cast him another rueful if appraising glance.

"Forgive me. I am not at my best. I have had a bit of a shock, you see. Actually, I probably would not have received you if I had read this correctly the first time, but since you are here, what might I do for you?"

"I apologize for the intrusion," Solomon said. "I was hoping you could help me understand the recent death of Mr. Terrence St. John."

The flashing change in her expression was so quick he could have missed it in a blink, and it had gone before he could properly recognize it.

She sat but did not invite him to do so. "What is that to do with you?"

"He was found on the back doorstep of my wife's property."

This time he recognized the flash. Simple and profound grief.

Only when he saw it, among all the gaiety of her dress, did he realize it had been missing from the purely shocked response of the St. Johns. He made little of that. Everyone grieved in their own way. But in this woman, it felt curiously poignant.

"Please, sit down," she invited him. "I have a kettle here, if you would like a cup of tea? Or something stronger, perhaps? I believe I will have a sherry."

"Thank you, I will join you if I may." He watched her pour from a beautifully decorated glass bottle, several of which festooned the table beneath a large mirror. Her hands trembled.

He took the crystal glass from her with a murmur of thanks and sat when she did.

"The policeman who informed me of Terrence's death was very vague about details," she said abruptly. "He was more interested in asking questions—impudent questions, at that—than in answering mine. And there has been nothing in the newspapers. How did Terrence die?"

"Apparently by opium poisoning, although he was also stabbed after death—one of the many mysterious circumstances."

"Opium?" A frown creased her brow.

"You find that odd? Did he not take it for any pain or ailments he was subject to?"

"Not that I ever heard, although it's perfectly possible he had toothache or something equally unbearable without relief. But he was not an idiot. He would not *poison* himself with it."

"In view of the stabbing, the general belief is that he was poisoned by someone else."

She was staring at him. "Who stabbed him afterward just to make sure? It makes no sense."

"Agreed. Another thing that makes no sense is that beside him on the doorstep was the equally dead—but unstabbed—body of a known vagrant by the name of Nevvy. Does that mean anything to you?"

She shook her head. "What else?"

"The doorstep was not far from Mr. St. John's home but was the back door to a discreet establishment of ill repute."

She blinked. "A brothel?"

"Of an exclusive kind. Run by a certain Constance Silver, of whom you might have heard."

Until the woman's shoulders relaxed, he hadn't been properly aware of her tension. "No. But then, such scandals don't interest me. To be honest, they don't—didn't—interest Terrence either."

"Because he had you?"

Her eyes widened, though she looked more bewildered than

insulted. Then she sighed. "I see you have made the same mistake as the police. I suppose you can't really be blamed, since the gossip has been peddled for years. Terrence and I were not lovers. We were friends and always had been."

"Does his wife know that?" Solomon asked.

"I should imagine she must."

"Why, are you on visiting terms?" he asked.

Her smile was lopsided. "Oh no. I didn't say she *liked* me, Mr. Grey. I am much too eccentric for her world, and she did rather resent when Terrence helped to finance my expeditions."

"Your expeditions?"

She waved her head to encompass the room full of exotic treasures. "To India, Africa, China. He would have come too if she had let him. Instead, he helped me raise money from learned societies and academics, to whom I reported back faithfully."

"You are an intrepid lady," he said with genuine admiration. Constance would like her, he knew.

"I have not had much time in my life for love affairs, you see."

He nodded, then realized she was watching him with faint curiosity.

"You believe me," she said, "that Terrence and I were merely old friends. The policeman did not, and made it perfectly plain that my answers to his questions were worth no more than those of any other proven liar."

"Ah. That would have been Constable Napier."

Her eyebrows lifted. "I believe that was the name."

"Take heart. I suspect he was sent because you were considered of little importance. In a murder inquiry, that has to be good."

She grimaced. "None of this feels good. Thank you for telling me the truth. What is it you think I can tell you?"

"First of all, I suppose, did you see Mr. St. John at all on the night he died?"

She shook her head. "No. I had not seen him for several days.

Not since last Sunday afternoon."

"Then tell me about his other friends. Who would he have been comfortable visiting after midnight?"

"Someone in your exclusive brothel? Not the ladies of the night but the servants?"

"Apparently not. No one knew him. Besides, there is a house rule that no one is admitted by the back door. For reasons of safety."

"I can imagine," she said.

"Apart from yourself, who were his friends?" Solomon asked.

"I know only of a few academics, artists, writers."

"Could you write down their names and addresses for me?" Solomon asked.

"I could," she said. "But you know, his wife will have a completely different set of friends to give you."

"Then he led something of a double life?"

"Oh, I wouldn't go that far," she said quickly. "Merely, he had a wide circle of friends who did not all mix."

"But he might, perhaps, have been more likely to visit the bohemian set after midnight?"

"I don't think he ever did. Apart from me."

"Why you?"

"Because we have been friends since childhood. Almost brother and sister. And I have no spouse to disturb."

"Miss Paul, was something troubling him in the last week or so of his life?"

She met his gaze, though hers shifted a little out of focus. "Do you know, I think perhaps something was? He didn't tell me what, and I never asked. I presumed he would tell in his own time if I could help." Again that flash of grief washed over her face and vanished. "One isn't always given that time."

"One isn't," he agreed. "Do you have idea what it was? Or when it began to bother him?"

"I don't know what the problem was," she said slowly, "but I suppose it began about a month ago."

"When was his daughter's engagement announced?" he asked on impulse.

Her lips parted in shock. "A little more than a month ago. But no, I'm sure you're wrong. He was delighted when he told me of it. He liked young Cordell, and in truth, it is a most suitable match. Bella was deliriously happy, and that made him happy."

"And troubled," Solomon pointed out.

She flapped one impatient hand. "That was after."

"How much after?"

"Oh, I don't know. A week or so, maybe, before I noticed he was a little tense and uneasy. But he still spoke happily about the wedding and the preparations that were keeping his wife contented, too, so I can't think it was anything to do with Cordell."

"With Cordell's family, perhaps? Do you know them?"

"Oh, we don't move in the same circles at all. They are very conventional, I believe, and would thoroughly disapprove of me. Not just because they think I am Terrence's mistress, but because I do unsuitable things for a woman."

"Do you suppose they disliked Mr. St. John because of his perceived connection with you?"

Her expression was tolerantly scornful. "You haven't quite grasped the hypocrisy of Polite Society, have you? Trust me, that is in your favor. No, they might disapprove of me, but Terrence indulging himself in discreet adultery would not raise an eyebrow. It would almost be expected."

"Funnily enough, I have encountered that kind of attitude all too often. What else happened in St. John's life in the last month? Anything unusual or new to him?"

"Not that he told me."

For the first time, her answer was too quick. She might have been bored with the questioning, or not quite truthful.

"Did you quarrel with him?" he asked.

She smiled, an odd, sad little smile. "Rarely. We could shout at each other when we were young. Recently, not so much, and we were quieter about it. Maturity does bring some good sense. We didn't argue much at all in the last month, no."

"Whom *did* he quarrel with?"

"No one, I suspect. He was a hard man to rile because he generally saw all sides of an argument and was very tolerant by nature." She swallowed and lifted her glass very slightly as though in a silent toast. "I shall miss him."

Solomon drank with her and allowed a respectful silence. "I met Mr. John on the board of St. Peter's Hospital. Do you know much about his charitable interests?"

"A little. The poverty of his fellow men concerned him."

"What about the homeless? Vagrants living on the streets?"

She thought about it. "I think he gave money for the building of a men's hostel. But he was not particularly involved, except on the matter of health, as in St. Peter's. Are you thinking of the vagrant who shared his doorstep?"

Solomon nodded. "If there is a connection between them, I would like to find it."

"It was probably made that night," she said. "If he saw someone in need, he would not pass him by." She frowned. "On the other hand, what was he doing in a stranger's back garden?"

"Precisely," Solomon said. He hesitated. "I think you were aware of the nature of that particular doorstep before I mentioned it."

She looked amused by his delicacy. "I was. The police constable told me with some relish. But I am not foolish enough to imagine Terrence was visiting the house. It was not in his nature."

"Perhaps not. And it's perfectly possible there is no connection at all between St. John and the tramp. The men could have been brought from entirely different places to be found there."

"Why?" she asked blankly.

He sighed. "I have no idea. Perhaps to impugn my wife, who owns the house." He set down his glass. "Thank you for your help, Miss Paul. If you should think of anything else at all that might help, you can always reach me or my wife through the address on the card. We would be very grateful."

"I would certainly rather tell you than the vulgarly offensive constable. But am I not obliged to tell the police?"

"We would be happy to do that for you," Solomon assured her. "They may come to you for a statement, but I shall suggest Inspector Harris calls himself. He is in charge of the case."

"You are very considerate." She eyed him curiously, rising with him as he stood to depart. "You are a well-travelled man, are you not?"

"All the way from Jamaica, by a somewhat circuitous route."

Her eyes sparkled. "Indeed? I would like to hear your story some time. I hope you will call again."

"Thank you. I would like to," he said truthfully.

"Bring your wife. She must be a very interesting woman."

CONSTANCE SPENT MOST of the afternoon making notes on the uses and abuses of opium, and then on the entire sum of their knowledge of the two dead men. There was depressingly little of the latter.

When Janey and Lenny returned to the office, crowing with delight because they had solved their theft case, she cheered up and celebrated with them, joining them in a cup of tea with cakes bought from the baker's shop round the corner.

Recklessly, she gave them each a bonus payment and sent them off for the rest of the day to enjoy themselves. She hoped Lenny would not simply go home and work on his carpentry.

She smiled as she watched them out of the window striding along the street arm in arm, talking and laughing. When they had first met Lenny, he had never even smiled, so lost was he in his personal tragedy. Janey had been good for him. Perhaps Silver and Grey was, too.

A hackney pulled up and Solomon alighted. Immediately, the world brightened further. She had to stop herself from rushing to the door and dragging him inside. After all, this was a respectable and professional office.

"Constance?" he called, closing the front door behind him.

"In here."

He strode down the hall to her office, filling it at once with his presence. Because she wanted to, she walked straight into his arms. She had grown too used to being there during the weeks of their honeymoon. It seemed to make even short separations more difficult. Though she was more than happy with their reunion kisses.

It was some time before they sat very close together on her sofa, his arm around her waist, ready to discuss the case.

"What have you learned about opium poisoning?" he asked.

It made her smile. They had always had odd conversations for lovers. "That a massive dose could not be easily disguised. The most likely situation I can come up with is that he was taking laudanum or some other form of opium anyway, and simply took, or was given, a larger dose on one or more occasions." She reached for the notes at her feet and passed him the relevant page.

"There seems to have been no hint of that," he said. "Unless he frequented some opium den. He was not ill or in pain that anyone knew of. Besides, if he felt ill, why go and sit on a stranger's doorstep?"

"We don't know that he did," she reminded him. "He could have died anywhere in the City and some wag chose to deposit him on my doorstep, perhaps in an effort to have the house closed down. Did you see Mrs. St. John?"

"I did. Not that I learned much from her. Questioning a bereaved widow without being thrown out of the house is surprisingly difficult when one has no authority. But I did have quite an interesting talk with her future son-in-law, Hanibal Cordell. I didn't take to him much at first—one of those arrogant, entitled men of the upper classes—but there is more going on beneath the surface. He liked St. John, seems devoted to the daughter, and he appears to be hiding from the family exactly whose doorstep St. John was found upon."

As Solomon talked, she added to her notes, with separate pages for Cordell and Zenobia Paul.

"You believe her when she says she was not St. John's mistress?" Constance asked.

"I do. I think she's an unconventional woman who simply follows her own path. And those who don't understand platonic friendships between men and women have simply labeled her and dismissed her. Including Cordell, incidentally. He thinks that if Mrs. St. John knows of the rumors, she simply pretends she doesn't, like so many dutiful wives. Zenobia, on the other hand, thinks Mrs. St. John understands the relationship perfectly well and just doesn't like her. They have met, though not by choice."

"Then we are ruling out jealousy from either of them as a motive for murder?"

Solomon hesitated. "I don't know. I *think* so. But there's something Zenobia is consciously not telling me."

"About what?"

"I'm not sure. Something to do with events in St. John's life in the last few months."

"She's keeping his confidences," Constance suggested. "In which case, perhaps she thinks it is nothing to do with his murder."

"Or just none of our business. Both she and Cordell seemed to find our business rather…quaint."

"Ha," said Constance. "Quaint or otherwise, we don't appear to have found a motive for murder so far. Everyone liked him. He had no enemies. No woman had cause to be jealous. His daughter's marriage was a matter for general rejoicing. He was not short of money or respect. Of course, if one really wants to know what's going on, one should speak to the servants. Perhaps we should send Janey to make friends. If they're not too haughty to speak to maids from my establishment."

"It's worth trying. We have no idea where he was going the last time he left the house. Presumably that was when he took the opium that killed him. No one ever noticed him being ill or strange, so I doubt he was a frequent user. I think perhaps I should investigate opium dens. Though my impression is that he was too respectable for such places."

"Don't take the stuff," Constance warned. "Not even to blend in. I've seen people become hopelessly dependent on it very quickly. Can that be what happened to our man? He just took too much accidentally?"

"Where would he have got it? Not from his doctor, or the police would know by now."

"You can buy it anywhere," Constance said. "It's cheap. Like gin. Mothers give it to their teething babies. Street girls take it to for pain, sickness, or just to forget for an hour."

Solomon was startled. "Anywhere?" he repeated. "In lethal doses?"

"Well, no, in little screws of paper. No doubt an apothecary would sell it with instructions. Tobacconists, news sellers, and corner-shop grocers often sell it too. But there's nothing to stop you buying several doses at a time. The only thing is, it stinks and tastes foul, so I don't see how anyone could have poisoned his food or drink without his noticing—unless they simply increased the amount he was used to."

Solomon nodded, frowning in thought. "Along with our other inquiries, we had better discover who is so outraged by your establishment that they are planting bodies at your door."

# CHAPTER SIX

ROUND COVENT GARDEN was a thriving industry of prostitution. The streets beyond, especially toward Seven Dials, were riddled with crime of all kinds. Constance had grown up in these neighborhoods and was still familiar with them. But before she went looking for anyone who was acquainted with Nevvy, she called on the woman who was all too often the fount of all knowledge on disreputable matters: her mother.

Juliet, one-time whore and fence of stolen goods, was just opening her shop when Constance called in. Gerry, who had been her mother's assistant since he was boy, in both the nefarious and the respectable, was putting out a tasteful little display of pretty knickknacks on a small table by the door. He paused to grin at her.

"Morning, Miss Connie! She's inside, polishing her treasures."

Juliet was sitting behind the main counter, and she was indeed polishing a rather fine set of engraved silver cutlery.

"Morning, love," Juliet said, her accent surely exaggerated. "Come to buy? Or to pick my brains?"

"The latter. For now. Do you know the local vagrants?"

Juliet blinked. "I don't invite them in here. In fact, I had to chase one out yesterday."

"This one seems to have been known to the local peelers, though not a troublemaker. Probably begged in the streets. His name was Gareth Neville, but he was known as Nevvy."

"Nevvy," she repeated, frowning. "I have heard that name.

What did he look like?"

"Rough. He'd been on the streets for years. In his forties or fifties, probably, receding hair. Unexpectedly gentle-looking face, though I've no idea if that was a reflection of his character. Apparently he owned a folding pocketknife with a mother-of-pearl handle. And he suffered from consumption."

"Ah! Nevvy," Juliet said with some satisfaction. "Yes, I've seen him around. Amiable cove. I slip him a sixpence every so often when I'm feeling flush. Or a cup of tea from Les's stall."

"You won't anymore," Constance said. "He died on my doorstep a couple of nights ago."

Juliet blinked. "What the devil was he doing there?"

"Your guess is as good as mine."

"Horrible disease, consumption," Juliet said bleakly.

"It is. Do you know anything else about him?"

"Nah, he was polite enough but never chatty."

"Do you know where he slept?"

"I know where I saw him most often, huddled under the nastiest blanket you ever saw." She looked Constance up and down, noticing for the first time that her dress was old and dull and not remotely fashionable. She scowled. "I suppose you're going there. Poking your nose in."

"I am," Constance said. "You could save my having to ask directions in the street."

Juliet sighed and tore a sheet of paper from her account book. With her pencil, she drew a rough map from the corner nearest the shop, marking Les's tea stall, and an alley opposite. "It ain't pleasant."

"Neither am I," said Constance, "as you have so often pointed out."

"Are the police not looking into this? I suppose they're not bothered because he's a tramp."

"They're more concerned about the body discovered with his. A Mayfair gentleman called Terrence St. John. Ever heard of him?"

"Course not. Unless he's old enough to have been a former customer. Sounds more like one of yours."

"But he never was. He seems to have been a virtuous family man."

"They all seem like that, dear."

"Old cynic." Constance turned to go.

"Be careful," Juliet called after her. "Take Gerry with you."

Genuinely touched, Constance threw a smile over her shoulder. "Thanks. I won't need him."

Her mother was right that the area wasn't pleasant, though. Through a maze of narrow, ever-filthier streets, she found a small courtyard at the back of a baker's shop, and an alcove with a vent where a vile blanket lay abandoned and disconsolate. Glad of her gloves, she picked it up and shook it out. Nothing fell out of it.

"'Ere! What you doing with that? Spot's taken, ain't it? And that's private property!"

A pile of hair and rags charged at her from a nearby doorway and snatched the blanket from her hold. The suddenness startled Constance, but although the man within the rags was clearly angry, she judged he wasn't violent.

She held up both hands placatingly. "I wasn't stealing. I'm just looking for Nevvy's friends."

"What for?" he demanded with natural suspicion.

"Do you know he died?"

The blanket fell to the ground. "No. I didn't know. Did he go to the hospital? I told him to go."

"No, he doesn't seem to have quite got there. He died on a doorstep during the night."

The man grunted, then bent slowly to pick up the blanket. "Suppose it's mine now."

"I suppose it is," Constance said.

"He said I could," the vagrant said defensively.

"Well, he would do, since you were friends."

The man nodded curtly, clearly about to shamble back off to his own doorway.

"It was my step he died on," she said quickly. "I'm trying to find out a bit about him and how he came to be there."

"Why?"

For a moment, there seemed no answer to that would impress Nevvy's friend enough to give her any information. Eventually, with inspiration, she said, "Respect."

He seemed struck by that, gazing at her seriously before giving another of his decided nods.

"Shall we have a cup of tea and you can tell me about your friend?"

"Very well."

She walked across the road to the movable stall and ordered two cups of tea and two pies from the man who was, presumably, Les. Then she went back to the yard and found her new acquaintance ensconced in Nevvy's spot, with two blankets and a ragged bag of what must have been his own possessions.

She gave him one of the mugs, and both pies, before crouching down beside him. "What's your name? Mine is Constance."

He looked suspicious for a moment, then growled, "Harry."

"Did you know Nevvy a long time, then?" she asked.

"Near fifteen years, off and on." There was a pause while he bit into his pie and chewed, and seemed to come to a decision, because he blurted the next words in a rush. "I showed him the ropes, so to speak, when he first had nowhere to go. Then we tramped into the country together. I couldn't take it there. He did some farm laboring for a time—backbreaking work, and I couldn't do it. Couldn't take the silence, neither, and then they tried to shut me up in the workhouse, so I bolted, made my way back to London. By myself. But he came back in the end, a few years later. Maybe he shouldn't have, 'cause he got ill. Went soft sleeping in barns, I reckon, and couldn't take having no roof. Older, too, I suppose." He sniffed, though whether with grief or because his nose was running wasn't clear. "Never thought he'd go so soon, though. He said he liked going to St. Peter's 'cause they gave him a bath. Funny old bugger, was Nevvy."

"What did he do before he lived on the streets?" Constance asked.

Harry shrugged. "Dunno." There was no interest in his face or voice. His existence was too immediate to dwell on history. He put the pies carefully away in his unspeakable pocket, presumably for later, and slurped his tea. "Think he come from the country. He liked it there."

"Why did he come back to Town, then?"

"Missed his friends, he said."

"Who were his friends?"

Harry raised both hands expansively, and some of his tea slopped over his knees. He didn't seem to notice. "Everyone. People like Nevvy. Good fellow."

"Did anyone come looking for him?"

He eyed her. "Like who?"

"Like someone who doesn't live rough like you. Someone with money, perhaps. People from the hospital, or reformers, other charities…"

Harry returned to his tea, as though losing interest in her conversation. "Don't know."

She tried another tack. "Did people make him gifts?"

"He got his share of coins. Better share'n me, but he'd never let me go short, old Nevvy." He sniffed again, gazing into his tea.

"Did someone give him a pocketknife with a mother-of-pearl handle?"

"It were his," Harry said aggressively. "Told the rozzers that. He never stole it."

"Then a rich man must have given him it."

"If you say so, lady."

"What do you say?" she said swiftly.

"He always had it. Before he went to the country and after. Used it to cut food up to share. Never hurt no one with it. Only time I saw him angry was when Jimmie Gantry tried to take it off him. Knocked him out cold."

"Where would I find Jimmie Gantry?" Constance asked.

Harry pointed upward. "God rest the old sinner."

"Did Nevvy often go to Mayfair?"

Harry cast her a scornful glance. "No point. Get moved on there." It was clearly a wisdom he had lived by and accepted as gospel. He scratched his head through his tattered, filthy hat. "Nevvy got a cup of tea there once or twice, though. Didn't go often."

"Tea on the doorstep," Constance murmured. "Is that where he went the last night you saw him?"

Harry shook his head. "Peelers said so. He couldn't walk that far. Could barely shuffle. I'd brought him food and drink the last two days and he scarce moved. Gave him my blanket that night, but then I found it over me when I woke, and Nevvy'd gone. I was happy. Thought he'd perked."

Constance gazed at him. "Did someone help, then? Take him away from here?"

"Dunno. Had a nice bottle some nob set down and forgot. Gave Nevvy a slug—must have done him some good—gave him half for tomorrow, and had the rest meself. Slept till it was light." He scowled. "Then the peelers came, said a lot of lies, like he stuck some nob with his knife. Nevvy'd never do that. Good man, was Nevvy." He stared at Constance, his red-rimmed eyes suddenly angry. "Tell you what's more! He'd never have left that knife anywhere, let alone in someone's back!"

AFTER SPEAKING TO a few more vagrants and beggars, Constance lingered in the area on more usual business, talking to some old acquaintances and looking for girls she might be able to save. There would be at least two places at the establishment if she took Bibby to the house, and someone else—maybe Hat—to work at Silver and Grey. And then Juliet had talked of taking on an assistant.

A couple of them knew Nevvy as well. All in all, she had a lot to think about as she made her way to the establishment. She went straight to the kitchen, where Mrs. Cate and Bibby were busy preparing delicacies for the evening's festivities. A young violinist was contracted to entertain them, and Constance intended to make this her first public appearance at the establishment since her marriage. So the girls had two reasons to regard it as special.

"I need a word," Constance said. Since everyone else was hard at work elsewhere on their own account, the three of them were alone in the kitchen.

They both paused in their tasks and gazed at her expectantly.

"Which of you," Constance asked, sitting down at the table, "gives beggars and vagrants tea on the back doorstep?"

Bibby dropped her vegetable knife with a clatter.

Mrs. Cate scowled. "I do. Not that we get many round here, but where's the harm?"

"I suppose you bring them in when it's raining, too?" Constance said mildly.

Mrs. Cate's eyes slid away. "Only once, 'cause he looked so ill, and there was no harm to him. He went after ten minutes and I never saw him again."

Constance switched her gaze to Bibby. "Did you?"

"Me?" Bibby squeaked. "What, ma'am?"

"Did you see this man again? I presume you did see him in the kitchen."

Bibby nodded miserably. "I did. And I did see him again, though I didn't realize it at the time. It was the dead man on the doorstep. They look different, don't they, with no life?"

Constance sighed. "Yes, they do."

"The dead man was my tramp?" Mrs. Cate said, catching up slowly. "Oh dear."

"When did you realize?" Constance asked Bibby.

"Later that day, after I told the policemen I didn't know either of them. So when I realized I did and I'd lied, I couldn't go back and tell them, could I?"

"Perhaps not," Constance said steadily. "But you could have told me."

Bibby's face turned a fiery red. "I should've, maybe, but you got enough to worry about, ain't you?"

Constance blinked. It wasn't the first time she'd come across the girls' protecting her, but it always surprised her. And took the wind out of her sails.

"Did either of you see him that night?" she asked.

They both shook their heads.

"We both went up to bed before midnight," Mrs. Cate said. "That weren't no lie. The lights were all off."

Constance nodded. "Look, I don't mind tea on the doorstep. And you know your friends are welcome to call. But we can't have strangers in the house. Ever. Everyone's safety depends on that. And you have to tell me important things, like recognizing the man who died."

"Sorry, ma'am," Bibby whispered.

"I know." Constance drew a breath. "So tell me about Nevvy."

"He appears to have been a man of few words," Constance said to Solomon later, when they finally met up in his office at Silver and Grey. "But when he did speak, it was quietly and politely. Bibby said he spoke a bit like me. Admittedly, I cultivated this accent for professional purposes, but why would a vagrant trouble to do that?"

"He wouldn't," Solomon said. "Nevvy was probably hiding his natural accent but it slipped out sometimes. So you think he was educated? From a respectable family fallen on hard times?"

"Maybe. There was the knife too, too fine for such a poor man, and yet he never sold it. And according to Harry and the others I spoke to, he might have begged, but he never stole, and the only time he was roused to violence was when of their own tried to steal his knife. It was all he had, apart from a blanket. But he liked the opportunity to wash at the hospital. Something remained of a better life. No one saw him leave his doorway that night, or noticed him passing in the street. Harry thinks someone must have taken him because he was too weak to walk the distance."

Solomon frowned. "Someone brought him here to die? Or picked him off the street when he did die and brought him to your doorstep? Why?"

"I don't know. Perhaps he asked to be brought. Mrs. Cate and Bibby just confessed to feeding him with tea and kitchen scraps in the past. On the doorstep largely, and always during the day. So he could have been sitting there, waiting hopefully, when St. John came across him."

Solomon sat up straight. "What if the hospital gave Nevvy opium? What if he gave it to St. John, who took too much?"

"What, just eating it, like a child will eat sugar? It doesn't seem to fit with what we know of St. John. Unless you've learned more."

"I went to his clubs," Solomon said, "but he wasn't at any of them after midnight on the night before he died. I spoke to a couple of friends who named a tavern he was fond of, but he wasn't noticed there either. He seems to have been a convivial fellow, but no one has seen him drunk or incapable. I asked around the hackney stands, too, without luck. None of our neighbors that I spoke to, either in the houses or in the mews, saw or heard anything that could have been people unloading bodies from a vehicle before five o'clock in the morning. Your own stable lads say the same, and Jeremy is still adamant."

Constance sighed. "Then we are left with the likelihood that they came on foot and voluntarily. Which doesn't fit with either Nevvy's physical weakness or St. John's habits. Why would he be creeping around other people's back gardens?"

"Perhaps he was in the mews and saw Nevvy come in that way, followed him to see what he was up to?"

"Possible," Constance said discontentedly. "But how would we ever know?" She drummed her fingers on Solomon's desk, impatient for answers, then forced herself to stop. "How did Janey get on with the St. Johns' servants?"

"I don't know. She isn't back yet. We really do need to get someone else to hold the fort if Janey is going to be making more inquiries."

"I thought of Hat. She can read and write and she's friendly. She thinks she wants to work in a shop, but she might like this. If she doesn't, I'll send her to my mother. If you like her, I can ask her."

"Will she be there tonight?"

Constance glanced at him in surprise. "Tonight? Do you mean to come to the party?"

"I thought I might escort my wife. She's fond of music."

Though conscious of a pleasurable warmth seeping through her, Constance said anxiously, "Are you sure? You don't want to be *too* associated with the establishment."

"I already am. Unless you feel I'm smothering you..."

She seized his hand, squeezing it hard. "Never," she said fiercely. "The more I'm with you, the better I like it."

"Then anything else has been said before."

He was right. She had spoken before of her determination not to drag him down into her world in the eyes of others. He had responded with highlighting the charitable aspects of the establishment to raise her respectability. Beyond a certain point, of course, that ambition could never succeed. But at the moment, it seemed the best compromise. Especially for the girls going into respectable work.

She consulted the watch she wore pinned to her dress. "Janey must have gone straight home. We can speak to her tonight, too. Neither she nor Hat will attend the party, but they'll be around in the early part of the evening. Everyone likes to hear the music."

# CHAPTER SEVEN

ANIBAL CORDELL, KNOWN to his family and friends as Han, could not make up his mind what to do. There were many reasons for staying well away from the crescent where Terrence St. John had died, not least of which being an unwillingness to get involved and, most of all, the possibility of being seen entering the house by someone who would carry tales to his beloved.

On the other hand, Solomon Grey had made an impression on him, and the man had been right. If Han had any intention of following his own ambitions, he needed to be involved with life in all its beauty and ugliness. And he needed badly to know the truth. He wouldn't be safe, and neither would Bella, until he did know.

In the end, he left his father's house in Brook Street without a word to anyone about where he was going—much as poor St. John had done on the night he died. He tipped his hat somewhat rakishly over his face to hide his features and walked around to the crescent without passing the house of his betrothed.

Stupidly, his heart thudded in what felt very like fear. He had not been in such a place since his student days, when his older friends had taken him to some squalid house, which they had thought great fun. He supposed it had been at the time, but afterward, he had felt grubby and never inclined to repeat the experience.

The infamous Constance Silver's establishment looked nothing like that. If it differed from its neighbors on the outside, it was only that it was so very well maintained. A man appeared to be patrolling the area below the front steps, occasionally emerging onto the payment to walk a few yards in either direction before descending again.

He tipped his hat to Han as they passed at the front steps of the building.

Han could walk straight past and go on to Grosvenor Square and spend the evening with his betrothed. It would be safest, and it was certainly the course his father would urge him to pursue.

He turned up the steps and rang the bell. The door was opened almost at once by a large young man in livery.

"Good evening, sir."

"Good evening," Han said with unwonted awkwardness. He was too wary to offer his card. "I am looking for Mr. Grey."

"Please come in."

The hall was as tastefully decorated as his mother's, as was the pleasant reception room another liveried servant showed him into. The room was empty of occupants, although he could hear the chatter of voices and the tinkling of glasses drifting down from the floor above.

While Han waited, he heard the arrival of other men, but though he tensed, none of them entered the same room. They seemed to be directed, or shown, upstairs.

At last the door opened again, and Han whirled around in some panic.

Solomon Grey stood there in immaculate evening dress. Although his skin was too dark for conventionally received handsomeness, he was undoubtedly a good-looking man. Yet it was not looks that drew the attention. It was presence. One could not ignore him.

Not that Han wished to, though suddenly he felt all the disadvantage of a youth at his first formal ball where he knew no one. Grey at least looked surprised.

"Mr. Cordell." The man moved like a panther, all dark grace and danger, and yet he offered his hand like a gracious host. "Did you wish to speak privately, or would you like to join the party upstairs?"

Han shook his hand. "I'm not sure. Both, probably. You said I would learn about some social realities here."

"Then why don't you come upstairs first? The music is about to begin."

Startled all over again, Han merely inclined his head and followed Grey. A footman waited in the hall. Another stood at the top of the stairs, directing people toward a large drawing room, from where the pleasant voices and tinkling glass came from. The occasional laugh rang out, bluff and male or gently feminine.

It could have been any drawing room in Mayfair, except that the gentlemen—one or two of whom he was alarmed to recognize—outnumbered the ladies. And, as one drew closer, the ladies' accents betrayed a lesser origin.

Then a woman detached herself from a vivacious group and came toward them, smiling. Han was stunned all over again. He had never seen anyone so dazzlingly beautiful. Her red-gold hair was a shining halo, her skin translucent, stretched tightly over a fine-boned face. Her lips in particular fascinated him—long and lush, with an extra little curve at each corner.

He knew who she was, of course, even before Grey spoke. "Allow me to introduce Mr. Cordell. Sir, my wife."

It should have been ridiculous, that a man with claims to be a gentleman—or at least a respected merchant—should be so proud to have a courtesan for a wife, however beautiful. Yet when she gave Han her hand and welcomed him in a warm, cultured voice as though, just for the instant, he was the most important man in the room to her...*he* actually felt proud.

"Mr. Cordell is interested in your charitable work," Grey added.

"Thank you for that," Mrs. Grey said, raising one finger to summon a maid, who brought a tray full of glasses. Still dazed, Han took one. "I shall be happy to introduce you to our work if you can stay for an hour? Our musical recital is about to begin. Excuse me."

Han could not take his eyes off her as she flitted through the crowd, exchanging a smiling word with patrons here and there as she went. No one tried to paw her. No bawdy jokes followed her. In fact, the whole room quietened as she met a young man holding a violin. Han recognized him, too. He had seen him play in a concert…Carl Darrow.

He barely heard her brief words of introduction, spoken with what seemed to be her characteristic warmth. He felt as if he were quite out of his depth and in acute danger of drowning, and yet he didn't mind in the slightest.

This was no condition in which to face adversaries. Or even to discover if that was what they were. With something very like desperation, he dragged his gaze away from her, trying to concentrate on the music, on the audience. He recognized a bishop and an earl. Other people had squashed into the room— servants and women dressed in ordinary clothing, all listening to the music. One girl was positively entranced.

Grey must have seen his lingering gaze. "She is a budding musician," he murmured.

Even more confusing, when the recital had ended, Mrs. Grey took the girl to meet Darrow before he could speak to any of her more important guests.

"Who were those other young women who have now vanished?" Han asked Grey, who was still with him. "Do they live and work here?"

"Yes, for now."

"They were not dressed to please," Han said delicately.

"They don't do that kind of work. You have to think of this place as a co-operative. Everyone contributes and everyone has their needs met as far as possible. Edith, the musician you noticed, is studying music; another is learning bookkeeping. One is about to become a clerk with a respectable company, and one is returning to her profession as a cook. Another is learning the same trade. The maids who serve this evening will go into formal service, either domestically or in hotels and eating houses."

"From *here*?" Han stared. "Why?"

"Because Constance found them on the street. If you wish to describe it so, they all have one thing in common—they are what the world smugly calls *fallen women*. Constance helps raise them up again in whatever way they wish."

"And if they wish to remain...?" He trailed off, reluctant to say the word for some reason.

"In the same profession?" Grey said coolly. "Then they are safer doing so here, with food and shelter and medical care, where violent men cannot beat them or abuse them. These women's stories are appalling. They should make us ashamed, angry, determined to help. And yet we turn our backs because they are *fallen women*. Some even regard that as their Christian duty, while the men who used and abused them—in some cases even caused their fall in the first place—walk freely amongst us as respected members of the church and Society."

"That is a novel way of looking at things," Han said slowly.

"It just requires a little thought. Who achieves more? The reformers who preach repentance for a heavenly reward? Or my wife, who provides them with food and shelter without judgment, and gives them a real chance to better themselves?" Grey gave a deprecating smile. "But you need not listen to me rambling on. You may speak to whomever you wish."

"Is that a euphemism?" Han asked, suddenly suspicious.

"No," Mrs. Grey said, suddenly appearing beside him. "You have to pay for the euphemism."

"W̲HY HAS HE come?" Constance asked Solomon in a private moment, while Cordell spoke to Carl Darrow, Sarah, and Hildie.

"Partly because he's genuinely interested. I think he's looking for a cause, lots of causes, to give him the courage to defy his father and go into politics. And partly…I think he wants to tell us something."

"About St. John?"

"Hopefully."

Before the guests had arrived, they had already heard about Janey's inquiries among the St. John servants. On the night their master had died, he had not used a horse or the carriage. The servants all seemed to have been genuinely fond of him, although they were warier of his wife. The son, Anthony, was a quiet, polite boy preparing for university in the autumn. The daughter, Bella, was a little full of herself since her engagement. Some of the servants were afraid Cordell would call the wedding off because of the scandal of their master's death.

"They claim he was a good man with no vices," Janey had said with blatant disbelief. "Always faithful to his wife. Although they slept in different rooms."

"Many couples do, if they have the space," Constance had said mildly. "Especially as they grow older. Did you get the impression they had quarreled?"

"No," Janey said doubtfully. She scowled, clearly struggling for the right words. "I had the impression they weren't…close."

"As a family?" Solomon asked.

She shook her head. "They both seem to have been devoted to the children—spoiled them, even. Both were thrilled by the engagement. The wedding gown and the full trousseau are already ordered from the most expensive dressmaker in town. The parents were happy, just not…with each other. They rarely did anything together, except for show."

"Was *she* unfaithful?" Constance asked.

"No such whisper from the servants," Janey said. "But then, there probably wouldn't be, would there? They're good, loyal people."

"Well done," Constance had told her. "Perhaps you should try neighboring servants tomorrow? Come into the office first, though. I want you to show Hat what to do in the office…"

Janey had certainly provided a better impression of the family's reality, but Constance looked forward to whatever they could learn from Cordell, who was almost inside it. The man had watched her all evening. She was not blind to his admiration. After all, inspiring such attraction had become second nature to her. He might have come from mere curiosity, but he was not here for the girls. On the other hand, would he know from her marriage to Solomon that she was off the menu? He had no way of knowing that she had never been on it.

"Let's take him for a short talk in private," Constance murmured. It was important for the business that she be seen here, but she did not want to stay late. She had thought she would miss this place, the company, the friendships, her lovely, private rooms upstairs, but she didn't. Or, at least, not nearly as much as she'd imagined. The new house, full of Solomon, had become home very quickly.

As Constance and Solomon approached, Hildie strolled off toward the bishop who was her regular.

"So how would I make a donation to this establishment?" Cordell asked as they led him from the room and across the hall to the currently empty small salon.

Solomon closed the door. "In any form you wish. A few coins, a bank draft, banknotes—all are welcome."

"And I can do this without being—er…a member of your club?"

"Of course."

"And do you report on how my money is used?"

"Indeed we will. As a formal charity, it has only just begun, but we now have a board with a duty to oversee accounts and so on. Basically, donations are kept separate from our other sources of income, and are spent on education, apprenticeships, suitable clothing and equipment, and rents to give girls a start in decent lodgings if they need them."

"And your own salary, Mrs. Grey?"

"Oh, no," Constance replied. "My income is quite separate. You need not rush into anything, you know. We shan't keep you here until you pay up."

He blushed. "I never suspected such a thing. But this is all new to me. I have never come across quite such an establishment before."

"I don't believe there is another," Constance said brazenly. "We are unique. Shall we sit and be comfortable? Have you learned what you wanted to this evening?"

"Some, certainly, in unexpected areas."

"Mr. St. John was not a member here," Constance said. "He never visited in any capacity."

"I never truly thought he did," Cordell said. "He was an innocent, in many ways. Unworldly. To be honest, I doubt he even knew what this house was, or if he had heard of its existence. Which makes it even odder, for me, that he was found on your doorstep."

Solomon sat down beside Constance. "I imagine you are acquainted with many people around Grosvenor Square. Have you ever heard of any ill feeling toward the inhabitants of this establishment?"

Cordell looked slightly surprised, but thought about it before shaking his head. "No, I don't think so. A few men regard it as something of an amusing joke, but no one ever admits to seeing it from the inside." His lips twitched. "Though some clearly do." He glanced at Constance and then back to Solomon. "To be frank," he said, "I did want to speak to you about poor St. John's murder. It troubles his family deeply, and I know you are curious on your own account to know what happened. I daresay you don't like this household living under police suspicion either."

With difficulty, Constance kept her face as politely expressionless as possible. "The situation is not good for anyone. Least of all for the two dead men."

"Exactly. Which leads me to my other reason for coming. You intrigued me, Mr. Grey, when you told me of your inquiry business. I would like to employ your firm to discover the truth about the murder of Terrence St. John."

"WHY DO YOU think he did that?" Constance asked suddenly. She and Solomon were lying in bed together, wrapped around each other in those peaceful moments before sleep overwhelmed them. Or, at least, it should have done. For some reason, she felt wide awake.

Solomon's eyes didn't open. "What? Employed us?"

"Yes."

"Probably because he thinks he can control what comes out of our investigation."

Constance propped herself up on one elbow. "He thinks he's *bought* us?"

Solomon pulled her down again and kissed her forehead and mouth. "He hasn't signed the contract yet. I'll make sure he understands the limits of our loyalty to our clients."

"It isn't just that… Whom is he afraid for? It must be his betrothed, Bella."

"Not necessarily. Families tend to rise and fall together. The ruin of one affects them all. And he could just want their innocence proved beyond doubt."

"Do you think he would jilt Bella if we couldn't prove that?"

"Such disloyalty would not look good for him either—unless we find proof that she or her mother or brother committed murder, in which case, the world might well be more understanding. His father appears to be a stickler for convention, but young Cordell is reaching for his own independence."

"You like him?" Constance asked.

"I might. If he didn't kill St. John."

"Why would he?"

"I can't think of a reason. Unless St. John was aware of some secret that made Cordell an ineligible son-in-law."

"Or St. John had a secret that made him an ineligible father-in-law." Constance wriggled. "What was he doing on our doorstep? If they weren't brought there deliberately, why were they together? What were they doing?"

"Waiting for a cup of tea from your Mrs. Cate or Bibby," Solomon said.

"The lights were out in the kitchen by midnight," Constance objected. "They must have known there would be no tea that night. But then, Nevvy must have used the last of his strength to get there. Perhaps he just couldn't leave."

"And St. John was dying too, so they just died in company? Why was St. John dying? Where did the poison come from?"

Several memories flashed into Constance's mind, scenes from her childhood right through to this afternoon. Ragged, homeless men huddled in doorways, drinking with friends, passing round a bottle. Arguing over a bottle. Fighting with a bottle.

"Drinking," she said. "I'll bet you all you have. Two men on a doorstep, both of amiable disposition though of entirely different worlds. Lonely men for some reason. They were drinking."

This time it was Solomon who loomed up on his elbow. "Drinking from a bottle laced with opium! Of course they were. And Nevvy was so riddled with tuberculosis that I'll bet they never looked inside his stomach. He could have been collecting opium from the hospital for months, saving it up for one last drink to end his suffering for good."

It made horrible, tragic sense. Apart from a couple of important points. "But why would he give it to St. John? Why would St. John drink it? Unless he was completely wheelbarrowed, he would have noticed it tasted disgusting. He'd never have drunk enough to kill himself."

"He was worried," Solomon mused. "He could easily have got vilely drunk after he sent his valet away, and then, in the way of drunks, decided to go out again."

"To my back garden," Constance said discontentedly. "Perhaps it made sense when he was so well oiled."

"And there is the fact that the police searched your garden as well as the bodies, and found no discarded bottles. Still, I think we might have something to investigate tomorrow."

Constance considered that. "I'll bet there are places in the garden they never thought of looking. We need to speak to Jeremy in the morning."

"Very early in the morning," Solomon said sleepily, "if we're to meet Cordell at the office…"

# CHAPTER EIGHT

Solomon and Constance alighted from the carriage in the mews, which were only just stirring with yawning grooms and the sounds of horses stamping for their breakfast, and entered the garden from the back gate. As they approached the house, Solomon could hear the distinctive sweeping of Jeremy's broom at the front.

"There should be someone up and making tea," Constance said cheerfully, marching toward the back door. The smell of horses seemed to be following them, which was odd. Until Constance halted so suddenly that Solomon walked into her and flung his arm around her to steady her.

"Give a man some warning," he said lightly.

She ignored that, raising her hand to point at the back door-step. "Look."

A large pile of horse manure steamed gently on its plinth.

"What the...?"

"Horses don't jump into gardens, reverse up to doors, and lift their tails," Constance said in a small, hard voice. "This is deliberate nastiness. Jeremy!"

As the big lad came running to answer her call, Solomon looked for footprints on the path or the garden, anything to give a clue. As with the appearance of the bodies, there didn't seem to be any. It was a pity it had not rained in days.

Uneasily, Solomon looked over at the houses on either side. There could be no doubt that this was malicious. Had someone got the idea of leaving unpleasant gifts for an unwanted neighbor from Tuesday morning's discovery? Or was it the same black-humored joker?

"I'll get a bucket and shovel, ma'am," Jeremy said, subdued. "Won't take a moment."

Tight-lipped, Constance watched him.

Solomon took her hand. She had never expected to be liked or welcomed here. She had never been naïve. But this deliberate nastiness with its implied accusation of "Filth!" delivered in secret after the shock of Tuesday's discovery…

It angered Solomon. Clearly, it had shaken Constance, and would do long after all physical signs of the outrage had gone. She clung to his fingers and took a deep breath.

"So much for civilized neighborhoods. I suppose you saw or heard no sign of the delivery, Jeremy?" she asked.

He shook his head. "Reckon it was before light."

"Maybe," Solomon said as another possibility struck him, "it's supposed to be a warning to us to stop asking questions."

Constance shook her head. "Even if we do stop, the police won't. They might if it was just Nevvy. But for St. John?"

"Respectable families don't want the police poking around," Solomon reminded her. "I doubt they want us either."

"A pity when they've just got my attention." Her voice was still hard, and for the first time he caught that hint of ruthlessness that had helped her build her business from nothing, besting rivals and enemies alike to reach her goal. This establishment was her achievement, her life's work, her pride. And she, who called herself all sorts of names without illusion, was insulted. And frightened.

"It's trivial," Solomon insisted. "Now, let's have a cup of tea inside and concentrate on the reasons we came. Jeremy, how thoroughly did the police search the garden the morning the bodies were found? Could they have missed a bottle, for example?"

Jeremy, filling a fresh bucket from the pump under the window, spoke over his shoulder. "I don't know. I didn't watch them. But I never found no bottles hiding under bushes, nor in the potting shed, nor the wood shed, neither." He carried his bucket to the step, threw the water over it, and brushed it clear before indicating they could now pass cleanly to the back door and tea.

CONSTANCE DIDN'T WANT to admit how shaken she was by what looked like a silly schoolboy prank. She wasn't quite sure what upset her so, whether coming so soon and in the same place as the bodies made it disrespectful, or whether it was simply the idea of someone actively hating her enough to do this.

She was used to being disapproved of. In many ways, she even gloried in it. But hate was different.

However, after a few minutes with Solomon in the familiar surroundings of the kitchen, she was ready to face the garden again, and they took their tea outside.

"Would drunks bother to hide their evidence?" Solomon asked. "Aren't they more likely to just abandon it or toss it to one side, out of the way?"

Constance sat down on the clean, drying doorstep and made throwing motions with her right arm, at first straight ahead in the direction of the herb garden, which Jeremy tended religiously, and the little lawn beyond. Then she tossed her imaginary bottle to the right and suspected it would have broken on the path or rolled into the wall. She tried to the left.

At best, it would probably have hit the potting shed door and probably broken on the path or…

Jeremy leaned his broom against the wall. "Sometimes things get stuck under the shed," he said, ambling toward it.

The shed was on a stone plinth but built to overhang it by several inches. Jeremy crouched down, peering into the space.

"It's not a bottle," he reported, much to Constance's disappointment.

But he stretched flat on the stone and thrust his hand under the shed. Constance and Solomon were on either side of him when he bounced back up and revealed his discovery.

Not a bottle, but a gentleman's leather-and-silver pocket flask.

For a second, all three of them stared at it.

"Oh, well done, Jeremy," Constance breathed, and the gardener shook a couple of insects off it and held it out toward them with distinct unease.

Solomon took it, checked the stopper was in place, and gave it a little shake. It seemed to be empty. He took out the stopper and sniffed it, then jerked his head back almost immediately, grimacing.

"Opium," he said, holding the stopper out to Constance.

She smelled it too, stale, but still distinctive, invoking distant memories from childhood that she hadn't understood at the time, and more recent ones of sickbeds and lost friends.

Solomon replaced the stopper. "Well, that's how he took the opium." He dusted some dirt and a clinging leaf from the flask and turned it over. "Smells like laudanum, only more intense. Definitely St. John's, I'd say." The engraved initials were clear enough: *TSJ*.

"Not new," Constance observed, touching the old scratches and the worn patches of leather. She glanced back at the step. "If he'd thrown this away, would it have slid under the shed like that? Or did he put it there deliberately?"

"Why would he do that?" Solomon asked.

She shrugged. "I don't know. To hide his identity? Conceal the opium? Perhaps Nevvy hid it, because the opium was his and he was afraid of a murder charge."

"And then sat back down beside St. John and inconveniently died? Wouldn't he have bolted to separate himself from the crime?"

"He was in no condition to bolt. The miracle seems to be that he made it this far. There's something going on here we don't understand."

"A good deal," Solomon agreed. "If they were having a jolly, foul-tasting drink together, how and why, and by whom, were the bodies shifted into the odd positions you found them in? If they were moved here by someone else, who?"

"And why?"

Solomon wrapped the flask in his very white handkerchief and pocketed it. "I suppose I should take this to Inspector Harris."

"He'll scold his men for not finding it."

"And so he should," Solomon said austerely, allowing her one of those rare glimpses into his life as a successful man who expected the best of all his employees. "But first, we need to meet Cordell at the office."

"We can take Janey and Hat with us…"

HANIBAL CORDELL PRESENTED himself at the Silver and Grey offices punctually at nine o'clock. The rather endearing uncertainty he had betrayed at the establishment last night had vanished and he was once again the self-possessed, almost arrogant young man of birth, wealth, and privilege.

Janey, showing Hat how it was done, announced the visitor to Solomon and Constance almost as soon as they had sat down for a cup of tea. Fortunately, Janey had thought to supply a third cup, so there was no need of interruptions once they were all seated around Solomon's impressive desk.

"Pleasant office," Cordell remarked. "It speaks of both comfort and efficiency."

"That was our aim," Solomon said. "The details are Constance's. Our usual contract, with our fees outlined, is in front of you—if you still wish to engage us. In full honesty, I have to tell you that while we treat private matters with unswerving confidentiality, we will never conceal crimes, whoever has committed them. So you must consider that before you sign the document."

The man's gaze had been on Constance. He had looked a lot last night, too. Solomon didn't blame him for that. Nor did it necessarily betoken a hidden agenda. But as his eyes met Solomon's, they were definitely thoughtful.

"I think," Cordell said slowly, "you would have gone on investigating without my engaging your services. I am not trying to buy your results, merely to ensure you don't give up in favor of some more pressing case. I need to know what happened to St. John, and so does Bella."

"Does Bella know you are employing us in the matter?" Constance asked.

"Not yet," Cordell said steadily, "but I shall tell her."

"And will you tell her who we are? Who I am?"

"That you own the house where he was found? Yes, probably. She doesn't know what the property is."

"Won't she want to meet us?" Constance asked curiously. "Will you allow that?"

Cordell hesitated, but only for an instant. "If you had asked me before last night, I would have said no. Now...I will not take her to that house, but I have no objections to your meeting."

It irked Solomon that the world did not accept her. It irked him more that he had once regarded her in a similar light. Fascinating perhaps, desirable most certainly, but not for Polite Society.

Constance only smiled. "Don't worry. I shan't appall anyone by calling on the ladies. And they have already met Solomon. It would be helpful if one of us could speak more frankly to Miss St. John at least, and preferably to her mother and brother."

"Why?" Cordell asked blankly.

"Because something in St. John's life, past or present, must have led him to our doorstep, and frankly, we are struggling to discover what. A greater knowledge of the man and his family might help."

Cordell licked his lips. "I'll see what I can do," he said at last, and picked up the contract.

Solomon was pleased to see that he read it thoroughly yet quickly, then reached for the pen beside him and signed his name clearly on both copies. So did Solomon.

"Tell us your impressions of the St. John family," Constance said. "Were they comfortable together? Happy?"

"As happy as most. I would say they indulged their children more than my parents did, but it has done them no harm."

"The children respected both parents?" Solomon asked, setting aside the Silver and Grey copy of the agreement.

"Oh yes."

"And were the parents a happy couple?" Constance asked more brazenly.

"I never saw them quarrel."

"Was that because they were in perfect, loving accord? Or because they were rarely in the same room?"

Cordell fidgeted. "Is that relevant?"

"We have established," Solomon said, "that in the last few weeks of his life, something worried Mr. St. John. Was it his wife?"

Cordell looked genuinely surprised. "Why, no, I would doubt it. They were amicable, never did anything to displease each other."

"What did they do to *please* each other?" Constance asked. "Did they give each other gifts? Did they laugh together? What did they do as a whole family?"

Cordell leaned back in his chair. Solomon could almost see him readjusting his thoughts to a different point of view, reconsidering.

"Actually," he said, "I never saw or heard them do anything to please each other specifically. Apart from St. John agreeing to escort Bella and her mother to some formal party, or to the theatre, or to be present at some gathering at the house. I never saw them give each other any gifts. They laughed—St. John more than Mrs. St. John—but now that I think about it, it was never together, except when Bella or her brother were being amusing. The whole family met at the dining table most nights, but otherwise, it tended to be one parent or the other. Apart from the formal occasions I already mentioned." He refocused his gaze on Solomon. "I don't believe that is unusual in couples of that age and class. They drift apart and enjoy their own lives."

It sounded just a little defensive. Perhaps his own parents existed in a similar kind of relationship. Solomon wondered if such apathy would ever overtake Constance and himself and could not imagine it.

"And there was no concern about either of the children?" Constance asked.

"No. Though Anthony is quite eager to get away."

"Why?"

Cordell shrugged. "I don't know. I always thought it was just a young man's need to spread his wings and be independent."

"Was there any conflict with his father?" Constance asked. "There often is between fathers and sons of that age."

"I never saw any arguments. St. John was proud of him, especially his academic achievements. They *did* laugh together."

Constance was busy taking notes. Cordell was watching her.

Solomon asked, "What did St. John do with his time? What were his interests?"

Cordell's mouth opened, and then closed as he frowned. "Actually, I don't know. He spoke amiably on lots of subjects, spent a great deal of time in his study with books."

"Books on what?" Solomon asked.

"Poetry. He was very fond of poetry. Classical literature. But he was also interested in modern science and engineering, bridges, railways, machines..."

"And when he left his study, when he went out, when he wasn't accompanying his family, where did he go?"

Cordell shrugged a little helplessly. "His clubs. Various lectures on geography, archaeology, science... I don't really know, to be honest." His face brightened. "He did go to musical concerts at lunchtimes occasionally."

"Do you know where?"

"No," Cordell sighed. "I always liked him, you know, but you've made me realize how little I actually *knew* him. He was a very private man."

A man with something to hide? Did he really go to all these lectures and concerts, or were they just cover for hours spent in an opium den?

As Cordell rose to leave, he said, "I don't want the truth to sully St. John's reputation, just remove the uncertainty to let the family grieve in peace."

Solomon thought of his own long search for David, of the oddities and tragedies that had come out of other investigations. "The truth isn't always what you want to hear. One last question for now…" He delved into his pocket and unwrapped the flask. "Do you recognize this?"

Cordell glanced at it. "Can't say I do. He picked it up and turned it over, his eyebrows arching. "TSJ? Is it St. John's?"

"We hoped you could tell us that," Constance said.

"I'm afraid I can't. I never saw it in the house, and I never saw him use it."

WITH CONSTANCE'S APPROVAL, Janey left Hat in charge of the office and returned to Mayfair. Hat was bright and orderly, once you got to know her, and providing she didn't try to speak in that refined accent that made Janey giggle, she was presentable too. Janey felt good about training her for the position she herself had held for several months now.

She was even more glad of the trust Constance and Mr. Grey had placed in her, and of her own step up to the investigative side of the business. It was as if she had found her own purpose in a world that had once daunted, baffled, and cowed her into a creature that was half animal. Now she was striding out, spreading her wings, doing good work. Sometimes she even got to work with Lenny…

But she knew better than to think too much about him. He was unattainable because of her past and his own tragedy, and most of the time it was enough that they were friends, even just on a superficial level, and that he liked her company. Oh yes, life was good.

The pleasure of seeing Constance happy added immeasurably to her sense of wellbeing. Not that she had been *un*happy before Solomon Grey, but Janey had watched the change in her and was curiously proud. Perhaps it also gave her hope. Constance, the best of them, had found love and a home. Maybe it wasn't impossible for Janey and the others either.

It infuriated her that someone was trying to hurt Constance, hurt all of them, with the nasty prank of the horse manure. And if the bodies had been a prank too, well, that was unspeakable.

For all of those reasons, she threw herself into the investigation, beginning in the mews with casual chat among the stable boys and coachmen. Since Janey had spent the last few months working at Silver and Grey, she recognized very few of the local servants, nor they her. Those nearest the establishment had already spoken to the police about the bodies on the doorstep, so she let them bring the subject up if they wished. The questions she asked were about their employers, and what they thought of the house of ill repute.

To most of the outdoor staff, it was a mere rumor. They had never seen anything untoward outside the house in question. Once or twice, a house servant stole a few minutes to join in the gossip, but no one invited her to the kitchen for a cup of tea until she was at the fourth garden along the crescent, where they were interrupted by no less a person than the housekeeper, who had come in person to pass a message to the coachman. Despite her vast seniority, she seemed prepared to listen from on high to lower-servant gossip.

"Hadn't you better run along back to your own work?" she said to Janey after they had discussed the vast number of carriages blocking the square last week during Lady Hardcastle's ball.

"Oh, it's my half day," Janey lied happily. "I got no family to visit, and no money to spend."

"So you thought to loiter in the mews distracting our servants instead?"

Janey grinned. "Well, most people can talk and work at the same time. I do meself. But I get lonely sometimes."

That was rather blatant manipulation that she had learned in her previous trade. Sometimes a fellow feeling was enough to make a man notice and take the bait. Some women too, apparently, for the housekeeper said, "Come and have a quick cup of tea with us, then. Just one, mind. I'm Mrs. Robertson, housekeeper for Mrs. Willow and her sister."

Janey did not have to feign her delight. All the servants seemed to have gathered for a short break under Mrs. Robertson's eye. There was no butler in this establishment, only one footman in livery, and another manservant who did everything from boot polishing to gardening. The other indoor staff were female, three maids and a cook.

"It's lovely to meet a friendly household like this," Janey enthused. "You must be lucky in your positions with a kind mistress."

Interestingly, a few glances were exchanged. One of the maids sniggered into her cup.

"They're good Christian ladies," Mrs. Robertson said repressively. "They lead us in prayer every evening and make sure we have all we need."

"Can't fault that," Janey said. She set down her cup, widening her eyes. "Here, though, they can't think much of *that* household!" She jerked her head vaguely in the direction of the establishment. "There was even a *murder* there."

"I heard there were two," one of the maids said. "And the

police even came asking questions, two doors down—my friend Millie, the parlor maid there, told me. It were awful."

"Yes, but in *this* house we don't talk about low subjects like murders," Mrs. Robertson said firmly.

"Don't talk about it much in ours either," Janey said, not entirely truthfully. "Bit gruesome and not at all polite. But when the police ask you questions, you got to answer."

"The police asked you questions?" Mrs. Robertson sounded shocked. Around the table, they all looked both appalled and eager. "Are they going to shut down that house?"

"Why would they do that? They're not even sure them bodies died there. They might have been brought, you know, to hide the truth. They asked me what I saw, which was nothing. Don't suppose you saw anything, neither?" She made it only a very slight question, as though she had already assumed the answer.

One of the maids giggled. "Saw her next door coming home at four in the morning. Ten minutes before her husband did!"

Mrs. Robertson scowled. "Decorum, Mavis!"

"Sorry, Mrs. Robertson."

"Drink up," the housekeeper commanded. "Time to get back to work."

"Idle hands," remarked a very different voice, and everyone jumped to their feet, including Janey.

A thin lady with neat gray hair, dressed all in unadorned black, stood in the kitchen doorway.

"Madam," Mrs. Robertson said, "what can I do for you?" As she spoke she was waving the servants back to work, and, abandoning their tea, they scattered like a flock of birds disturbed by a dog in the park.

The lady, who was presumably their employer, regarded this flurry of motion with clear satisfaction. "I am just returning the inventory of..." Her sharp, beady eyes had found Janey, the cuckoo in the nest who had been edging reluctantly toward the back door. Janey froze.

"Oh, this is a neighbor's girl who joined us for a few minutes on her half day. She is just going."

"Yes, she is," thundered the lady. "And she won't be back! Get you hence, girl, back to that den of iniquity that has been foisted upon us! And tell your evil mistress to begone from the sight of decent people."

*Rumbled,* Janey thought, trying not to laugh. And yet, as she swaggered out of the suddenly silent kitchen and across the back garden to the mews, she found her legs were shaking.

# CHAPTER NINE

L EAVING THE CARRIAGE for Constance's use, Solomon took a hackney to Scotland Yard, where he was lucky enough to catch Inspector Harris in his office. The man rose to shake hands over his desk, eyeing Solomon with his usual mixture of displeasure and interest.

"I was wondering when you would appear. Sit down."

Solomon took the handkerchief-wrapped flask from his pocket and laid it on the desk before he sat. "We found that this morning, under the garden shed, where it might have been kicked by accident or by design. It reeks of opium."

Harris's eyebrows flew up. Silently, he unwrapped the flask, examined it, and sniffed it. He grimaced. "It does. The question is, was it always there and my fools missed it? Or did someone plant it there for you to find later?"

"I can't see what their objective would be in that," Solomon said. "On the other hand, someone is definitely trying to cause trouble for Constance." He told Harris about the manure piled on the back doorstep.

The policeman looked only vaguely interested. "I don't have the men to investigate quarrels between neighbors."

"Even if your murdered bodies are an extension of that quarrel?"

"Murdered *body*," Harris corrected him. "Singular."

"Really? Was there an autopsy on Nevvy? If they weren't put on that step from different places, isn't it likely they were drinking together?"

"There's no proof of that."

"There's no proof of anything very much," Solomon retorted. "But Constance did say Nevvy's fingers were curled as if he'd been holding something."

"He can't have been holding it *and* kicking it under the shed."

Solomon sighed. "I know. And I see no reason for St. John to have been drinking with vagrants. He seems to have been a refined sort of fellow, and had no shortage of friends."

"On the other hand," Harris said thoughtfully, "the doctor at the hospital did give Neville some opium a couple of weeks ago. And a month before that. If he saved it up and put it all in the flask full of brandy, I suppose it could have killed both of them. But why would St. John have drunk anything so foul? Unless he was in the habit…"

"Was he?"

"Not according to his family or his servants. There was a bottle of laudanum in the house for emergencies, but the housekeeper swore it hadn't been touched since the boy broke his arm falling off a horse in the park two years ago."

"Did you speak to the family physician?"

"We did. He had no concerns over the health of any of the family. Hadn't seen St. John since he came to treat the boy's arm. His family, his friends, all thought he was in perfect health."

"But worried…" Solomon drummed his fingers on the desk. "Still no witnesses?"

"Not to murder, and not to the loading or unloading of bodies."

"The same with us," Solomon said restlessly. "So far. Tell me, when they were interviewing neighboring households, did your men find any ill feeling toward Constance's establishment? Outrage, I mean, rather than mere disapproval."

Harris shook his head. "No. My instinct is the bodies died where they were. Though why they were there…"

"Constance's cook occasionally gave vagrants a cup of tea to drink on the doorstep," Solomon admitted. "She may even have let them in, which is strictly against the rules, so she never admitted it. Her assistant remembered Nevvy's face, though only after she'd calmed down enough to think. Neither of them were lying. Mrs. Cate never saw the bodies."

Harris grunted. It changed nothing important in his eyes.

"What about his finances?" Solomon asked. "Did you get access to his bank?"

"Yes, through his solicitor. He was very well off, no troubles, although he was shelling out extraordinary amounts of money for his daughter's wedding. Gowns, champagne, an elaborate breakfast, new jewelry. In all, more than the rest of us are likely to earn in our lifetimes. Present company excepted."

"Could he afford it?"

"Apparently so."

"Any payments that were odd? Unaccountable to you or the solicitor?"

"If you're thinking blackmail," Harris said, "I'd be surprised. I found nothing to suggest it. In fact, the man appears to have been beyond reproach. No one has had a bad word to say about him. No affairs—unless you count the Paul woman, which seems to have been an open secret—and nothing to hold over his head. His wife knows about it. So does Cordell, the girl's prospective father-in-law."

"Have you met Cordell senior, then? What is he like?"

"Very upright and rigid. Not quite a caricature, but a decent man, well respected."

"Does he approve of the marriage?"

"Heartily."

Solomon smiled wryly. "You know, in most of our cases, we have so many suspects that we have trouble ruling them all out. In this case, we can find no one who wished the man ill, or would benefit from his death—I suppose that would only be his son?"

"In trust until he is twenty-one. But yes. The family is all taken care of, and the servants have small legacies according to how long they have been with the family. Charities benefit too to some degree."

"What did you think of the marriage?"

"Cordial. No complaints on either side."

"You see?" Solomon said. "No damned suspects. Dare I ask what lines of inquiry you are pursuing?"

"Looking at Nevvy the vagrant, but there's no obvious connection, except for the hospital. It may be that it was just a horrible accident. One sick man and another in his cups, finding some kind of solace in each other's company."

"Do you believe that?" asked Solomon.

"I'm beginning to," Harris said morosely.

FROM SCOTLAND YARD, Solomon delved into the darker regions along the Thames, heading eastward toward Limehouse. In his convoluted voyage from Jamaica, which ended in London, he had visited Hong Kong and mainland China. He had seen opium dens and knew roughly where to look in London. But even the most opulent he had seen in the East had depressed him. The hot, airless, stinking dens of East London were almost unbearable. And quite useless, since the owners were close-lipped to the point of pretending not to understand him, and the patrons mostly too addled to be reliable.

After his third visit to a den, he found a hackney to take him back to the office. He was convinced he had wasted his time. He could not imagine the fastidious St. John in such a place, even to buy opium to smoke somewhere else later. Besides, wasn't the preparation of the drug for smoking different from that used in laudanum, and the powdered variety bought from apothecaries?

*Perhaps St. John and Nevvy simply swapped, and St. John bought the opium with his entire wallet.*

But why?

Increasingly discontented, Solomon returned to the office to think. He read through the notes that Constance had begun, and then added the minor snippets he had learned from Harris. He felt frustrated by how little they were learning. What they needed was Constance's view of the family. And that was impossible.

On top of which, the malicious manure incident bothered him far too much. Since Constance's poisoning in Venice, he had grown vastly overprotective of her and had to force himself to bite his tongue and stay his hand, especially if he allowed the possibility that it was something to do with the murder of St. John.

A knock at his office door heralded the unfamiliar face of the new girl, Hat. He was so used to Janey that it took him a moment to realize who she was.

"A lady to see you, sir." She darted over to give him a visiting card. "Miss Paul."

Surprised, he said, "Show her in, if you please."

"Should I make tea?" Hat asked nervously.

"Yes, please."

She vanished, only to announce, "Miss Paul, sir," a moment later.

Zenobia Paul's outdoor dress was as eccentric as he could have imagined, all bright, flowing shawls and something remarkably like an orange turban on her head. He was struck once again by the contrast between her fantastical appearance and her civil but down-to-earth manners.

"Mr. Grey," she greeted him, holding out her hand. "Thank you for seeing me."

He took her hand and bowed over it. "Please sit down. Hat will bring tea."

"Oh, there is no need. I merely brought you the list of Terrence's good friends that we spoke of previously." She rummaged inside a large cloth bag that had blended with her shawls, and emerged with a slightly crumpled piece of paper, which she handed to him before she sat in the comfortable chair by the low table. "I have added addresses where I know them, and occupations to give you a clue. They are rather a motley collection of artists, writers, naturalists, even radical thinkers. Some of them are very old friends, from childhood, like me. I've marked those too. The people I've spoken to didn't see him the night before he died, though."

"Thank you," Solomon said, accepting the list. "This could be just what we need. To be honest, we are struggling for direction in this case."

"What do you mean?"

"I mean…Mr. St. John remains elusive to us. Everyone seemed to like him. Or, at least, no one *dis*liked him enough to murder him. We are beginning to think it was an accident, although the circumstances remain obscure."

He cast his gaze over the list, while Hat brought in a tray and seemed unsure where to put it. He indicated the space in front of him without looking at her. "Here is fine."

"Shall I pour, sir?"

Her anxiety finally penetrated his thoughts, and he glanced up at her with a quick smile. "No, we'll manage. Thank you, Hat."

The girl smiled with relief and hurried away.

"New staff?" Zenobia asked.

"Her first day with us."

"You are a kind man," she said with the odd abruptness he recalled from their previous meeting. "One can generally judge people quite accurately by how they treat their servants."

"How did St. John treat his?"

"Like people."

It was a telling phrase, and it struck a chord. Inequality was a fact of life, just or otherwise. But his early life among wealthy plantation owners, slaves, paid workers, rebels, and soldiers had taught him the importance of seeing the humanity in all, good and ill. This woman saw it too. Born into a privileged class, she must have battled for her independence in a man's world and paid for it in many ways. She saw clearly, but there was no resentment in her.

Solomon poured the tea, politely offering milk and sugar before asking, "Did he ever dismiss servants?"

"I imagine that was his wife's business, but he would not allow it if it was unjust."

"I am thinking of the last month, when you said he was concerned about something. Did he confide anything about his servants to you?"

She thought about it. "Nothing bad."

Solomon returned to the list, struggling to turn his instincts into words. "These people—including yourself—were whom he *chose* as his friends, not those who were his mere neighbors or natural allies in the world he was born into. Free thinkers, free *doers*, who don't live according to custom but to their own views and whims. Was that what he truly wished to be? Was he *crushed* by the conventionality of his public life?"

Color flooded her face, which he was at a loss to account for. Embarrassment? Shame, because she had inadvertently given away her friend's confidences? For a moment, he wondered if she would bolt or just snatch the list of names back from him.

She did neither, merely reached for her teacup. "In a way, yes. But never think he did not love his family. He did. They were the world to him."

"And *this* world," Solomon said slowly, with a flick of the list, "this was his escape?"

"Yes, I suppose it was." But she wasn't looking at him now. She was drinking tea, her shoulders tense.

"What are you not telling me?" he asked abruptly.

Surprise often worked, but she seemed to be ready for the accusation. She even looked and sounded faintly amused. "My dear sir, I am trying to help you discover what happened to my friend. I want you to succeed."

"And if what we need is whatever you are hiding?"

"I have kept back nothing that is relevant."

"Are you the best judge of that?"

She smiled serenely. "Yes, I am."

Along with his frustration at that blind confidence came the thought, *Where the devil is Constance when I need her?*

CONSTANCE, IN FACT, was at the dressmaker's.

In an effort to learn more about St. John's family, the women in particular, she was seeking a source of gossip. She began with her own favored modiste, who had not dealt with Mrs. St. John, but directed her to a more likely establishment. It was at the fourth of those that she finally found what she sought.

Madame Veronique herself clearly recognized a lucrative customer when she saw one, for she stopped an assistant from rushing up to Constance and approached her in person.

"Is madame seeking something in particular?" she asked. Her accent was very subtly French. Genuine or not, it was perfectly done. "Whatever it is, we shall have something uniquely ravishing for such an elegant lady."

Constance spared her a glance—a smartly but modestly dressed woman of some forty years, her figure trim, her manner submissive, and her eyes hard and assessing. A businesswoman who had struggled upward from very little and had no intention of going back down. Constance understood that well enough.

"Nothing in particular," she said. "I am merely considering a subtle change in style and looking about for inspiration. Someone recommended you, so I thought I would look in."

"May I know who?" asked Veronique, preening slightly.

Constance shrugged carelessly. "I can't remember. One of my friends with whom I was discussing the matter… Mrs. St. John, perhaps? Yes, I believe it was, for you are making all the gowns for her daughter's wedding, are you not?"

She had used the same line three times that afternoon, but it finally struck home.

Madame Veronique's eyes positively sparkled. "Indeed, Mrs. St. John is one of my most valued customers."

"Not so *immediately* valuable, I imagine," Constance said, minutely examining the gorgeous golden silk evening gown in front of her, "if the wedding is postponed."

"Oh, but it is not," the dressmaker said smugly. "Such an appalling tragedy, of course, but madame and mademoiselle come for their next fitting tomorrow. Madame confides in me that her late husband would wish the wedding to go ahead without postponement. Mademoiselle persuaded her."

"I am so glad for their sakes," Constance said. "You know, this gown is gorgeous, but I rather doubt it is my color, and the style is too busy for me, with all those flounces and trims…"

"You will be surprised, madame. You will carry the style most beautifully, and I have other colored silks that might please you more. Why don't you try it?"

She condescended to try the gown and let Veronique fuss about her for some time while Constance flitted from subject to subject before bringing the conversation back to the St. Johns, wondering how many gowns there were to be for Miss St. John's trousseau.

"At least Mr. St. John can't balk at the numbers and veto any," she added callously.

Veronique didn't bat an eyelid. "He never did," she said simply. "He liked to be generous." Perhaps she caught Constance's look, for she added hastily, "To his family."

"Such a kind man," Constance agreed. "Did you know him well?"

If she had hoped to surprise a betrayal of an illicit liaison between St. John and the dressmaker, she was disappointed.

"I never met him," Veronique said. "I know him only through the affectionate chatter of his daughter and his wife."

"I do like to hear of affectionate families," Constance said. "Do you know, you are right about this gown? I really can carry this style. Perhaps you could show me the other silks you mentioned."

Unfortunately, another customer entered the shop, and though Veronique was happy to leave this person to her assistant, there was too much possibility of being overheard to hope for further confidences.

Still, having ordered the gown in a bold scarlet silk for an extortionate amount of money, Constance returned to the Silver and Grey offices with new theories buzzing around her head.

Catching sight of Janey at the end of Chandos Street, Constance alighted early from the hackney to greet her.

"Wotcher, ma'am," Janey exclaimed. "Know anything about the two old biddies four doors up from us? She's called Willow and lives with her maiden sister. They're the sort who give churches a bad name, making their servants pray all the time and faces as prim as a duck's—"

"Janey," Constance interrupted. "I understand."

Janey grinned. "Course you do. Well, the servants are pleasant enough; the housekeeper herself asked me into the kitchen for a cup of tea. Only then she—Mrs. Willow—appears unexpectedly and throws me out like I'm…whoever it was Jesus threw out of the temple. Anyway, the point is, she *recognized* me."

Constance saw the significance at once. "Which means she's been paying attention to the household and knows who and what we are…"

"Can't see her shoveling sh…"—again, Janey caught Constance's eye and changed her mind—"shoveling dirt, though, and trotting round to our back door with it."

"Is she frail?"

"No…"

"Then she could have. Or got a servant to do it for her."

"True," Janey allowed. "It'd take several servants, though, to lug two dead bodies there."

"We're beginning to think they died where they were and their position was altered only slightly."

"Why?" Janey asked.

Constance sighed. "That is another question." She inserted her key in the lock and was glad to see Hat bob immediately out of the reception office she still thought of as Janey's.

"Tea, ma'am?" Hat said brightly. "I just made some for Mr. Grey, so the kettle won't take long. He's with someone, by the way."

"Who?" Constance asked, for there were no appointments. Had Cordell come back to change his mind and dismiss them?

"A Miss Paul." Hat lowered her voice. "Very bright, colorful lady."

"Ah." Constance was intrigued. "We'll talk later, Janey. You go and see how Hat's been faring."

With a brief knock, she entered Solomon's office.

"Constance." Solomon rose immediately and turned to face her with such laughter in his eyes that she was startled. It wasn't a joke he'd been sharing with his visitor, either. It was for her, and over in a flash. "Miss Paul, this is my wife, Mrs. Grey, the Silver part of our partnership. Constance, Miss Zenobia Paul, Mr. St. John's friend."

Zenobia was regarding her with blatant curiosity. She held out her hand. "How do you do? You do unusual work for a woman."

Since she offered, Constance shook hands with her. "So do you."

Zenobia's lips curved upward. She had a strong-featured face that had its own beauty. But her main attraction seemed to be character, which blazed out of her eyes and her every expression. After a moment, she delved into a capacious bag and came out with a card, which she presented to Constance.

"I shall be at home tomorrow evening with a few friends. I would be honored if you would join me."

Constance blinked. "You know who I am? You understand about my establishment?"

"I admire your work there," Zenobia said calmly. "Yes, I too can make inquiries. And you need not fear being ostracized by less liberal-minded guests." Her eyes danced. "My dear, I even entertain *actresses*."

# CHAPTER TEN

BELLA ST. JOHN felt as if she would explode. Oppressed by her own misery as well as by her mother's and Anthony's, she found the relentless stream of condolence visits unbearable without the sustaining presence of her betrothed.

But Han had remained frustratingly absent all day, while Bella and her mother drank endless cups of tea with people she regarded as mere acquaintances, most of them come for purposes of curiosity and gossip. She wanted to scream at them all to get out, but she had been too well brought up to allow herself to do more than grit her teeth and wait for it to stop.

When the vicar finally left after his third call of the week—at least Mama seemed pleased to see *him*—she hoped the afternoon was finally over. But no, the maid who came to show the vicar out had two more visitors in tow, and it was too late to deny them.

Bella only just stifled a groan. It was the pair from the crescent that she always thought of as the sour-faced spinsters, though in fact Mrs. Willow was a widow. She and her sister, Miss Morton, haunted the square, exuding smug judgment. Or so Bella and Anthony imagined, although they had only exchanged civil words with them, and that on just two occasions.

She gritted her teeth once more and affixed a suitably sad smile to her lips. She resented that smile, which was for their sake, not hers. She *was* sad, so why was it considered not necessary that she *look* it?

She rose and curtseyed to the ladies then listened with low-ered eyes to their platitudes of sympathy. She was probably being unkind. Mrs. Willow had lost a husband, so she probably understood.

*Oh, Han, why don't you come? It's so much more bearable when you are here...*

"So kind of you to call on us," Mama said, as she had so often in the last couple of days.

"How could we not?" said Miss Morton. "Such a terrible thing to happen. We do feel for you so. Of course, my sister suffered the same kind of loss—"

"Not quite, dear," Mrs. Willow interrupted. "Poor Mr. Willow died of natural causes. I can't begin to imagine what you are going through, Mrs. St. John, you and your family. So very terrible."

From the little Bella knew of Mrs. Willow, it was not like to her to allow that anyone, ever, had suffered more than she. Mama looked suitably impressed by the kindness and inclined her head.

"Mr. Willow died at home, of course," his widow continued. "I had that comfort. And we did not have to deal with the annoyance of the police, or such scandal..."

"There is no scandal," Mama said with sudden sharpness. "My husband was taken ill suddenly while he was out. I daresay he had no time to seat himself more respectably at a *front* door!"

"Oh, my dear, the front door would have been worse!" Miss Morton exclaimed.

"I don't see why," Bella said, stung. "My father would be no less dead."

"But everyone would have seen him there," Mrs. Willow explained, lowering her voice as though it were a secret. "At *that* house."

Anthony, looking suddenly alarmed, opened his mouth, but Mama had already spoken.

"What house?"

And that was their moment, Bella realized. This was why they had come.

Mrs. Willow put up a hand to her mouth, as though shielding her words from Bella. "Why, the house of immorality that respectable people should not even have to know about. I cannot begin to imagine how you feel."

*The house of immorality.* A whisper among neighbors and servants, a salacious chortle among Anthony's friends... Bella had very little idea what went on there, but she understood spite when she heard it.

"How is it, Mrs. Willow, that you are so well acquainted with this house?" she demanded, much to Anthony's clear horror, and her mother's violent shake of her head. "*We* could not even tell you where it was."

There was an appalled silence. Miss Morton fidgeted uncomfortably, gazing hard at her gloved hands clasped in her lap. Mrs. Willow's face grew mottled with ugly red patches.

"Why, because I had cause, only this afternoon, to throw one of the creatures out of my kitchen. Such underhand insolence to get herself invited in by my gullible servants, who were merely being kind, with no idea who she was!"

That might have been true, but it wasn't the reason Mrs. Willow knew where the house was. She had looked for it.

Perhaps she saw the knowledge in Bella's face, for her eye twitched at one corner and she delivered her final blow.

"And if you want to know where it is, you need only ask Mr. Cordell. Come, Marguerite. Let us leave this poor family in peace to grieve and reflect."

Bella barely noticed them depart, though she must have said and done the right things. She came to only with Anthony gripping her shoulder.

"They're malicious old cats," he said urgently. "Han would never go to a place like that, and neither would Papa."

"Anthony is right," Mama said distantly. "But there was no need to antagonize them, Bella. Now they could tell everyone."

Bella straightened, staring at her mother's back as she walked to the door. "Is that really all you care about? That people might *know*?"

"Men have feet of clay, Bella," Mama said wearily. "It's as well you know now. Just remember never to notice."

The door closed behind her.

"I won't need to, will I?" Bella said. Her voice did not sound real either. "I will never see him again."

"Oh, don't be an ass," Anthony said impatiently. "Don't condemn a man on the word of those two! Papa may have died on that doorstep for reasons none of us can fathom, but I'm dashed sure he never stepped over the threshold of the house, as they implied. Which means there's every chance Han did not either. There's nothing worse in this world than supposedly godly scandal-mongers."

She needed time and peace to absorb all of that, the accusations and Anthony's surprisingly sensible reasoning. She could not think in this state.

But of course, *now* was when Han deigned to call.

As a frequent visitor and her future husband, he was not even announced, simply walked into the drawing room and came toward her, both hands held out. She backed away from him, unable to bring herself to touch him. A frown of incomprehension tugged at his brow. His hands dropped slowly to his sides.

"What is it?"

"I'll leave you to it," Anthony said hastily. "But Bella? Don't do—or say—anything you'll regret."

"Come, sit down," Han said gently as the door clicked shut. "Tell me what has upset you so."

"I can't sit," she said, her voice oddly stifled, while her emotions ran riot. "Did you go that house, Han? That house of immorality? Did my father?"

He understood. A flash of enlightenment, even annoyance, showed in his eyes. Eyes she had trusted.

"I very much doubt your father went there," he said quietly.

"I should be very surprised. But it was that back doorstep he was found upon."

"And you?" she challenged.

A rueful little smile just touched his mouth, and her world truly fell apart. "I did go there once. Last night, for the first time."

The blood drained from her face, leaving her skin cold. "I want you to go."

"I won't," Han said with unexpected firmness. "Not until you've heard why I went there, what I did, and what I learned."

CONSTANCE, SOLOMON, JANEY, and Hat all squashed into the carriage to return to the establishment. It was to be a mere drop in and out, just to make sure there was no more trouble and that the girls and their protectors were in good spirits.

In fact, there was outrage in the crowded kitchen. All the occupants of the house had gathered there, staring down at a large sheet of paper.

"What is it?" Constance asked with foreboding.

Sarah picked it up and handed it to her. Solomon peered over her shoulder. It was written on in bold black ink, all in capital letters.

WHORES, BEGONE.
    THERE IS NO PLACE FOR YOU AMONG DECENT PEO-PLE. GO BACK TO YOUR GUTTERS FOR ASSUREDLY YOU ARE ALL GOING TO HELL, ESPECIALLY THE WHORE OF BABYLON HERSELF.
    LEAVE THIS HOUSE NOW BEFORE WORSE HAPPENS.

Constance had heard it all—and much worse—many times before, and yet it took all her strength to make herself laugh.

"I really don't think so," she drawled, still smiling. "If this is meant to frighten us, it was not written by anyone who's faced what we have. Where did you find it?"

"Nailed to the back gate," Jeremy said. "When we came in for our supper."

"I'll bet you anything you like it came from that bloody old witch Willow," Janey said with contempt. "Here, Jeremy, why don't you and me take a shovelful to her door?"

"No," Constance said sharply. "No retaliation. No one will arrest them for this kind of thing, but you are more vulnerable. We shall remain the perfect neighbors."

"Did you see either of these women or their servants in the mews?" Solomon asked. "In the later part of the afternoon?"

But of course, no one had.

Constance made light of it, while urging everyone to be vigilant, to observe without fighting back. "Our continued existence here might depend on that," she said seriously, and was relieved to see the reluctant nods. These people were fighters because they'd had to be, and showing weakness did not come naturally.

"In this case, it's showing strength," Solomon added. "And frankly, such nonsense harms none of us."

*Us.* Once, she had fought against her feelings for Solomon because she did not want him associated with the sordid side of her business and knew that he did not wish to be. And yet now, he identified with it, and his words as well as his support soothed her.

She left the household much calmer and happier than she had found it, but once alone in the carriage with Solomon, she said restlessly, "Perhaps I should go back this evening, just in case there is more trouble."

Away from the others, Solomon was looking uncharacteristically grim. "I don't like it," he said. "I don't like that this harrying has started now."

"You think it's the same person who killed St. John, or at least brought the bodies to our doorstep?"

"Or it's someone taking advantage of the event to spill their own venom—perhaps even to distract us."

"Well, at least it's a clue," Constance said. "Though I must admit I've had more than enough of anonymous letters after the affair at Sutton May."

"This was no letter. This was a notice, designed to be seen by more than the occupants of the house. Everyone was supposed to see it and revile you."

"To drive us out," Constance said. "I suppose it was always a risk setting up in such a place."

Solomon put a finger under her chin, turning her face up to his. "You will give in?"

"Not without a fight. But I do have to consider the safety of my girls. And our clients," she added ruefully. "Most of whom do not want their presence with us advertised to the world."

"At least they have the excuse of charity."

"That is true. What an excellent idea of yours that was…" Even if someone, or several someones, were doing their best to destroy the rise of her respectability.

THAT EVENING'S PARTY was not as well attended as the night before, partly because there was no lauded musician, Constance's presence had not been guaranteed, and the charity donors rarely came twice in a row.

But the girls were their charming selves, and Constance, as she had always done, pushed worries to one side in order to be the perfect hostess, making sure her guests were comfortable, entertained, and never lonely.

Supper had just been served when Max murmured her in ear that there was trouble.

She excused herself to her companions and accompanied Max into the hallway. "What?"

"In the back garden again. Jeremy saw someone creeping about."

"Thanks. You watch at the front. Where is Mr. Grey?"

"I don't know, ma'am."

Of course, he was the first person she saw in the garden, standing very still just beyond the doorstep. She slipped her hand into his. Their communication was silent, a touch of the fingers, the faintest of shrugs against her shoulder.

*Who is there?*

*I don't know.*

After a moment, he led her toward the bench on the lawn, and they sat down together. Her skin prickled, because the raspberry bushes on her left were stirring when there was no wind. Shadows moved on the other side of the garden, and at the back, near the gate. One of them might have been a cat, but her heart beat faster.

Solomon put his lips close to her ear. "I think there are two of them. Jeremy heard one man slip through the gate while he was walking round from the front. He's behind the raspberry bush. I saw another whisk in before he saw me at the door. He's skulking in the shadows behind the apple tree at the back. They seem spry and quick."

She pressed her cheek to his, so that they could speak in the inaudible whispers of lovers. "Then not the old ladies themselves. What are we waiting for?"

"For Jeremy and Max to get round the mews to the back gate, while you and I stroll to the raspberry bushes."

"Shouldn't we have a lantern to see their faces clearly?" Constance suggested.

"Jeremy has one and Janey will bring two from the kitchen."

"How efficient you are in this house."

"In this life," he murmured with mock complacency. "Shall we?"

Along with the clop of horses arriving home to the mews for the night, she could hear the soft, distant voices of grooms and, closer, accompanying a moving light, Max's unmistakable laughter. He was used to acting and good at it.

She and Solomon strolled down the narrow path as though

interested only in each other. Solomon paused beside the raspberry bush, but as he spoke, Constance slipped her hand free and advanced another few feet to cut off their intruder's path to the gate.

"You had better come out, you know," Solomon said to the raspberries.

The gate opened, flooding the dark shadows and the apple tree with wildly swinging light. There came a startled grunt and sounds of intense scuffling.

The raspberry bushes waved and rustled, and a female voice commanded, "Don't hurt him! Don't dare hurt him!"

Janey's two lanterns, held up to shine on the speaker's face, clearly blinded the female intruder, who emerged with one arm held across her eyes.

Even so, Constance could see she was young, no old harridan. She was sure she had never seen this person in her life before. But Solomon had. His intake of breath betrayed startlement as well as recognition.

"Let him go!" the young woman insisted, panic in her voice.

Jeremy and Max held the other intruder by the arms, marching him up the path to the others. To be fair, he no longer struggled. Constance doubted he ever had, for there was not a hair out of place on his handsome head, or a crease in his well cut evening coat.

Hanibal Cordell.

Constance began to laugh. "Sir, how unexpected. Then this must be Miss… But no doubt discretion is the better part of this revelation. You may release him, gentlemen, and return to your duties."

She regarded Miss St. John in some consternation. Under no circumstances could the girl be seen inside the house. Yet there was little privacy out here, where anyone could be lurking beyond the garden walls.

Miss St. John reached up somewhat defiantly and pulled a thick mourning veil from the top of her hat to cover her face from brow to throat.

"Well," Constance said, "you had better come in."

The girl seized Cordell's freed arm, and Constance waved Janey and the lanterns forward in front of her. Solomon, presumably, brought up the rear.

There was no privacy in the kitchen, where servants came and went all the time while supper was served. Without instruction, Janey abandoned the lanterns at the door and led the way through the kitchen to the stairs. At the top, she pushed the baize door open a crack and peered out. A male voice and a female gurgle of laughter faded, and Janey led the way through to the small parlor, where she turned on the gas lamps.

"Thanks, Janey," Constance said, and her assistant reluctantly departed. "Do sit," she invited her guests, "and explain."

"Must we?" Cordell asked, with a trace of his familiar arrogance. "I am, after all, your employer."

"We shan't dispute terminology," Solomon said without softening. "But I never heard that any employer had the right to invade an employee's private property."

"We couldn't come to the front door, could we?" Cordell said reasonably.

"Because of me," Bella St. John said.

"You," Constance said without sympathy, "should not be here at all. And you, sir, should not have brought her."

"He was meant to go in alone and bring you out to the mews," Bella said. "But I went in before he could stop me."

"Why?" Constance asked, baffled. "Do you imagine a brothel is an interesting or romantic place?"

Bella's face heated to a fiery red. "No, of course not."

"Perhaps you were seeking adventure?"

"I was seeking the truth!" Bella burst out.

Constance blinked. "About me?"

"About me," Cordell said with a crooked smile. "I was seen by the Willow creature a few houses up from yours, entering this establishment yesterday evening, and of course she and her crow of a sister could not wait to impart the news to Bella and her mother. They also revealed that Mr. St. John was found here, something we had been keeping from the ladies."

"We?" Solomon asked.

"Anthony and I. Even the police inspector understood that."

Bella's large, mournful eyes were fixed on Constance. "*Did my father come here?*"

"Never," Constance said steadily, "until the night he died. Even then, he was never over the door."

The girl's gaze did not shift.

"She doesn't believe me," Cordell said, unable to keep the bitterness from his voice. "I told her—"

Bella stopped him with a quick, silencing gesture. "Let her speak. I presume you are Mrs. Silver?"

"More properly, I am Mrs. Grey. But yes, the establishment is mine."

"And how do you know Mr. Cordell?"

"My husband met him in your home. They talked together on leaving, and Solomon gave him a card for our investigation business, Silver and Grey."

The suspicion remained in Bella's eyes. She was not yet convinced.

Solomon stirred in his chair. "We also discussed other aspects of this establishment. My guess is that Mr. Cordell was curious—and perhaps too impatient to wait for morning to visit the Silver and Grey office."

"Exactly," Cordell said, but Bella did not look at him.

She flashed a glance at Solomon. "What other *aspects* are there?" she asked contemptuously.

"There are the people who live here." Constance allowed a shade of scorn into her smile. "Yes, we are people too. Not all of us were born to wealth and safety. Some of us were born into poverty. Some of us fell there from poor decisions or bad luck. Either way, we are still entitled to life."

"Like *this?*" Bella said, gesturing to encompass the whole

disreputable house.

"Why not? My profession is as old as time, Miss St. John, though not all of us choose it. Some do. But what do you think happens to the ladies of your own class who are seduced—or worse—by so-called gentlemen? What happens to the maids who are made pregnant because they're too frightened to resist their masters, and are then dismissed without a character? Without help, their fall is relentless and inevitable. Some have to provide for children."

"So you take them in and put them to work here," Bella said disdainfully.

"Oh, I take in the few I can help, and yes, we are all responsible for some work. Some choose to be courtesans in a safe place—"

"Safe!" There was anger as well as derision in the girl's face.

Solomon said, "Brothels are rarely safe for women, who can be beaten, abused, and even murdered without anyone batting an eyelid. They deserve it, don't they, for being fallen women? It does not happen here."

"Nor," Constance added, "are we going to kidnap you and hold you captive without food and water until you are broken enough to agree to lie with whoever is brought to you. Because, yes, that happens too, to women of all classes unfortunate enough to be in the wrong place without the right protection."

"That's enough," Cordell said, clearly appalled at such subjects sullying the ears of his betrothed—who, in fact, was looking both astonished and revolted.

"It is," Solomon agreed. "More than enough. So, Constance takes in as many such women as she can, providing shelter, medical treatment, and good food, all without judgment. She helps them give birth and have their children adopted by decent people where appropriate. She sees to their training in various trades and professions they have chosen—if that is their wish. It is a recognized charity, which Mr. Cordell has chosen to support after his visit last night."

"With cash donations," Cordell added deliberately, in case, presumably, his betrothed chose to suspect any other kind of transaction. "Many respectable people do."

"This morning," Constance continued, noticing that the girl's flushed face had whitened, "Mr. Cordell called at the Silver and Grey offices by appointment, and contracted us to investigate the death of your father. Who was not, by the way, known at any other of the establishments I'm familiar with. We will hear in time if he ever visited any, but my impression of the man is that he did not."

Bella was still staring at Constance, as though trying to force the truth out of her. "*You* were not born into poverty, deprived of wealth and education!"

"My dear, I am a mere example of dragging myself up by the garters," Constance drawled. "You can choose to disbelieve everything I, my husband, and Mr. Cordell say. Or you—having rather forced yourself into my house—can help us find the truth about your father. Mr. Cordell seemed to believe it would help you."

Bella's gaze fell at last. It was a lot to grasp and understand, and no doubt contrary to everything she had ever been taught. But the defiance, the outrage, had drained out of her.

"How can I help you find the truth?" she asked in a small voice. "I know nothing about his leaving the house that night, or about opium, or anyone who could conceivably want to hurt him."

Solomon leaned forward. "You could begin by telling us all about him. And by allowing us into his study to see his private papers."

# CHAPTER ELEVEN

BELLA'S MOUTH DROPPED open. "I can't do that! It's up to my mother, and she has locked his study door. She won't let anyone in there."

Constance and Solomon exchanged startled glances.

"Haven't the police been through his papers?" Constance asked.

Bella shook her head. "Mama forbade it. Inspector Harris did not insist."

"Does she spend much time in there?" Solomon asked, rather deliberately keeping any unease out of his face and voice.

But Bella shook her head. "No, she cannot face it yet. But she won't let anyone else in either."

Constance said carefully, "We know of no one who wanted to hurt your father. But we also believe that he was anxious over the last couple of weeks, something he did not reveal even to his closest friends. Did he talk to you about it?"

"No. No, he seemed just the same to me." Bella's frown showed as much guilt as concern. "Did I miss something? Too caught up in my wedding to notice my own father was in pain!"

"He would have hidden it from you," Constance said. "Men often do. Was he a *happy* man, Miss St. John?"

Bella opened her mouth, then closed it again. "No," she said slowly. "I don't think he was. Oh, he was *at times*. On birthdays and at Christmas, when we did well in our studies—particularly Anthony, who is very clever. Also, when we went on excursions, or when he'd heard a lecture that impressed him. But there was always a sadness in his eyes. A sort of…" She trailed off, shaking her head.

"Discontent?" Solomon suggested. "Restlessness? Some past tragedy, perhaps, that he shared with no one?"

"I don't know. All of those perhaps. Sometimes I thought—" She halted, pressing her lips tight together to stop them blabbing.

"Your opinion is the most valuable of all," Constance said gently. "You were his daughter, and if you want the truth, we need to know what you think. Mr. Cordell will tell you we are bound to discretion in all things except the criminal."

Bella drew a sharp breath. "Sometimes, I thought there was no love between my parents, and it made them both unhappy."

A first fringe of suspicion brushed against Constance's mind. She dismissed it for later. "When did you first think this? Recently?"

"No… A few years ago."

"Why?"

"They spend no time together that is not formal. They rarely argue because it seems neither of them cares enough. But occasionally, I could see that they irritated each other. And then, when Han—Mr. Cordell—asked for my hand and we became engaged, they were so delighted that I thought I was mistaken in such a foolish belief. They actually discussed the wedding together and began to plan… That too was part of my own happiness." Bella looked down at her hands. "And now it is all gone."

"No," Constance said. "It's just a little lost in grief. It will find its way out again. Now, how can we get into your father's study?"

Cordell said, "You and your mother are going to Veronique's tomorrow, are you not?"

"I don't know if there is any point now," Bella said, with a return to petulance.

Ignoring that, Cordell persevered. "If you can somehow get the key from your mother and give it to me, I'll let them in. The servants are quite used to my running tame in the house and will let me wait there with friends."

Constance bit back that there was no need. She could pick most indoor locks. But a key would certainly speed matters on and make their intrusion less likely to be noticed.

Bella didn't look at her betrothed but glanced doubtfully from Constance to Solomon and back. She knew that agreement meant breaking her mother's trust. The question she had to consider was if the end justified the means. No one could answer that for her, but Constance was already contemplating the alternative method of breaking and entering.

"If you think that it's important," Bella said in a rush, "and that it will help, then I'll try."

HAVING AGREED TO meet Cordell in the gardens at Grosvenor Square at half past ten the following morning, Constance and Solomon left the opening of the office to Janey and Hat while they called at the establishment to make sure all was well.

They alighted from their carriage before nine o'clock, and Constance was ridiculously relieved to see the front doorstep clean and pristine. On impulse, she set off down the area steps, and Solomon followed her. The path was swept and the borders tidy all the way around the side path to the back garden.

Here, they discovered Jeremy, his broom abandoned anyhow on the path beside him. He stood facing the back door, both hands grasping his cloth hat and pulling it so hard down on his head that his knuckles were white.

"Again," he said in anguish. "It's happened again."

Constance went to him at once. Solomon brushed past them both and finally saw what was upsetting Jeremy. The body of a man lay spread across the back step.

UNLIKE THE LAST time, there was no doubt that this man was dead. The flies were already buzzing around him. And the smell was such that Solomon had to raise his handkerchief to his mouth and nose.

But the next steps were distressingly familiar. Jeremy was taken into the house through the area door. The back door was locked while a stable lad was sent for a constable. Constance and Solomon forced themselves to examine the scene.

It had been raining last night, and there were muddy footprints on the path.

"They look like workman's boots, not a little old lady's," Constance remarked.

"And then there is this wheel track across the grass," Solomon said, pointing. "If I'm not mistaken, the body was brought in a wheelbarrow."

They both had cause to recognize such tracks from the case of the girl found in the lake at the home of Constance's friend, Lady Maule.

Constance pointed to other marks on the path just under the step. "That's where he laid the barrow down, before tipping the body out onto the step."

Solomon nodded. The body lay on its side, slightly curled, probably exactly as it had fallen.

"Not posed," he murmured, "but definitely moved. This man has been dead for days."

"And whoever brought him was careless. Or just unlucky." She raised her eyes to his. "Is this part of the campaign to drive us out? Or meant to distract us and the police from looking into St. John's life?"

Solomon put his arm around her and urged her away from the scene. They had both had enough. "What are you thinking?" he asked.

"That Bella knows what we're about. And that there's every chance she told her mother."

"In which case, we can't rule out Cordell either," Solomon said. "Or Zenobia Paul. Isn't it more likely to be the minions of the old ladies?"

"Whoever it is must have brought the body some distance. It wasn't just waiting at the bottom of the garden to be discovered. They must have allies. Either way, I shall be interested to observe Cordell's manner when we meet him—supposing we can escape the police's clutches before then."

IT WAS AFTER ten before Jacintha St. John managed to shepherd her daughter into the carriage. Which was annoying. It had been Bella's idea, after all, to keep the date of her wedding and merely draw back on the lavishness of the celebration. Jacintha had given in only reluctantly, for she would have preferred proper mourning to be publicly maintained.

On the other hand, why should Bella's happiness be compromised because of her degenerate father? In fact, it made sense to have her safely married into the Cordell family as soon as possible just in case scandal ever broke over Terrence's death.

For now, she thought they were safe. The police had found nothing—thank God—and she must make sure they never did. If all went according to plan, Terrence's death would be ruled an accident and the police investigation halted. There was always the possibility of a suicide ruling, of course, which brought its own shame, but the solicitor had assured her that juries were unlikely to bring in such a verdict unless the evidence was overwhelming. And in this case, everyone knew Terrence was a happy fellow. Even Zenobia Paul would not dispute that.

"There you are!" Jacintha exclaimed, finally running her daughter to earth in the little-used morning room, where she appeared to be having a spirited argument with her betrothed. "Oh, good morning, Han. I did not know you were here. Bella, do put on your hat—the carriage is waiting. It is you two who insist on proceeding, remember?"

"Of course, Mama," Bella said, a little stiltedly, which made Jacintha peer at her.

"Enjoy your morning," Han said in his easy manner. "I shall call again later, if I may…"

He kissed Bella's cheek, and the silly girl looked outraged, as if she would have preferred to keep quarrelling. But he escorted them from the house, handed them into the carriage, and strolled across the road toward the garden.

"Don't quarrel with a man who loves you," Jacintha said as the carriage pulled into motion.

"How does one know?" Bella asked. "How did you know that Papa loved *you*?" Jacintha was glad not to be looking at her daughter as the question burst out, and fortunately Bella did not seem to want an answer. "Words don't mean anything, do they?"

"Actions mean more," Jacintha said, suddenly distracted. The carriage was held up by a queue of vehicles in front, and she found herself gazing down the crescent. A policeman in his uniform and tall hat stood on the pavement beside the front steps. "Now that is interesting. They must be investigating there again…"

"There?" Bella said, following her mother's gaze.

"That is the house of immorality Mrs. Willow was kind enough to mention yesterday afternoon."

Men in street clothes came up the area steps and stopped beside the constable. Jacintha imagined they were the same policemen who had first called on her, but she couldn't tell at this distance. It didn't really matter. If they were focusing on that house, they weren't focusing on hers.

The carriage bumped into motion again and whisked them onward to Veronique's.

THE WHEELBARROW THAT had presumably brought the body to the establishment's back door had clearly come through the back gate from the mews. However, the trail vanished there under the passage of hooves, other wheels, and other feet. It was impossible to even tell which direction the barrow had come from.

Constance and Solomon, having agreed with Inspector Harris's assessment, told him about the manure and the notice on the gate the day before, and pointed him toward Mrs. Willow and her sister as a possibility.

"He doesn't look pleased," Constance said as they left the house and strolled up toward the square where they were to meet Cordell. As they walked, she drew the veil of her hat down over her face. Since she was wearing black, it was a reasonable disguise against recognition going into the St. Johns' house.

"I'm not pleased either," Solomon said. "If that poor man was stolen from a paupers' grave, as Harris seemed to think, then that is a considerable amount of malice. Especially if they were responsible for bringing the other bodies."

Constance stared at him. "How many people can there be in such a small area, able and willing to lug dead bodies around and pose them at houses of ill repute?"

"This poor devil wasn't posed," Solomon pointed out. "He was tipped, and in something of a hurry too. No care was taken to erase footprints or barrow marks. And unlike the first bodies, there can be no doubt that this fellow did *not* die on our doorstep. It wasn't necessarily the same person."

Constance frowned. "But someone is making it commonplace to discover bodies on our doorstep. A distraction from the previous murders? Or a simple attempt to drive us out? Perhaps it was *all* intended to drive us out."

"Murder seems a step too far for such a campaign," Solomon protested, opening the gate to the garden in the center of the square.

There, an elderly gentleman dozed in the morning sunshine. A maid walked a panting pug who sniffed at every plant. Constance and Solomon gazed about them, searching for two elderly ladies without success.

Cordell rose from a bench near the middle of the square and walked toward them. "I was about to give up on you," he murmured as he doffed his hat to Constance.

"Excuse us," Solomon said, and told him about the latest development.

To Constance, Cordell's shock was genuine. "That's outrageous! Not to say dangerous—who knows what the man died of? There must be something more to this. I cannot imagine two old ladies going so far in their moral quests. It puts them quite in the wrong."

"Many people believe the ends justify the means. In all matters. I presume you have the key?"

Cordell grimaced. "I do. But I don't think she has forgiven me. It is you she trusts, not me."

"She is shocked and grieving," Constance said. "Give her time to adjust her view of the world."

Cordell glanced around, as though to be sure he would not be overheard even by a stranger. "What if we do find out something reprehensible about her father? That is hardly going to improve her trust in men in general, or me in particular."

"You said you wanted to know," Solomon reminded him. "And that she *needs* to know."

Cordell nodded, though he still looked unhappy as they left the gardens and crossed to the St. Johns' gracious house.

The bell was answered swiftly by a butler, who looked vaguely surprised, though he opened the door wider to admit them. "Mr. Cordell."

"Good morning again, Hutton. Is Miss Bella returned yet?"

"Oh no, sir. We don't expect them for another hour at least."

"That long, eh? I was sure they would be back... Mr. and Mrs. Grey here wished to pay their respects to the family."

"That is most kind."

"I'm sure you're wrong about a whole hour, Hutton. Perhaps we could just wait in the drawing room, and you can inform Mrs. St. John as soon as she returns?"

"Very good, sir," Hutton said, with such a sympathetic glance at Cordell that Constance suspected the servants all knew the young couple had quarreled. Which was good. They would assume Constance and Solomon were his excuse to call again and make amends. "Mr. Anthony is not up yet, but perhaps he won't be long either."

Hutton took Solomon's hat, inclining his head with recognition, and left Cordell to lead them up to the drawing room.

"No need for tea yet, Hutton," Cordell called over the banister. "We'll wait for Mrs. St. John."

"Very good, sir."

Constance walked past Cordell into the drawing room, which was a little more cluttered than she would have liked, but both tasteful and expensive, with its too-long velvet curtains, bright carpets, and the most elegant of modern furnishings.

Cordell left the door open and walked toward him. "That is the study door, directly opposite us." He took a key from his pocket and passed it to Solomon.

"What of Anthony?" Constance asked.

"He never appears before midday."

Although Cordell had passed the key to Solomon—perhaps to shrug off the guilt of prying—he accompanied them across the passage and into the study. There were no servants nearby.

"Leave the door open a crack," Solomon advised in a low voice, "and listen. If anyone approaches, go out and close the door, and be seen in the drawing room by whoever passes. Pretend to be talking to us if you can."

The study was lined with books and contained a comfortable sofa and a table with fine glass decanters. But its main focus was the large mahogany desk, well polished and clear of any documents or correspondence.

Solomon went to one of the matching cabinets that flanked it against the wall, and Constance opened the first drawer in the desk. It contained only a box of good-quality notepaper, headed by this address and that of a country house in Berkshire, three spare bottles of ink, a selection of pens, a penknife, and a book full of addresses.

Constance spared the time to flick through the address book. She looked under *W* for Willow, and also under *M* for the unmarried sister. On impulse she also checked the *N* names, but was hardly surprised when neither Neville nor Nevvy appeared. Even if they were unlikely acquaintances, there was no point in recording *No fixed abode*.

She placed it back in the drawer and closed it. The middle drawer was locked. Excited, because this had to be the treasure trove, Constance extracted two hairpins and set to work. She could feel Cordell's shocked eyes boring into the side of her face, but he did not try to stop her.

The locked clicked easily and she slid it open. On one side of the drawer was a collection of tradesmen's accounts, all marked as paid. On the other, tied with narrow black ribbon, was personal correspondence St. John had chosen to keep.

"Sol," she said, knowing this was what they had come for.

Solomon joined her, and they went systematically through the correspondence, allowing themselves only quick glances. To be fair, none of them were worth much more. There were no love letters from his wife, nor from anyone else. There were childish letters from his son Anthony, written from school, and a couple from Bella, written from her sickbed in the country to her father in town. They all seemed affectionate and comfortable. There didn't seem to be any from friends, unless Solomon had all of those.

Keeping his children's letters betrayed a sentimentality that made this odder. Surely such a man would have kept letters from Zenobia, particularly from the travels he had helped to finance.

Setting her pile of letters down, Constance examined the

ribbon. She could see easily where it had just been folded to wrap around the letters. But when she looked more closely, fainter creasers, and the position of previous knots, showed that the ribbon had once confined something all of an inch larger.

"Someone got here first," she said in frustration. "The letters have been purged."

Solomon glanced at the ribbon and set down his own letters. "So Mrs. St. John *has* been busy. Why? Let's have a look at the accounts."

Abandoning the letters, she took out the pile of paid accounts and passed half to Solomon. She flicked through them quickly, finding only what one might expect of a wealthy man with two households and a daughter about to be married. Madame Veronique was horrendously expensive, as were the wine merchants and caterers to whom he had paid a deposit.

All most disappointing. "What is in the cabinets?" she asked Solomon without much hope.

"Past years' household accounts and copies of estate books. Records of investments, that kind of thing. Nothing untoward, at a glance, but then, if there were, the bank would have noticed, and Harris has been there."

She gathered the accounts back together, with Veronique's latest at the top, as she had found them. Again, the eye-watering amounts caught her attention. One hideously expensive evening gown in blue watered silk cost twice what Constance had paid for her most expensive garment ever, and sundries—presumably matching gloves and reticules—cost almost the same amount again.

Startled, she flicked to the next Veronique account and the next. On each, after the main garments purchased, sundries were listed for equally high amounts. On impulse, Constance extracted two of Veronique's bills from lower down and put them in her own reticule.

Solomon watched her, his eyebrows arched, while he reached for the third and final drawer. Which was unlocked and contained only an engagement diary.

While Solomon examined that, Constance re-bundled the letters. As she picked up Solomon's pile, which had been beneath her own, she saw that here, at last, were a few from friends. One fell from the middle of the pile and landed on the desk. Hastily, Constance retrieved it and was about to shove it back into the midst of the others when one word out of the scrawl leaped out at her.

*Neville.*

"Someone's coming downstairs," Cordell hissed. "I think it's Anthony."

There was no time to place the letters in the ribbon according to the previous creases. Having swiped the Neville letter into her reticule with Veronique's accounts, she tied the quickest of bows, then shut the drawer. There was no time to manipulate the lock again before she darted out of the room, Solomon at her heels.

They only just made it back to the drawing room. Constance only hoped Cordell had had time to lock the study door before a young male voice hailed him.

"Good morning, Han. You're too early, you know. Bella won't be back until luncheon."

Solomon touched Constance's hair. "Pins," he breathed, and she passed them over without a word.

In the passage, Cordell was saying smoothly, "So Hutton informed me. I was silly enough to disbelieve him—and to bring in visitors to wait. You remember Mr. Grey, who called before?"

He wandered into the room just as Solomon, having re-pinned Constance's loose hair, dropped his hands to his sides.

"Of course." A young man around the same age as Bella wandered into the room. He looked a little weary, as though he had had his fill of condolence visitors and was already at the end of his tether.

Constance couldn't help smiling sympathetically at him.

He looked slightly taken aback but quickly shook hands with Solomon. "How do you do, sir? How kind of you to call again."

"I would not have so intruded, except that my wife wished to pay her respects to your mother. She too is involved with some of the same charities as your father."

The boy bowed, flushing slightly as though caught out in rudeness. He seemed exhausted by grief. "How do you do, Mrs. Grey? We are most grateful for your condolences."

"One feels obliged to keep traditions," Constance said, "and some people find it a comfort. For myself, I feel it an imposition and somewhat insolent that strangers purport to understand one's own immeasurable grief. Be assured we are thinking of you, though. I believe we should impose no longer, Solomon. But we shall attend the memorial service, of course."

"It's tomorrow afternoon," Anthony said, "in Hanover Square."

"Please pass our sincere sympathies to your mother and sister too," Constance said, pulling on her gloves. She had never intended to inflict her presence on the St. John ladies, though she could not help a powerful curiosity about the lady of the house. "Goodbye, Mr. St. John."

Cordell escorted them to the door, without disturbing the servants, and returned Solomon's hat. "Well done," he breathed.

# CHAPTER TWELVE

CONSTANCE COULD NOT wait to get back to the office to read the purloined letter, so she dragged it out of her reticule as soon as the carriage began to move.

"There was no time," she said without looking up, though she felt Solomon's gaze upon her. "Here," she added, holding out Veronique's bills to him. "What do you make of these?"

The letter was dated in the autumn of the previous year and came from someone called George Lorimer, who appeared, from the lack of formality, to be an old friend and neighbor in the county of Berkshire. Most of it was homely news about his family and an amusing tale about the village innkeeper. The name Neville was only mentioned once, and as if in answer to a query previously sent by St. John. It wasn't all she had hoped for, but it was better than nothing, so she read it aloud.

"*Sadly, I have heard nothing of Neville for over fifteen years, but do let me know when you find the old reprobate. When do you come down to the country next? We all look forward to seeing you and the family. Ever your friend, George Lorimer.*"

She looked up to meet Solomon's interested gaze. "So he *did* know Nevvy!"

"If it's the same Neville, which does not seem terribly likely on the face of it. It's a common enough name."

"Worth investigating, though," she said, slightly deflated.

"Absolutely," he agreed, and flapped Veronique's invoice between his fingers. "What am I looking for in this? It looks like daylight robbery, but presumably the St. Johns agreed to it, since it's been paid."

"What are all these sundries? A few gloves and reticules should not cost as much as one already ridiculously expensive evening gown. And *all* Veronique's bills are like that, so it's not just a one-time payment for all the hats and gloves in Bella's trousseau."

"Are they indeed?" Solomon stared at it again. "Do you go to fashionable dressmakers like this Veronique?"

"No." She sighed. "I have my own woman who is not remotely fashionable, but she is very good at following my ideas and does excellent work. But you're right, I don't know what the wealthiest expect to pay. The dressmakers I spoke to yesterday, including Veronique herself, certainly threw around eye-watering prices in my hearing, but nothing like this. We need to speak to a wealthy aristocrat…"

"And Bella," Solomon said. "We need to be sure before we start accusing someone of blackmail, but if it's true, it's a clever way of doing it without leaving any evidence. At worst, Veronique has overcharged, which is hardly a crime."

"She could have been blackmailing any of them," Constance said excitedly. "Most men just seem to wince and pay the bills. This was a special occasion, and we know St. John was happy to indulge his daughter. What if he was killed to stop him going to the police about Veronique?"

"Veronique herself?" Solomon said consideringly. "Or…surely St. John's own family could not have done it simply to avoid the possibility of scandal coming out?"

"You'd be surprised the lengths people will go to in order to remain outwardly respectable. Though, to be frank, I can't imagine what Bella could have done in her short and sheltered life that would be worthy of blackmail. She doesn't seem the type to seduce the footman or try to elope with the stable boy."

"Some affair of her mother's?" Solomon suggested dubiously.

"And she poisoned her husband to prevent him from finding

out? Or from revealing the whole thing to the police?"

Solomon passed the account back to Constance. "Veronique would not murder her funding source, so I doubt she killed St. John."

"But even a visit from the police could badly affect her business. She depends on her reputation and the goodwill of Society's powerful patrons."

"Wouldn't cutting out the blackmail have pacified St. John enough? Why risk murdering him?"

"I don't know," Constance admitted. "But we need to find out where Veronique was on the night St. John died."

Solomon nodded. He was silent for the rest of the journey to the office until, just as the carriage was pulling up, he said, "It's not right yet. Why stab him when he's already dead?"

"To cast the blame on Nevvy," Constance said, gathering up her bags.

"Why was Nevvy even there? Who *is* Nevvy, and what has any of it to do with this morning's corpse and the other attempts to intimidate you?"

"We haven't solved it yet," Constance said defensively, "but at last we have some kind of motive and a few more paths to look into."

Solomon alighted and handed her down. "We have something important," he agreed, "and it's just as well you spotted these things. We'll discover how they all fit together."

His praise and his optimism still warmed her ridiculously, and her own slightly flattened spirits lifted again. In the office, a burst of hilarity emerged from Janey's preserve at the back, but both she and Hat stuck their heads out of the office to greet their employers.

"Conference, Janey," Constance called, and the three of them trooped into Solomon's office. "How is Hat getting along with everything?"

"I wouldn't have picked her out, to be honest," Janey said. "But she's bright and got the hang of it without a problem. She's even stopped being scared to answer the door. She'll do."

"Good." Solomon took the case notes from his desk and passed them to Constance, who had always been the chief keeper of their lists. "We need to go over every aspect of this case together and decide on our next steps."

They started at the beginning with the discovery of the body, and Constance added to the notes as they went along, particularly Janey's full impressions of the Willow household.

"Can you really see the old ladies physically bringing bodies to our door?" Constance asked. "Without help? Would they really soil their hands in person?"

"I can see them *wanting* to," Janey said. "Even ordering it."

"And who would obey them?" Solomon asked. "What of the menservants? Are they brawny fellows?"

"One of the stable lads is. It was him I first spoke to, but he seems too amiable to do anything so awful—even the manure incident."

Constance felt her lips twitch at the almost primly spoken *manure*. Not so long ago Janey would have called it something much earthier, and Janey's quick grin at her confirmed she was well aware of it.

"Well done," Constance murmured. "So, you don't think he could be made to do such things?"

Janey considered. "Maybe. His job depends on his obedience, after all. But I don't think he *did* do it. Not the two bodies, anyway. He wasn't in the least embarrassed to talk about it. None of them were, not even the housekeeper, Mrs. Robertson. She paid lip service to us being unfit subjects of conversation, but it was clear she was as interested as everyone else. No one was looking furtive."

Constance made a note in the Willow column. "So before your visit to the house, we already had the two bodies and the manure," she said. "After, we had the note on the gate, and the other body. It could all be part of the same campaign to drive us out, and yet nothing to do with the actual deaths of either St.

John or Nevvy. What if the bodies died in the Willow house or outside it? What if Mrs. Willow and her sister poisoned St. John?"

"Why?" Solomon asked blankly. "No one disliked him."

"What if they knew whatever it was Veronique did? And, instead of blackmail, resorted to murder? Being overly self-righteous, from what Janey says, they'd have to be mad as hatters, of course..."

Solomon and Janey looked thoughtful, but Constance sighed.

"We still have the difficulty of removing the bodies to our doorstep without leaving a sign," she said ruefully. "And Janey's seeing no guilt among the servants who might have done the moving. Besides the fact that we don't even know if Veronique was blackmailing St. John. Moving on..."

By the end, they had a list of fresh inquiries. Janey was sent to discover what she could about Veronique.

"Especially what she was doing on the night St. John died," Solomon said. "Try making friends with her assistant and discover their relationships with other customers. If she was blackmailing one of the St. Johns, she could have been doing the same to others. Take Lenny with you if he's free."

"He's busy nearly every day now," Janey said proudly. "But I'll see if he can spare an hour or two. What are you going to do?"

"Call on a duke's daughter," Solomon said, "and learn what we can about the St. Johns, and about Mrs. Willow and her sister."

"And the price of aristocratic weddings," Constance added. "This evening, we'll be at Zenobia Paul's gathering, where we're hoping to learn if the Neville in St. John's letter is our Nevvy, and if so, what the connection is."

Janey nodded at the pile of letters on Solomon's desk. "You've got them to answer too," she said somewhat smugly, and swaggered off to fetch her hat.

IN THE END, since they hadn't thought of calling on duke's daughter Lady Grizelda Tizsa while they were actually in Mayfair, Constance and Solomon went home to change and eat a quick dinner first.

They found the Tizsas enjoying a quiet moment in their little house in Half Moon Street Lane. Their offspring had just been put to bed, and they welcomed Constance and Solomon with flattering delight.

"You look very smart," Lady Griz said when they were all seated in the pleasant study-cum-drawing room. "I can't imagine it is for our benefit."

"Am I overdressed?" Constance asked ruefully. "We've been invited to an evening party at Miss Zenobia Paul's."

"Oh, then you are *perfectly* dressed. Everyone is."

"You know her?" Solomon asked quickly.

"No," said Dragan Tizsa, one-time revolutionary in his home country of Hungary, and now doctor and refugee—and son-in-law to the Duke of Kelburn.

"Yes," Griz said. "She's an explorer. I like her, though I haven't seen her since the Great Exhibition. She knows lots of interesting people, too. You are bound to enjoy the evening." She looked from one to the other. "Or are you working?"

"On the death of Terrence St. John," Solomon said.

To Constance's surprise, Griz's expression changed to one of dismay. Or was it grief?

"You knew him?" Constance asked quickly.

"He was a very good musician," Griz said. "He played the violin with our amateur orchestra when it first began. He left us not long afterward but came to most of our concerts still."

"Why did he leave?" Solomon asked.

"Family commitments, I think. Which probably meant his wife didn't like us."

"She wasn't musically inclined?" Solomon said lightly.

"No."

"You don't like her?" Constance guessed.

Griz shrugged. "I don't think I ever met her. He just seemed…" She gave an apologetic little smile. "He seemed to *need* the music. Was there something untoward about his death? I only saw the announcement in the paper."

"He was found on the doorstep of my establishment," Constance said. "Along with a vagrant called Nevvy, or Gareth Neville."

Griz's eyebrows rose above the frame of her spectacles. "He was not a client of your establishment, though, was he?"

"Why do you say that?"

"No reason," Griz said vaguely, and again the suspicion Constance hadn't yet mentioned to anyone slid into her mind.

"What do you know of him?" she asked.

"A good man, a cultured man, devoted to his children."

"And his wife?"

"I know nothing to the contrary."

"Then you don't know anything about his marriage?"

"Such as?" Griz asked.

"Was it a love match? A marriage of convenience?"

"I don't know," Griz said. "It must have happened twenty years ago, when I was in the schoolroom. How did he die?"

"Opium poisoning. Did you ever see or hear about his taking opium for any purpose?"

Griz shook her head. "Was he ill?"

"Apparently not. He was also stabbed, after death, with the vagrant's knife."

Griz frowned. "That is certainly a mystery. Especially when the vagrant is dead too." She looked up suddenly. "Actually, I met St. John a few times at Zenobia's. He was a friend of hers."

"Just a friend?" Constance asked, then added apologetically, "Rumor has her as his mistress."

"I should be surprised."

"Because he was faithful to his wife?"

Griz nodded.

"What about his wife?" Solomon asked. "Was *she* faithful?"

"Oh dear, I have no idea. I never really moved in such circles. My sister might know. Or my mother. I could ask them." Her lip twitched. "Subtly, of course."

"Thank you. I don't suppose you are acquainted with an elderly widow called Mrs. Willow? And her sister, Miss Morton? They live in Grosvenor Crescent, near Constance's establishment."

"I don't think so," Griz said cautiously. "I never really went out much in Society, you know. I'll add it to my questions for my sister. I should see her tomorrow. Anyone else?"

"Gareth Neville," Constance said, and Griz wrote that down, too. "Also…" She fished the purloined dressmaker's account from her reticule and passed it to Griz. "Would you say this gown is reasonably priced?"

Grizelda's mouth fell open. "No," she said emphatically.

"Even at Veronique's?"

"I'll add it to my list for Azalea." Griz paused, her pen still poised. "Neville. Nevvy… I used to volunteer at a soup kitchen in the East End. There was a Nevvy that came in there sometimes."

"What was he like?" Constance asked eagerly. "How did he speak?"

"He didn't much. Quiet fellow with a sweet smile, never any trouble."

"He died of consumption," Solomon said to Dragan. "I don't suppose you ever treated him? He went to St. Peter's Hospital, where apparently they gave him opium."

"Not to my knowledge. I have no connections to St. Peter's, I'm afraid. The opium would probably have eased his passing. Lung disease is tragically common in people living or working on the streets."

"If he was about to die of it, could he have walked from St. Giles to Mayfair? Without help?"

Dragan lifted his shoulders. "Anything is possible. I have seen people achieve the supposedly *impossible* with wounds that should already have killed them. Some of it is down to spirit and sheer determination."

"*Spirit and sheer determination,*" Solomon repeated in the carriage as they went on toward Bloomsbury. "Why was Nevvy so determined to reach your doorstep? Or wherever he went first?"

"Perhaps he is related to the Willows or the Mortons and they didn't want to own him…" She threw up her hands in mock surrender. "I know, sheer speculation again."

"He could have been trying to get to St. John." Solomon said, joining in. "Though, if they did know each other, it makes more sense that they were together. Perhaps the St. John family moved them both from their own doorstep."

"Bella and Anthony?" Constance considered. "It's true Bella was somewhat ambivalent about our investigation, and she's definitely angry with Cordell, though whether for employing us or coming anywhere near me is debatable. Anthony is a bit of a dark horse. Clever by all accounts, and probably stronger than he looks. He probably *could* have moved the bodies. And he could easily have left the house in the middle of the night without the servants or anyone else knowing. Only…"

"Only they both seem genuinely grief-stricken," Solomon said. "Which leaves their mother, and frankly, I can't imagine her heaving bodies around. She could never have done it alone."

Constance sighed. "Let us see what we can learn from Zenobia…"

IN MANY WAYS, the gathering in Zenobia's rooms reminded Solomon of evening parties at the establishment. There was a similarly eclectic mix of people, from actresses, artists, and radical free thinkers to scientists, politicians, and academics. However, they were squashed into a much smaller space than Constance's gracious salons, and there appeared to be a mere scattering of the nobility present. Solomon guessed they and the politicians were less powerful than those who flocked to the establishment, often for more nefarious purposes.

Zenobia welcomed them with genuine pleasure, poured them each a glass of wine, and indicated where little bowls of nuts and fruits could be found. By then, one of Solomon's acquaintances from the Royal Geographical Society had found them, and Constance was introduced. After a few minutes, he felt Constance relax into her usual social manners, quickly finding her feet in a company she expected to shun her. If anyone knew her as Constance Silver, they did not judge her for it.

He still found it rather touching that, as herself, she could still be hurt by such things. If she had been in her own establishment, or if she had been playing a part—as she was on their first case together—she would have sailed through this experience with panache.

When she felt confident enough, she drifted away from him to learn what she could. Solomon followed gentlemanly accents until he heard St. John's name mentioned.

"...St. John! You could have knocked me down with a feather. I count him one of my oldest and best friends, you know. I'm devastated."

The words came from a stout man in his forties, rather soberly dressed for this gathering, apart from his bright, flowered waistcoat.

"My condolences, sir," Solomon said as the rest of the group made sympathetic noises. He held out his hand to the man who had spoken. "My name is Grey. I knew Mr. St. John slightly through the board of St. Peter's Hospital. A sad loss."

The man took his hand. "Elton Granger, one of the Berkshire members."

It took Solomon a moment to realize he meant member of Parliament. "Honored to make your acquaintance," he said.

The other men, perhaps embarrassed by death and grief, wandered off.

"I believe the funeral service is tomorrow," Solomon said.

"I shall be there, of course."

Solomon nodded. "I've been trying to locate another friend of his. One Gareth Neville? Perhaps you also knew him?"

"Oh, yes," Granger said at once. "We've all tried to locate him, without any success at all."

"Really? How long has he been missing?"

"Oh, he's not *missing*, exactly," Granger said with sudden awkwardness. He grimaced. "Well, I suppose he is, but he did it himself. Had a spot of bad luck, ended up bankrupt, and wouldn't accept help from any of us. He told us all he was going away, and went, and nobody's seen him since. He'd like to attend the memorial service, though. Maybe he'll see it in the newspapers and come. That will be something."

But increasingly unlikely, Solomon thought. "How long is it since Mr. Neville—er…went away?"

"Goodness, it must be fifteen years."

"And you've heard nothing from him since?"

"Not a cheep," Granger said sadly.

"Might I ask how you know him and Mr. St. John?"

"Oh, we were all friends and neighbors, growing up—Terrence, Gareth, Zenobia, and me."

*Gareth. Gareth Neville.* Surely it had to be the same man?

"To my regret," Granger was saying, "I drifted apart from them all a bit when I went into politics. But then I ran into St. John again by accident, and it was just like before. We were all at his wedding. And shortly after that, Neville's bit of bad luck began."

"Was he married?"

"Neville? Not when he left. Confirmed bachelor, old Neville. And I don't suppose he had the means after he went away. Unless his luck changed." His voice turned wistful. "It would mean a lot to Zenobia and to me if he came to the funeral. I may be sentimental, but I feel we all need to be together."

Solomon drew in his breath. "Let's sit down for a moment. I think I might have some bad news for you…"

# CHAPTER THIRTEEN

I N SPITE OF her focus on the case, Constance found the two actresses quite refreshing. She recognized one of their names, but they both seemed to have won considerable acclaim on the stage and were ambitious for more leading parts. They were intelligent, independent, and somewhat bohemian, never selling their favors but granting them according to their own desires and whims. One lived openly with her lover, a wealthy gentleman. The other was contemplating taking the same step with hers, a young writer of plays who was also present.

"Do you never think of marriage?" Constance asked curiously.

"Lord no," said the writer's lover. "Then I'd be stuck with him, and I might not wish to be in ten years."

"Or ten months," said the other cynically. "Live and love in the present, is my advice. Why did you marry, Mrs. Grey?"

"Love," Constance said, and laughed.

"Not surprised," came the reply as they both looked across the room at Solomon in a manner that was almost predatory. "There must always be exceptions…"

Zenobia reappeared before Constance's rising indignation could spoil the budding friendship, and drew her away from the others. "I wanted to ask you how your investigation progresses."

"I wanted to ask you about Gareth Neville."

Zenobia's prominent eyebrows flew up. "Gareth?"

"Then you know him?"

"An old friend I have not seen in fifteen years. What has he to do with this? Have you found him?"

"In a manner of speaking," Constance said. "A man of that name was the other body on my doorstep."

Zenobia's hand jerked, almost spilling her wine. "Oh, no," she whispered. "Oh, no, that is too much. Gareth too?" She sat abruptly on the hard chair behind her, staring up at Constance with swimming eyes.

Constance moved another chair close to her and sat down. "Then he is the same Neville?"

"It would seem too much coincidence if he wasn't."

"Who was he?"

"We all grew up together—Terrence, Gareth, Elton Granger"—she nodded across the room to the man seated beside Solomon—"and me. Terrence found him." Her voice cracked. "I'm so glad he found him… But how can they both be dead? You said the other man was a vagrant!"

"He was. Known on the streets as Nevvy. I wish we had thought to tell you his name before this. I'm sorry for the shock."

"Pride is a terrible thing," Zenobia said shakily. "How could he have fallen so low, living on the streets, begging, and never come to us? Dear God, we could have walked past him and never *looked*." She took a steadying breath and a sip of her wine. "Terrence was looking for him. We all were, of course, at one time, but we had given up. In the last year, Terrence took it up again, writing to everyone who had ever known him, traveling out of town to follow old clues and look at parish records. How could he have found him and never told us?"

"Perhaps he had only just found him."

"On your doorstep? That in itself is bizarre."

"Not as bizarre as I once thought, since my cook was not above giving tea and food to vagrants there. Miss Paul…"

"Zenobia," the explorer said distractedly.

"Zenobia," Constance agreed, inclining her head, "can you think of any reason Mr. Neville would not go to any of you in his trouble?"

Zenobia shook her head, her eyes unfocused. "Only pride."

"Then there was no quarrel among you that might have made him wish to avoid you? Nothing that he had done that might make him ashamed?"

Zenobia blinked at her, a frown dragging down her brow. "Of course not!"

"Why would someone kill both of them?"

"Why would anyone kill *either* of them?" Zenobia said bleakly. "But wait—did Mr. Grey not tell me that the vagrant had died of consumption?"

"He was certainly about to," Constance said. "No autopsy was conducted on him for that reason, and I believe he was buried immediately. But it's my belief they both drank from a poisoned flask."

"Then someone murdered Terrence, and Gareth was just unlucky…" Zenobia's lips twisted. "It still makes no sense. Who would murder Terrence?"

"He does seem to have been the kindest and most liked of men," Constance said. She waited until a couple walked past them toward the wine bottles, deep in some literary conversation. "But no one is perfect. Was there anything in his past that was less savory? Some slight, some foolishness of youth that someone might have borne a grudge about?"

"I cannot think what. He was never a rake or a gambler or a great drinker, never knowingly hurt people. I don't recall anyone ever falling out with him."

"Might Gareth Neville have? Could that be why he left you all?"

Zenobia's jaw dropped. "And when he came back, he poisoned his old friend with opium?"

"It might have been accidental."

"It is definitely far-fetched."

"And yet Nevvy's pocketknife was found in St. John's back."

"Pocketknife," she repeated blankly. "Oh no, that is not

Gareth. Poor Terrence was already dead!"

Constance sighed. "It is baffling. Let me ask you something else. Are you acquainted with a Mrs. Willow and her sister Miss Morton?"

Zenobia thought about that quite hard, as though grasping with relief at a question that finally did not hurt. "Daughters of Sir Gregory Morton?" she suggested at last. "The eldest was married to a fellow called Willow—very rich but not top drawer. Non-conformist, not Church of England. She was widowed during my one disastrous London Season, I believe."

"Why disastrous?" Constance asked.

"Because I infuriated my parents, who had spent a great deal of money on me. I was shy and awkward, too tall, and too blunt when I did speak. Frankly, I wasn't interested, and neither were the young men lined up to court me. We all agreed it was a wasted experiment, and I began to plan my first trip abroad... That was when my parents cut me off. My brother still won't speak to me."

"You seem remarkably cheerful about it."

"I barely knew my brother. I don't regret the decisions I made then. Do you know, I think I might plan another expedition? I have been thinking about South America—such vast lands, so little explored..."

With an effort, Constance returned to the case. "You knew the Morton family, then?"

"I may have met them," Zenobia said without obvious inter-est. "I can't remember them, though, or picture any faces."

"The daughters might have been deeply religious."

A light seemed to go on. "Willow was. A non-conformist with very fixed views. Charitable but stern. Why are you interested in them?"

"Do you think Mr. St. John knew them? The sisters live near Grosvenor Square."

"I shouldn't be surprised. He knew many people. And if he didn't, his wife probably would."

"Is *she* religiously inclined?"

"Not particularly, I don't think. But she likes to do the correct thing. I suppose that includes church and charity… She's not a non-conformist, though, strictly Church of England."

Constance thought about that. She wasn't sure it helped, but she stored it all away for later.

"You have a wide mix of friends," she remarked at last. "I don't suppose one of them is a dressmaker known as Madame Veronique?"

Zenobia looked blank, then shook her head. "Neither socially nor professionally." Her lips twitched and she gestured with her hands toward her person. "I do not indulge in fashion. I can't afford it and I don't like it. Not that *you* do not look perfectly charming. Is this Veronique your dressmaker?"

Constance replied, "I have ordered something from her." And she would be interested to learn the cost.

"SO THEY DID know each other," Constance said in the carriage going home. She sat very close to Solomon, her head against his shoulder, his arm around her. She wasn't sure why she needed the comfort, but she did. "Not only that, they were old friends. Close friends at one time. What does that mean?"

"That they did not meet by accident, and so very probably they did die on the establishment doorstep. And the grief of their friends is genuine, don't you think?"

"I do… Such a waste. Gareth Neville walked away from friendship and affection, and wasted fifteen years in poverty and hardship…"

"A gentleman does not sponge off his friends," Solomon said mildly.

Constance shook her head impatiently. "It wasn't a simple choice between vagrancy or charity, was it? Among such people there are always networks of favors and strings to be pulled. If Neville's business failed, other positions would have been found where he could flourish, or at least not have to live in the streets, or off friends' handouts. He *chose* to go. Some people do—the call of the open road and freedom. And then he chose to come back from the country and live on the streets of London. Again, why?"

"His friends don't appear to know."

"I think…"

Solomon used his free hand to turn her face up to his, and her heart melted. The moving light from the streets played over his beloved face and the thought of never seeing him again dried her mouth with fear. Life could change in an instant, within and without one's own control. An accident, a bad decision, and suddenly…

"What do you think?" Solomon asked urgently.

She shivered, trying to throw off the sense of doom. "I think Zenobia knows."

"Why Neville went away? Or why he came back?"

"Perhaps they're connected."

Solomon considered that. "Why wouldn't she say? She was their friend and she feels their loss badly. She must want the killer brought to justice."

"Perhaps her reasons have nothing to do with their deaths. Or she thinks they don't."

Solomon was silent, searching her eyes. "What is it you think you know?"

"That I don't want ever to lose *you*," she whispered, throwing both arms tight around him and reaching for his mouth.

When they made love that night, it was fiercely, almost desperately, and it made her want to weep because love came in so many forms, and they could all turn tragic in an instant.

IT WAS MIDNIGHT before Esther Willow could bring herself to speak to her sister. Ruth's frightened face and vocal twittering annoyed her almost more than the insolent policemen who had visited this morning and spent the rest of the day catechizing her servants.

At last, when even the servants had gone to bed, Esther said abruptly, "We cannot go out tonight."

"Oh, no, no, of course we must not," Ruth agreed fervently. "So frightening!"

"So outrageous!" Esther corrected her, still fuming. "Vile suspicions about us—*us!*—while That House continues to exist! What can one expect from such people? Of course there will be all manner of crimes there, a swirling, ugly mess of immorality, hatreds, and petty jealousies. Violence is the inevitable result. But do the police look there for their culprits? No, they come to us, to *me*, to the occupants of a godly house who live according to all the rules of decency. When all they need to do to stop this wave of atrocities is to shut down that house of sin. Drive them out, as Jesus drove the moneylenders from the temple."

"I know," Ruth sighed. "I know. And yet it is we who have been confined. The sin goes on unchecked."

Slightly mollified by her sister's understanding, Esther stood and said, "Put out the lamps, Ruth. We can at least keep a short vigil at the window."

A carriage passed in the street, pulled by two ambling horses. Inevitably, it stopped a few doors down—at That House. There was no crest on the carriage doors, of course, and the man who leapt into it only a few moments later was unrecognizable.

"Shame on him," Esther said.

"Shame on *them*," Ruth added.

Comforting sentiments. Comforting words in their familiarity, if nothing else. Esther began to feel she could go to bed and sleep after all.

"We shan't allow ourselves to be cowed," she declared. "We must maintain our dignity. Tomorrow we shall order new gowns. And in the afternoon, we must support the poor St. John family by going to the memorial service. How easily man is led astray."

Including Joshua Willow, her husband of blessed memory. A good man, a godly man. And yet even he had been led into the sin of adultery by such women as inhabited That House. Their very presence in the crescent was a personal insult, and they deserved every ill perpetrated against them.

"Perhaps we could take just a short walk," Esther said at last. "I see no signs of watching policemen."

"Even if there are," Ruth said eagerly, "two innocent ladies have every right to take the air before bed."

With a triumphant thrill, Esther went out into the dark hall and seized her coat and hat.

DESPITE THE INTENSE passion of last night—or perhaps even because of it—Solomon was aware of something troubling Constance deeply. Something she was not yet ready to discuss with him. Whatever it was, it had made her afraid of losing him.

It was hardly the first time such fears had struck either of them. The life they had chosen together was full of risks and dangers they had faced alone and together. But this was an odd case to be quite so fearful about, with little more than dotty old ladies and jealous wives to fear. Probably. He had to wonder if it was something other than the case, and that worried him more.

But since it was a confidence that could not be forced, he tried to be patient, making no demur when she suggested she go to the establishment alone to see if any more "presents" had been left on the doorstep, while he went on to the Silver and Grey office.

Janey and Hat were already there, drinking tea and opening post, but Janey brought him a cup into his office immediately.

"I spoke to the dressmaker's assistant yesterday afternoon," the girl said cheerfully. "She's called Anne Morris, and she's not stuck up at all."

Solomon gestured to another chair, and Janey sat down. "Does she like her position?"

"She does. Some of the customers are demanding to the point of rudeness, and God help you if you stick a pin in 'em when their own wriggling caused it."

Solomon grunted, shuffling the letters already left on his desk. "What about Veronique?"

"Tartar, expects perfection, and if she don't get it she can melt your ears—language no better than mine, by the sound of it, though fortunately some of it's in French so Anne don't understand it all."

"Isn't Anne tempted to leave?"

"No," Janey said. "She's a good employer in other ways. Wages are good, and she gets breaks for luncheon."

"How good are these wages?"

"Good enough that she can afford to eat in that very nice tea shop on the corner. Which reminds me, if you want me to go back there today, I'll need more money."

Solomon nodded. "Do they have happy customers?"

Janey nodded. "Seem to. She has a gift, this Veronique, so Anne says, and her customers appreciate it. I asked her about Mrs. St. John and her daughter—said I used to be lady's maid to a friend of theirs."

Solomon regarded her skeptically. "Did she believe you?"

"Oh yes," Janey said, toning down her accent deliberately without sounding too obvious. "I can be refined when I want to be. If I stop swearing long enough."

"You're a lot better at that, too."

"Bloody am," Janey said, grinning. "Anyway, Anne's dealt with them only under Veronique's supervision. They're very valued customers. I didn't ask any more in case she got suspicious, but I'll get more details today. Veronique lives above the shop with her husband, but she's talking about moving to a bigger place."

"Retiring?" Solomon said quickly.

Janey shrugged as the doorbell rang. "I'll try to find out." She stood and moved toward the door before she clearly remembered it was Hat's job to answer now and turned back. "Where's herself?"

"At the establishment."

"All quiet today—I looked out the back before I left the house."

Hat knocked on the door. "Inspector Harris, sir," she said nervously. Policemen made most of Constance's girls nervous.

"Show him in, Hat," Solomon said.

"Shall I get on with that?" Janey said, edging further toward the door and effacing herself as soon as Harris walked in.

If he was aware of his effect, Harris did not show it.

"Just passing," he said briskly. "Thought I'd step in and tell you what we know about yesterday's body on the doorstep. It was removed from a paupers' grave in Holborn which was due to be filled in. One of the workers was bribed to lift the top one and put it on a cart."

"Bribed by whom?" Solomon asked. "And when?"

"By an old lady muffled up as if it were winter, at about five in the afternoon when the men were finishing up for the day. Couldn't get much more out of the man. He couldn't tell her accent because of the scarves around her face, and I don't think he looked very hard either. A shilling's a shilling, and he thought she'd be selling it to anatomists anyway."

"Mrs. Willow? Or the sister?"

Harris sighed. "Your guess is as good as mine, but I wouldn't be surprised if it was one of them. They're positively vitriolic about Mrs. Silver's house. Some people get completely addled by religion and lose sight of the point. In any case, I can't pin it on either of them. They were both out at the right time, claimed to be on church business, but frankly, I don't have the men to confirm that right now. Just as well, for they have friends in high places."

Solomon stood up, frowning. "You're going to let them get away with it?"

"I have no evidence," Harris retorted. "I am already investigating several murders. And frankly, you can't have it both ways with the police—no attention one minute and every attention when it suits you. I gave them both a severe lecture on the law, disease, and nuisance, and though they were absolutely livid, I believe they took it to heart. If it was them, I doubt they'll do anything like that again."

"You will have no objection if we continue our own investigation?"

"None. As long as you don't cause your own breach of the peace. I seriously doubt they're involved in the earlier business, though. They don't have anything to do with drugs or even herbal remedies."

"Did they tell you that?" Solomon asked skeptically.

"No, the housekeeper did, and the lady's maid confirmed it."

There was a short silence. Solomon sat down again.

"What have *you* learned?" Harris asked at last.

"That St. John and Neville knew other. Nevvy was a gentleman fallen on hard times. They grew up together. And died together, oddly enough, by accident or design. Also…we think St. John or his family might have been blackmailed by the dressmaker Madame Veronique. Is she known to you?"

Harris's eyebrows had almost reached his hairline. "I'll look into it," he said. "For what it's worth, St. John's flask definitely contained opium in quantity, probably laudanum, and brandy. The flask itself was made about two decades ago, but he doesn't seem to have used it much in the ten years before the night he died. I'm thinking stupid, but accidental death."

"Only he wasn't stupid," Solomon said ruefully.

Harris rose this time and headed for the door. "Keep us informed."

"Likewise," Solomon murmured.

He was far from satisfied that the old ladies should get away with nothing more than a lecture. They would keep up their nuisance campaign, probably as soon as police attention moved on from the area. He could not allow Constance—or her girls—to be menaced or even hurt. In his experience, ill feeling only ever escalated.

He was still sitting deep in thought when Constance came in, reporting, as Janey had, that all was well with the establishment. "But all the same, I think I shall go back tonight, perhaps organize some kind of watch."

She looked rather carefully at Solomon, as though she expected him to object.

"Good idea," he said. "Harris more or less told me that they've ruled the Willow household out of the murder and they're giving up on the 'nuisances,' as he calls them. So it is up to us."

By the time he had reported everything about Harris's visit, Hat came in and said a young lady was asking for Mrs. Grey.

# CHAPTER FOURTEEN

I NTRIGUED, CONSTANCE LEFT Solomon's office and went to see who was in the waiting room. The very fashionable young lady, who sat there with all the poise of a princess, lifted her veil.

"Miss St. John," Constance said in surprise. "Is Mr. Cordell with you?"

"No. I am quite capable of hiring a hackney on my own."

"Then I presume your mother doesn't know you're here either."

A smile flashed across the girl's face and was gone.

"Hmm," said Constance. "Did you wish to be private with me?"

Bella hesitated. "Partly."

Constance closed the door and sat beside her.

"You understand men," Bella blurted.

"I have reason to," Constance said evenly.

The girl met her gaze. "Would you tell me if I was wrong to trust Han Cordell?"

"Yes," Constance replied.

"Even though he's your client?"

"Not in the manner of his life. He really was never a client of *mine*. He is not that type of man, and I think you know it."

"Then why am I still so angry with him?" Bella demanded.

"Because he came to us behind your back?"

Bella stared at her, then suddenly laughed. "You're right."

"I imagine he was protecting you," Constance said, "but you

need to be clear between yourselves about honesty before you marry."

"Were you and Mr. Grey?"

"Yes," Constance said, before she remembered the insight that had been creeping up on her and that she had not yet shared with Solomon. There were many forms of protection.

"Then I shall speak to Han," Bella said. "Mama has very fixed rules about what a lady should and should not discuss with her husband, let alone a mere husband-to-be."

"Did she keep to these rules in her own marriage?"

"I expect she did. Which is possibly why they never spoke of anything that mattered. Do you know he was a musician? My father played the violin quite beautifully."

"So a friend told me."

"He stopped playing in public to please my mother, but they never spoke about it. He never told her what music meant to him. And she never explained the reason for her disapproval. Or her disappointment..." Bella straightened. "Have you learned any more about my father's death?"

"A little. In fact, if we could join Solomon, there are several matters you could help us with."

"Of course."

A few minutes later, when they were all settled in Solomon's office with tea, Constance asked, "Did your father ever talk of an old friend called Gareth Neville?"

Bella sipped her tea thoughtfully. "Not that I can recall."

"What about Zenobia Paul?" Solomon asked.

Bella wrinkled her nose. "Very occasionally. Mama did not care for her. From her distaste and Anthony's and Han's evasions, I suspect she was my father's mistress."

"I don't believe she was," Constance said, "but she was certainly an old friend."

"What about Elton Granger?" Solomon asked. "The member of Parliament."

"Oh yes, we know him. He and his wife come to dinner

sometimes, and we occasionally dine with them. I like him. So does Han. In fact, I think Han has similar ambitions."

"Then your father never quarreled with Mr. Granger? Or with Miss Paul?"

"Not that I ever heard. Papa was much too well mannered and tolerant to quarrel with anyone."

Constance went to the desk drawer and drew out the purloined invoices from Veronique. "Has Madame Veronique always made your clothes?"

"Only since I came out. But I believe she's dressed Mama for about ten years. Why?"

"Because even by the standards of fashionable modistes," Constance said, "she charges a formidable amount of money."

"It is expected," Bella said with a little shrug, glancing at the accounts Constance laid before her on the table. Her eyes widened. "Whose—?" She broke off the question as she took in the name and address at the top of each. She swallowed. "That does seem an awful lot of money."

After a blank moment, she suddenly frowned and snatched one bill off the table. "Blue silk evening gown… We never bought such a gown. The color does not suit me or my mother. And the date…" She straightened the other account and cast her gaze over it too. "There's a mistake. These are someone else's accounts. The last of my trousseau was delivered two weeks before this date. And there is not a blue evening gown nor a coral walking dress amongst them. Why would Papa have paid for them?"

She lifted her gaze to Constance and then to Solomon. "Did you find these in my father's study?"

Constance nodded.

"Perhaps he just paid everything without consulting Mama."

"Veronique always sends accounts directly to your father?"

"I suppose she must have. I never thought of it. But such an exorbitant sum he would surely have queried… Oh, I have it! Mama must have bought these dresses for herself."

"Can you find out?" Constance asked.

"Yes. Why does it matter?"

"No particular reason. It just seemed odd to us."

Solomon asked, "How did your mother come to patronize Veronique? Was she recommended to her?"

"I really don't know. Does it matter?"

"I'm not sure," Solomon said. "Have you ordered anything else from her?"

"Only black mourning gowns. They were delivered this morning."

"Could you intercept the bill when it arrives? Or at least take note of it?"

"Yes, if you think it's important. What is it you suspect?"

"We're not sure yet," Constance said. "We're just following oddities that have anything to do with your father."

"You said your mother had locked the study and couldn't yet face sorting your father's papers," Solomon said. "Is that still the case?"

"Yes, I think so. Why?"

"There was a bundle of letters in his desk—personal letters, mostly those sent by you and your brother when you were children, and a few from old friends. But the bundle seemed to be thinner than at one time, as though someone had removed a few letters."

"It must have been my father. No one else goes in there when he is not present." Bella's voice wobbled and she swallowed.

"Do you remember anyone visiting him in the study in the week or so before he died?"

"Only Anthony and me."

"Not an old friend—like Mr. Granger, perhaps?"

"Not that I can recall, but sometimes he stayed at home when Mama and I were out, so it is possible. But Mr. Granger would never poke into Papa's possessions! He is a gentleman."

"Of course not," Solomon soothed her. "Tell me, would your father have any reason to be worried about Anthony?"

The question seemed to surprise her—it surprised Constance

too, for she had never really considered Anthony—but Bella thought about it. "Only about his going away from home to university, but I wouldn't say he was worried, precisely—just the usual concerns parents have, I suppose, that he wouldn't go wild and get into all sorts of trouble. But Anthony isn't really that kind of boy. Papa was proud of him."

"Of course," Solomon said.

Bella stood up. "I must go. Mama will need me… The funeral is this afternoon."

Hat was dispatched to fetch a hackney, which she did speedily. Finally alone again, Constance looked at Solomon. "Anthony?"

"A boy gets up to mischief without considering the consequences. St. John sounds the sort of man who would do anything to protect his son."

"It would have to be something wretchedly serious for him to be blackmailed over it! Besides, how would Veronique find out find out about it?" Even as she asked the question, she knew it was foolish. Like a servant, only without the loyalty, dressmakers would overhear a lot of private conversation, rumor, and gossip. She drew in a breath. "Perhaps that is what Zenobia is not telling us, from loyalty to St. John. If she knew about Anthony's trouble, but not about the blackmail, then she would see no reason to pass it on."

"I would like to speak to him," Solomon said. Then he shook his head. "But even if this is true, I don't see how it helps us find St. John's killer."

"Neither do I," Constance said bleakly.

JANEY HAD TIMED her visit to the tea shop perfectly. Veronique's assistant was allowed half an hour for an early luncheon late in the morning, just before the busy period for the shop, when the wealthy ladies of leisure were most likely to call.

From her position opposite the tearoom window, Janey could also see if Anne Morris walked past and be able to follow her. She had the coin for her tea in her pocket, ready for a swift departure. But Anne, clearly a creature of habit, came in almost exactly when expected.

Janey smiled and waved to her. The girl's face lit up in recognition and she changed direction to come up to her.

"Join me if you like," Janey said cheerfully. "I was just debating whether or not to have a cake and another cup of tea. Now, I will."

Anne sat down. "Much more pleasant to have company," she agreed. "Since you have the time, I'm guessing you were not engaged by that lady yesterday?"

Being interviewed for a position nearby had been yesterday's excuse to be idling in the tea shop. Janey wrinkled her nose. "The old bat had already given the position to the girl before me. A waste of my time. So I got to thinking…" She broke off to let Anne order her sandwiches, and then, with a thrill of daring, Janey also ordered cakes and another pot of tea. Well, she had to do her job properly, and Constance rarely quibbled…

It would be even more pleasant if Lenny could join them, she thought wistfully, but she didn't really expect him until the afternoon.

"What were you thinking?" Anne asked when the waitress went away.

"About *your* place, the dress shop. Maybe I should think about a change. I got no experience, mind, but I can sew neatly enough to be a lady's maid, so I might be some use to the likes of your mistress. I don't suppose she's thinking of taking on anyone else?"

"She does mention it from time to time, because we're terribly busy. But she never actually gets around to it. If you like, I'll mention you to her this afternoon."

"Would you?" Janey asked eagerly. "I'd really like to work with you. We'd have a laugh, wouldn't we?"

Anne smiled shyly, and Janey felt an uncharacteristic twinge of guilt. The girl was quiet and didn't seem to have many friends, and here was Janey taking advantage of her for her own ends.

*Silver and Grey's ends,* she comforted herself.

"Would Madame Veronique like me, though?" Janey asked, as though anxious. "Would I suit her?"

"Well, she insists everyone is well spoken and polite, which you are."

*Hear that, Mrs. S?* Janey gloated.

"I don't see why she wouldn't like you," Anne said.

"Then I'd fit in? What's *she* like? You said she's a bit of a tar-tar."

"You have to do just what she says, take the scolds, even when they're unreasonable, and never, *ever* answer back a customer who's rude."

The last was well beyond Janey's capabilities, but since it didn't really matter, she said brightly, "I can do that."

The waitress brought a fresh pot of tea, a plate of sandwiches, and another of cakes. Anne seized a sandwich at once while Janey tested the tea. Since it was still a little pale, she swirled it a bit.

"Would I have to work long hours?" she asked.

"Sometimes. Not so much in the shop, but when she needs sewing done, even the less-skilled needlework, you've got to do it."

Janey poured the tea. "Do we get paid extra for those times?"

"No, but the wages are still pretty good."

"What about men?" Janey asked, as though suspicious. "I bet there are men that come in."

Anne smiled. "A few, who like to help their wives or daughters...or whoever...to choose. Some to buy gifts for their ladies."

"Here, did that nice Mr. St. John ever do that?"

Anne blinked. "No, I don't think so." As if sensing she had disappointed her new friend, she added hopefully, "He did used to pay all the bills on time, though. In fact, latterly, they were all addressed to him."

"Just latterly?"

"All the wedding clothes."

"I knew he was a good man." Feeling she had asked enough on that score for now, Janey shifted slightly. "But no men work there?"

"Sometimes, for deliveries. And, of course, there's madame's husband."

Janey grinned. "Monsieur Veronique."

Anne laughed. "Mr. Kenny. He's as English as you and me."

"Isn't *she*? I thought she just made up the French bit because people think Paris is the center of all fashion."

"No, I think she really is French. The accent never slips."

"What's he like?"

For the first time, Anne looked uncomfortable. "He's not so bad."

Janey fixed her gaze on Anne's. "He's not one of those with *hands*, is he? Because I can't be doing with that."

"Oh, no." Anne blushed. "He's just a little bit...scary at times."

Janey widened her eyes. "Scary? In what way?"

Anne gave an uncomfortable little laugh, shaking her head. "Oh, I don't know. It's probably just me. He's one of those big, tall men, you know. It's probably just his size that's intimidating, but he did throw the delivery boy across the yard one day."

"What for?" Janey asked.

"I don't know. Maybe he crushed a dress or forgot one, I don't know. The boy never came back, though."

"I don't think I like the sound of Mr. Veronique."

"Mr. Kenny!"

"Whatever."

"He has a temper," Anne admitted. "But mostly he takes no notice of the likes of us."

"Is he around much?" Janey asked, as though having second thoughts about working there.

"In the back, mostly, so you rarely see him except in passing. Honestly, I wouldn't worry about him."

Janey was more worried about Anne. He sounded the sort of man she had left well behind when she gave up the old life and entered the establishment with Constance. They talked about other things for the rest of Anne's break, and when the girl asked for the bill, Janey paid for the tea and the cakes.

They left together, and Janey walked back to the shop with her. She was trying to work the conversation back round to the St. Johns, or other "special" customers always seen by Madame Veronique in person, when Anne said suddenly, "Do you still want me to speak to madame for you?"

"Oh, yes, please," Janey said. "I can meet you at the tearoom again tomorrow and you can tell me what she says." They were almost at the shop now, and time had run out. Unless she could persuade Anne to linger for a moment or two.

She couldn't.

Without warning, Anne gasped, "Goodbye!" and whisked herself into the shop.

Perhaps she was late, Janey thought. But Anne was holding the door for two exiting customers whom Janey recognized with shock.

Mrs. Willow and her sister.

Janey halted by the window, gazing with what she hoped was longing at the single gown and reticule on display. She made sure her face was turned away from the old ladies, who hurried off in the direction of the teashop. They did not speak, and Janey wondered uneasily if they had seen and recognized her.

*Surely not.* Surely there would have been some disparaging comment spoken to each other, if not to her. In fact, when she risked a surreptitious glance after them, they did not walk with the stiffness of outrage she had frequently seen when they walked past the front of the establishment, or even when they passed each other in the Grosvenor Square gardens. In fact, walking very close together, they looked so curiously old and vulnerable that Janey almost felt sorry for them.

A shadow fell over her, darkening the bright window display

with the large figure of a man.

Janey met every challenge face to face. She could not simply stay where she was and wait for the menacing man to get bored and move. For one thing, he could probably hit her quite agonizingly without being seen by any passersby. So she spun around to face him.

Oh yes, this was a bully in a well-cut suit. Large, cold-eyed—he had to be Veronique's husband. No wonder his very presence frightened Anne. Janey, on the other hand, was used to the type.

"Trying to see the pretty dress, sir?" she said cheekily.

"Seen it. What are you about here?"

She put on her patient expression. "Looking at the pretty dress."

He looked her up and down with contempt. "It's not for the likes of you. What you doing with my girl?"

"I don't even know your girl!"

Impatiently, he jerked his head toward the shop. He still stood far too close to her, probably blocking her from the sight of most passersby. But she knew better than to try to edge away— he would win that game.

"Her in there. Anne."

"Oh, her," Janey said carelessly. "She's my friend. We had tea together."

"Two days in a row," he said. "What's your game?"

"I don't have one. What's yours? You want to step back, mister? I can smell your breakfast. Yesterday's."

She'd hoped that surprise at her cheek would give her the instant she needed to dart free, but his gaze never left hers and he actually lifted one beefy arm. Whether he meant to strike her or lean his arm on the glass above her head, she never found out, for the arm suddenly jerked backward instead.

"Watch it, mate," Lenny said mildly, and the bully turned to glare at him instead. "You nearly knocked my hat off. There you are, love. Sorry I'm late."

He had Janey by the arm, and they sauntered unhurriedly

away together.

"What the devil," Lenny said in an entirely different voice, "was that all about? Open your mouth too wide?"

"Yes," Janey said shakily. "Anne's right. He *is* scary."

Rather to her surprise, Lenny's manner changed again. His hold gentled, he slid her hand through the crook of his arm, and his expression was concerned. "Who is he?"

"Veronique's husband. His name's Kenny, though I don't know if that's his surname or a Christian name."

"We'll find out," Lenny said grimly. "And you're not going back there without me."

Janey should have scoffed, of course, and made it plain he could not give her orders. But it struck her suddenly that his spurt of anger had been fear for her. He had stood up for her, protected her. Only Constance had ever done that for her before. It made her feel oddly…good.

Because it wasn't just about chivalry, although that was his nature. There was something deeper in his eyes. He cared.

She smiled up at him because she couldn't help it, though she said cheerfully enough, "He'd be an excellent blackmailer's minder. And I suspect he is."

# CHAPTER FIFTEEN

CONSTANCE AND SOLOMON sat discreetly at the back of the church. In addition, to avoid distractions and any appearance of disrespect, she wore a veil. Which meant she could stare at people without anyone knowing.

Mrs. St. John—also veiled and decidedly elegant in her mourning black—walked in leaning heavily on the arm of her young son. Bella came behind, escorted by a middle-aged gentleman who might have been an uncle. She looked dazed again, as Solomon had described her on their first meeting. Funerals were never easy.

This one was very well attended. Solomon pointed out several prominent figures from the government, and the worlds of trade, philanthropy, and academia. She recognized a few more gentlemen who frequented her establishment, and then Lady Grizelda and her sister, escorted by Lady Azalea's husband, Lord Trench. Constance hoped there would be a chance to speak to them.

Hanibal Cordell accompanied both his parents and sat just behind the chief mourners. Elton Granger arrived with his wife and son. Household servants sat at the back, on the opposite side of the aisle from Constance and Solomon. Mrs. Willow and Miss Morton arrived, the former very stiff and haughty, her sister looking half frightened.

*Of what?* Constance wondered. *Me?*

But then, they would never expect her to have the nerve to

come here. Did they know Solomon by sight? Did they know he was her husband? Or simply misjudge him as a customer? She gazed after them as they walked up the aisle and took their seats. From the back, they looked unexpectedly frail, which surprised her somehow. It was harder to imagine their creeping about in the middle of the night with a shovelful of manure, let alone supervising the transport of a body in a wheelbarrow.

But then, perhaps the frailty was an act. It was how people were supposed to behave at funerals.

"Excuse me," a lady whispered, and Constance shuffled over to make space for her before she realized it was Zenobia, dressed in somewhat narrow garments, but all of them black, as though she had made a special effort for the family while she mourned her old friend in her own way. She appeared to recognize Constance and Solomon at the same time, for she gave them a quick, fugitive smile.

And then the service began.

Zenobia's presence, while welcome to Constance for professional as well as personal reasons, made it harder for her to slip out before the family, as she had fully intended. But then, Zenobia too was something of an outcast in this company. Many people, those who believed she was St. John's mistress, would be scandalized by her presence here.

But Zenobia showed no signs of bolting, and the moment passed as the clergyman led the chief mourners down the aisle to the door. Outside was bright sunshine, so there was less chance of Mrs. St. John being hustled straight into a carriage.

Bella had been weeping. Anthony's eyes were suspiciously bright, contrasting with his serious, almost stolid expression. *Poor boy...*

No doubt it was Solomon's tall, distinguished figure that caught Lady Grizelda's eye, but she nodded acknowledgment to both of them as she walked past. Constance harbored some hope that being last out of the church—the servants at the back had already bolted, no doubt back to their duties—would ensure Mrs.

St. John was fully occupied with other, more distinguished mourners. But she was still there just outside the church porch, beside her son and daughter, exchanging a brief word with everyone.

Zenobia led the way, looking directly into the widow's veil. Perhaps Mrs. St. John gave her hand from habit, but there seemed no outrage or stiffness in the murmur of words they exchanged.

Then Constance was facing the veil through her own. "I am so sorry," she murmured, taking the hand that would never have been offered if she had embroidered her name on her hat.

"Thank you," Mrs. St. John returned, and turned to Solomon. "So kind of you to come, Mr. Grey. I hope you will both join us in Grosvenor Square."

Constance repeated her condolence to the stiffer figure of Anthony, who, she guessed, was held together by a very tight thread. He did not shake hands but inclined his head and thanked her.

Bella, who had moved slightly further away with Zenobia, was saying, "Come back to the house. My mother does not believe the nonsensical rumors, you know. We understand you are one of his oldest friends."

"I am," Zenobia said, "so I know he will understand why I won't come. And I know you and your brother were the joy of his life. Bless you." She gave Constance and Solomon a vague, flapping wave and hurried away to where Elton Granger and his family waited for her.

By then, Cordell had joined his betrothed, who grasped his hand gratefully as she addressed Constance and Solomon. "I'm so glad you came. There are no new gowns in my mother's wardrobe that fit the descriptions on those accounts."

"What are you talking about?" Anthony asked, staring at his sister as if she had gone mad.

"We told you," Bella said. "Han hired Mr. and Mrs. Grey to find out the truth about Papa's death."

The boy's eyes widened. "I did not associate the name. What

is this to do with wardrobes? Or my school troubles, come to that."

"Did you have any?" Solomon asked mildly.

"No! Well, except the time Fairclough and I climbed onto the roof for a dare, and I fell off."

"And the lamb," Bella reminded him.

"I don't think it's really that kind of trouble Mr. Grey means," Cordell said wryly. "Suffice it to say, there was no vice in Anthony's schooldays, merely mischievous pranks. He was never expelled or even sent home in disgrace."

Anthony's nostrils flared as he stared at Solomon. "It was my father who was the victim of murder. Why are you trying to blacken his name and family?"

"We are not," Constance said quickly. "Everyone has things in their past they regret to one degree or another. Your father was singularly well liked and we are having difficulty identifying any motive for what happened to him. We know he would have protected you at all costs, so we needed to discover any indiscretions associated with you, too."

"And now you've done so," Cordell said. It wasn't a question, but Constance answered anyway.

"I believe we have."

Bella said, "We should go back to Mama."

Han escorted her back, Anthony at their heels. The boy glanced back once.

"Well, my sleuth-hounds?" murmured Lady Griz, and they turned to face her and her sister. "Azalea has something that may interest you."

They walked a little further away from the slowly melting throngs in the churchyard.

"I heard it, of all unlikely places, from my mother," Lady Azalea said, "but I had to ask very specifically, and I would not like the gossip to spread, particularly at such a time as this when the poor woman has enough to deal with."

"Which poor woman?" Constance asked.

"Mrs. St. John," Griz murmured.

Lady Azalea looked about her once more. "Apparently, before she was even out, she fell madly in love with an unsuitable and entirely unscrupulous man. She eloped with him, though her family caught up with them and brought her home before they could be married. It was all hushed up and she was duly presented at court, and within the first few weeks of the Season was engaged to Terrence St. John."

"If it was hushed up," Solomon said, "how does your mother know about it?"

"Because she's the duchess," Azalea said wryly. "And because she was part of the hushing-up process. Jacintha was said to be with her while she was, in fact, with Madly."

"Madly?" Constance repeated. She had heard the name before.

"Jason Madly, a younger son of Lord Darroway. Though young himself, only twenty or so, he was going to the devil long before he met Jacintha, but apparently he could be a charming dog when he made the effort. There were no duels, but Madly did vanish from Polite Society."

"Do you know where we can find him?"

"He was never—er…rehabilitated into Society," Griz said. "But my least-reputable brother has come across him once or twice in low gambling dens where you're as likely to get your throat cut as your purse. So he's probably still in London." She fished inside her reticule and came up with a scrap of paper, which Constance took from her. "These are the places Forsythe encountered him, but I wouldn't go without someone to watch your back."

Constance did not say she had been inside both places on the list, though not for some years. Nor that she recalled now how she knew Madly. She had refused him access to her old establishment, and the current one.

"Apart from that youthful indiscretion," Azalea said, "her life has been a model of rectitude, according to Her Grace. So has her husband's. So please be careful how you use this."

"We will," Constance assured her.

"One more thing," Griz said. "About the cost of those gowns? Azalea says no one would pay such a price without genuine diamonds sewn thickly into the fabric."

⟫⟫⟫≪≪≪

"Veronique could somehow have got hold of the old scandal," Constance said eagerly as the carriage trundled back toward the Silver and Grey office. "St. John paid to protect his wife's reputation, and his children's futures."

"Then why kill him?"

"Perhaps she didn't. Perhaps she confronted Madly and Madly did it."

"Why?" Solomon repeated.

Constance scowled. "I don't know. From what I remember of Madly, he was more of a beater than a poisoner."

"You know him?" Solomon said, startled.

"I saw him around in the old days, one of those roaring rakehells who came to the squalid backstreets for thrills and ended up more of that world than his own. I wouldn't let him near my girls. His one saving grace was that he accepted each refusal without a fight."

"How many did you give him?" Solomon asked, truly appalled now, although he strove not to show it.

"Two. One in Mayfair. I think he recognized me, because he laughed as he retreated. I don't quite see how he fits into any of this, but we need to speak to him."

"I do."

"Solomon, he is not of your world."

"Nor of yours," Solomon said implacably. "And I have seen more of life than you imagine. Besides, you are too…recognizable. I can go to such places without notice—"

"No you can't, Sol."

"Less than you," he amended.

"Perhaps, but Griz was right. You really can't go alone."

"I'll take David," Solomon said, suddenly inspired. "I think he needs something to do."

"Take one of the establishment men, too."

"I'm not going to pick a fight, Constance," he said patiently. "I'm not even going to gamble. If I have to, I'll just leave word I'm looking for Madly and leave our office address."

"He might come from curiosity," Constance allowed.

She lapsed back into silence, and he watched her, loving her. *Now. Now, she will finally tell me the suspicion that's troubling her.*

"Perhaps he knows Veronique," she said at last.

And Solomon looked out of the window.

At the office, Janey, with Lenny in tow, hustled them into Solomon's room and closed the door, telling them everything she had learned from Veronique's assistant, the existence of the dressmaker's large and threatening husband, and the discovery that Mrs. Willow and her sister were also customers.

"Now that is interesting," Constance said. "I've no idea what it means, but it's definitely interesting."

"They were odd," Janey said. "Not like themselves at all."

"I thought that at church," Constance said.

Solomon caught his breath.

He lifted his gaze from the growing pile of case notes in front of him. "Veronique has lost her golden goose. She's catching another."

BEING AN OBSERVANT man, Solomon had learned to suit his posture and his manner to his clothing. With David, it seemed to come much more naturally. As he donned his old sailor's clothing, with a secondhand coat and a new hat, he actually became the swaggering sailor with money in his pocket and ambitions for more.

He had jumped at the chance to accompany Solomon on the adventure—another sign that he was bored in his new life. As they left Constance at the establishment and headed eastward into St. Giles, Solomon was thinking desperately how to relieve his brother's boredom.

"So, we're not going to play, and we're not going to pick up women," David said. "I've just to watch your back and listen for the name Jason Madly."

"A dull night out, I hope," Solomon said lightly. "Play if you want, but the dice will be crooked and the cards marked, and if you take your hands out your pockets, you'll get them picked."

"That kind of place. But you know, if you want to be inconspicuous, you should choose another bodyguard. Two not-white men who look exactly alike are going to be noticed."

"I don't mind that."

David's lips quirked. "I'm here to pacify Constance?"

"You're here *instead* of Constance."

David laughed.

Not without difficulty, they found the first den on Lady Grizelda's scrap of paper. Inevitably, it was halfway down a dingy alley where every opening in the greasy walls seemed to have eyes, and metal flashed among the shadows—not coins but blades. Solomon walked beside David as far from the doorways as possible until they found the one they sought, flanked by two large and watchful bullies.

Rather to Solomon's surprise, they were nodded straight in and down some dark steps to an only slightly better lit room below. There was everything Solomon had expected: tables for cards and dice, the clank of coins and glasses, screeches of female laughter, and a whole variety of voices, from the broadest London accents to the most cultured. Many slurred; some shouted. The place stank of smoke and tobacco, which also helped to obscure one's view of what was going on there. Scantily dressed females toured the room, looking for business and no doubt emptying pockets while pretending to bring luck to the players.

An oily specimen greeted Solomon and David, rubbing his hands. "Good evening, my fine gents! What's your pleasure? Cards or dice? How about a glass of fine brandy to begin with?"

They sat down where the man indicated, and he sent a girl to fetch their drinks. "Actually," Solomon said, "I'm looking for someone. Jason Madly."

"Never heard of him," said the oily man, adding only a moment later, "What do you want him for?"

"I think I owe him money," Solomon said, as the quickest route to a man of uncertain fortunes.

The oily man cackled. "Well, I wouldn't owe it too long. But you're still out of luck 'cause he ain't here."

"No matter," Solomon said amiably.

The girl with the drinks swayed toward them and Solomon placed a coin on her tray, distracting her hand from its furtive journey toward David's coat pocket.

"Looking for Madly," Solomon said, adding another coin.

"He ain't in tonight."

Solomon put his Silver and Grey business card on the tray. "Drop him a word I was looking."

"'Cause you owe him money," the girl said derisively.

Solomon smiled slightly. "Well, you wouldn't want to be the reason he didn't get it, would you?"

Her laughter vanished. The card and the coins disappeared into her costume—somehow—and she vanished.

David was watching him with a mixture of fascination and amusement.

"What?"

"I never expected you to be good at this. I thought that's why *I* was here."

"Oh no," Solomon said. "I just wanted the company."

David laughed and clinked the bottom of his glass against

Solomon's.

The brandy was anything but fine. It tasted as if it had been made in a coal scuttle from old socks. They nursed the glasses without drinking, waiting to see if Madly emerged from the woodwork. Solomon looked about him. As he got used to the dimness and the smoke, he saw there was indeed a group of gentlemen in that night, making no effort to blend in with the lesser mortals. They were loud and drunk but liable to get into more trouble than they ever caused. But they were also in their early twenties, far too young to be Madly. In fact, anyone of about the correct age looked anything but dangerous.

After half an hour, Solomon said, "Let's try the next."

The next was off a back court and up a set of outside stairs, but otherwise it resembled the previous establishment, including the disgusting brandy.

"They must make it in a vast communal tub," David observed, as a girl sat in his lap.

"But it's probably safer than the water."

The girl said, "What you playing, gents? Dice is fair."

"We'll watch first," David said.

The girl half slid off his knee, tugging him by the hand while her other hand crept into his pocket. "Come and bring me luck, then."

"No luck in there, darling," David said apologetically. "But this kind man will give you a coin if you tell him where to find… What's his name, Sol?"

"Madly," Solomon said. "Jason Madly."

The girl pouted. "He ain't here. And we ain't supposed to answer cheeky questions. You could be peelers. Though you talk too nice. You ain't from round here, eh?"

"No, we're from Jamaica," David said.

"Where's that, then? Got to be better than here."

Solomon put a coin on the tray she'd abandoned on the table. "A reminder. About Madly. I owe him money, you see."

"Oh. You want to try George's place around the corner. I'll

take you for another of them coins. Keeps the guv'nor happy and gets me some fresh air."

Solomon, wary of being led into places he couldn't find his way out of, wished he had a huge ball of string or a pocket full of breadcrumbs to mark the path. But in the end, it wasn't far, before the girl introduced them to the lookouts as "gents wot are friends of mine." She skipped off grinning with her extra coins, only one of which was for "the guv'nor"—Solomon hoped.

He wondered if Constance ever recruited from places like this and felt his flesh crawl in fear for her.

This den was marginally cleaner than the first two. It even had one open window, high up in the wall, so it smelled slightly better, too.

Solomon saw him at once, partly because he was the sort of man who did draw attention. Broad of shoulder, with a shock of black, curly hair, graying at the temples, he was handsome in a sort of harsh, almost brutal way that gave one pause. His black eyes seemed to glitter, though whether from excitement or drink or sheer volatility was not immediately plain. He sat at the head of a busy table, surrounded by coins and throwing dice. A bottle of decent brandy and a half-empty glass stood at his elbow while he threw the dice. A girl fawned over his other arm.

"Who's that?" Solomon asked the man who was showing them the way.

"We don't ask names here."

"But I'm sure I know him," Solomon said.

"Then what you asking me for? If you want to play, sit down. You want to ask questions, sling your hook."

Solomon and David moved toward the dice table and watched the game. Most of the gamblers were looking furious and glaring at the man Solomon was sure was Madly. He held the bank and was clearly winning. Just as clearly, the other players were suspicious of his luck.

The banker's laugh was jeering. "Suit yourselves. Split the dice. Go on, I've finished for the night anyway."

"And if they're loaded?" one man growled.

"Take it up with the management, old man. They're not my dice."

"Then it's not your money," the man insisted.

The banker jumped to his feet and roared, "Hammer!"

As though it was a frequent occurrence, a scantily dressed girl brought him a hammer that looked as if it weighed more than she did. There was a sudden surge away from the table as the banker swept the hammer upward—and brought it crashing down on both dice, one after the other.

Some of the glasses foolishly left on the table fell to the floor and shattered. The man threw the hammer onto the table among the detritus of bottles, cups, and coins, and began to clear his winnings into his pocket.

His accuser was inspecting the pieces of dice, all of which he threw down with disgust.

"Madly wins," he uttered. "Again."

"Cheer up," Madly said. "You should have seen me last night. Now, my sweetheart," he added to the fawning girl, sweeping her up like his coins, "at the end of a hard night, a young man's fancy turns to—"

"Mr. Madly?" Solomon interrupted. "Might I have a word?"

The beetling brows and the hard, glittering eyes turned on him. Madly seemed surprised, though he only shrugged. "Stay with them—they love to talk. I'm on to other business."

The girl giggled as he fondled her.

"It concerns an old friend of yours," Solomon said optimistically.

"I don't have any old friends. Precious few new ones, come to that."

"A lady," Solomon added.

"I *definitely* have none of those."

"Perhaps not," Solomon said, "but I had hoped the lady might."

Madly, who had been nuzzling the girl's neck, raised his head and regarded Solomon with a very steely gaze.

"Damn you," he said between his teeth. "You have five minutes. Less, if I get bored."

He abandoned the girl, snatched up his bottle and glass, and strode off toward the back of the room, so Solomon and David followed him to a solitary corner, where he threw himself onto the only comfortable chair with an air of insolence, leaving them to sit on the hard benches against the wall.

Madly was looking from one to the other. "Have I had too much brandy? Am I seeing double?"

"No," Solomon said. "We're twins."

"Twin whats? Peelers? Footmen? Lawyers?"

Solomon lifted one brow. "Brothers," he said gently. "We want to talk about Jacintha."

"Never heard of her." Madly poured himself a large brandy and swirled the liquid around the glass.

"We think someone is trying to hurt her," Solomon persevered.

"Whoever she is, it isn't me."

Solomon held Madly's gaze, which seemed to surprise him, for he lowered the glass from his lips.

"Actually, it probably is you," Solomon said. "One way or another. We think someone is blackmailing the lady about an elopement twenty years ago."

Madly knocked back his brandy with a quick, fierce jerk. "Nothing I can do about that. I've told you, I don't know who you're talking about, and I will never say anything different."

It took Solomon a moment to recognize that for what it was. Honor. Thin, and perhaps hanging by a thread behind many years of selfish, hedonistic, and probably brutal behavior, but it was there, and its presence felt curiously warming.

"I need to know who else was aware of this elopement," Solomon said carefully. "Because this blackmailer has already caused a great deal of damage and probably committed murder. The lady and her children could be in great danger."

"Surely the lady has a husband," Madly drawled. "Or…are you his servants?"

"No, and he can't help her, being dead."

Madly's gaze flew back to Solomon's. He jerked his head around to a man who was approaching their table.

"Bugger off!" he growled, and the man slunk away.

"Who did you tell?" Solomon asked steadily.

"No one. How could I when I don't know what you're talking about?"

It could have been evasion. He'd had years to practice such arts, but for some reason Solomon believed Madly's honor had stretched to silence both then and now.

"Did she tell?"

"Women always blab, don't they?"

"Who to? Her mother?"

"God no, though I'm sure the old bat was in for the kill. Look at the maid."

Dear God, could it be that simple? "Veronique?"

"Never heard of her," Madly said blankly.

Solomon almost groaned, for this time, it sounded like truth. Still, the maid could have told Veronique…

"Did you know Terrence St. John?" he asked on impulse.

Madly shrugged. "Sure. I didn't move in his circles, but I knew who he was. Amiable cove, preferred the more refined aspects of life, music and learning. Not this"—he waved an arm to encompass not only the room but the entire lifestyle—"filth."

"You don't have to live in filth," Solomon said.

"I don't have to live," Madly retorted. "You're in danger of boring me."

"Sol," David murmured.

At almost the same moment Solomon looked up, two men playing cards shouted out, "Kenny!" and Solomon saw a large, floridly handsome man stroll across the room as though he owned it.

Surely, Veronique's husband.

# CHAPTER SIXTEEN

T HE BIG MAN greeted as Kenny wore an expensive dark suit, with what looked a very fine wool overcoat over his arm. He walked with a swagger, soaking up the fawning admiration of his acquaintances, his violent face smug as though he realized the honor he was conferring on this squalid den of iniquity by his mere presence. A pace or two behind him came his friends or minions, lean, whippet-like men who looked both malnourished and vicious.

Two men at the largest drinking table in the middle of the room—which also boasted the most comfortable chairs—sprang up and effaced themselves to let the great man sit at what was, presumably, his customary place. Kenny enthroned himself without acknowledging their courtesy.

Solomon glanced back at Madly and found the man watching him with a sardonic curl to his sensual lips.

"A friend of yours?" Solomon asked.

"Why, do you want an introduction to the newly great man?" Madly's contempt was more pronounced now, though whether for Kenny or Solomon and David was not clear.

"Newly?" Solomon prompted him. "Who is he?"

"Minor criminal like so many around here, hired muscle like those on the doors—until a year or so ago, when he came into a wife with some money."

"Does he live around here?"

"Not anymore. He has a place near Bond Street, so he says.

What's your interest in the great man?"

"Is his wife called Veronique?"

Madly's eyes changed, though Solomon could not quite read their expression. "That name again. Is he responsible for the troubles of this lady of yours?" He spoke very softly.

"He's one of several possibilities."

Madly stared at him, then barked out a laugh. "As am I? Who the devil *are* you two?"

Solomon passed a card across the table.

Madly looked at it, then at David, who smiled. "Not me. I'm only here for pleasure."

"This foiled elopement of yours," Madly said. "The father would never have told. And a duchess vouched for the young lady herself."

"Which leaves the maid."

"And the husband. An honorable woman would have told her husband."

*And he had died for it…?*

"HE'S AN ODD duck," David remarked, when they finally sat in a hackney. It felt like three o'clock in the morning, although in fact it wasn't quite midnight. "A gentleman gone to the devil who doesn't even miss his old life?"

Solomon shrugged. "I don't think it's so very different from his old life. Except he doesn't feel obliged to shave every day. And I expect the bed's less comfortable. By all accounts, he was a nasty piece of work in both lives."

"It's odd, isn't it?" David mused. "We can all lead several lives, one after the other…except you, who seems to lead them all at the same time. What made you this way, Solomon?"

Startled, Solomon peered at his brother through the darkness. "What way?"

"You move among the ladies and gentlemen, dispensing charity from your massive, self-made fortune. You married a courtesan and investigate other people's problems for money. You deal with low-lifes and dangerous situations as though you've done so all your life. You're my brother, and I don't know who you are."

David had never talked so personally since he had come back into Solomon's life. For once, Solomon didn't know what to say. A light rain had begun to fall, pattering on the carriage roof, reflecting the moving street lamps as they passed by the windows. The streets were quiet, the clop of their horse and the rumble of carriage wheels loud in the silence.

"What is it you're asking me?" he said at last.

"I don't know… I suppose… We've talked about me, what I remember and what I've forgotten, what I can do in my life going forward. You've told me about Father's death. You've never told me about your life on the island. Tell me what you did, Solomon, what it was like for you when slavery ended, why you left, where you went, why you stayed here in London."

*It's not important.* The words died in his throat. Compared with what David had suffered, perhaps it really was nothing, but who wanted to be reminded constantly of their own wounds? They had both been formed by their experiences together and apart. It had just never entered Solomon's head that David might want to know.

"Is there any wine in your house?" he asked lightly.

IT REALLY *WAS* three in the morning by the time he knocked quietly at the area door of the establishment. The door was opened almost immediately by Constance herself, though a large footman called Ally lurked not far behind. Seeing Solomon, he effaced himself.

Constance almost dragged Solomon inside. *"There* you are! What happened?" The fright and relief in her face amazed him.

He touched her cheek in contrition. "Nothing bad. I'm sorry. I just went back to David's to talk. I didn't mean to stay so long, or I'd have sent word. Is all quiet here?"

"So far. What did you learn?" she demanded as he sank down by the kitchen table. She poured him a cup of coffee from the pot. Her own cup was half full.

"That for a duke's son, Grizelda's brother frequents some filthy dens."

"We always knew that," Constance said impatiently. "Did you find Madly?"

"Eventually, yes," he said, and told her of the encounter.

She listened avidly, occasionally frowning or nodding, and he knew she was committing every word to her phenomenal memory. Tomorrow, she would write it into her notes, not to remind herself but to straighten her thoughts and look for the patterns that might lead to the truth.

"So you don't think Madly is our blackmailer?" she said in frustration.

"No, I don't. He wouldn't talk about her because he never has. He's fallen low, and doesn't much care, but there's still a speck of honor there. Love, even."

She raised an eyebrow. "You think he genuinely loved Jacintha St. John?"

"You find that hard to believe?"

"Well…I suppose she doesn't seem a very lovable person to me. So rigidly ruled by appearances and convention that she stopped her husband playing his violin except behind closed doors. She kept him from his old friends. Even this afternoon… Behind her veil, she wasn't exactly overcome by grief, was she?"

"A discontented woman," Solomon said thoughtfully. "Possibly forced into marriage by her parents because of her youthful indiscretion with Madly. A loveless marriage with a man she did not understand, and who did not understand her…"

She waved that hurriedly aside. "Perhaps. So you don't think Madly's involved?"

"Not with blackmail. I wouldn't put murder past him, though."

"After twenty years?" Constance said doubtfully. "Why? He's finally ready to settle down with a rich widow?"

"Except I don't really see him as a poisoner. Though experiments with opium are unlikely to be beyond him. No, on the whole, I believe he's no more than the *cause* of the blackmail. Though he did suggest we look more closely at her maid of that time—who, sadly, was not Veronique. On the other hand, the surprise of the evening was the sudden arrival of one Kenny, who has a rich wife in the West End."

Constance sat up straighter. "That *is* unexpected…"

While Solomon told that tale, too, she looked increasingly excited. "All these disparate people from different worlds, but we're finding connections all the time. St. John and Neville, Mrs. St. John and Veronique, Mrs. Willow and Veronique, Mrs. St. John and Madly, Madly and Veronique through her husband Kenny… It must mean something, Sol."

He met her gaze. "What do you think it means?"

"I wish I knew," she said ruefully. "Because you're right. I really don't see blackmailers killing the source of their wealth."

"Unless…" Solomon said, setting down his coffee cup with a dangerous crack. "St. John had had enough and refused to pay anymore. They were bleeding him dry, after all, and paying hadn't got them off his back. Perhaps he decided to stand up to them, and they made an example of him."

"Because they had Mrs. Willow and her sister waiting in the wings," Constance said thoughtfully. "I wonder what sin these impossibly self-righteous ladies committed? Snaffling the church collection?"

"It can't be that trivial."

"You think not? For blackmailers, it's not about the actual sin, is it? It's about how their victims *perceive* that sin. Mrs. St. John is obsessed with respectability and conformity—of course she is, after her youthful adventure almost ruined her. Mrs. Willow and Miss Morton have so hemmed themselves in with righteousness that any trivial, one-off folly would cause them to be mocked and jeered out of Town by all, from duchesses to maidservants to whores."

She sounded eager, and yet he knew she didn't really believe it.

"Constance—"

The kitchen door was opened with a key and Ally the footman came in. "Trouble in the mews."

Solomon leapt to his feet and Constance reached for her shawl. "What sort of trouble?" she asked.

"Someone creeping about, peering over walls and gates. He's carrying something heavy, too."

"Oh, God, not another body…"

"Why don't you wait here?" Solomon suggested, and just as he'd expected, she sailed first out of the back door. He tried not to grin as he followed her.

"Where exactly was he when you saw him?" Solomon murmured to Ally in the doorway.

Ally pointed diagonally to the left, and then swept his arm right to explain the direction of the man's movement.

"Did you recognize him?"

Ally shook his head and locked the back door.

Moving as fast as they could without making a noise, the three of them crept across the garden to the well-oiled gate. Interestingly, the object of their suspicion seemed to have walked straight past the establishment gate, for faint, slow footsteps sounded to the right. Solomon opened the gate and peered in that direction.

A lean man slouched toward the house two doors down, carrying something wrapped in cloth. At least it was far too small to be a body—an adult body, at any rate. He paused to peer over the gate and moved on. The moon was bright enough to show his dark figure pass the next garden too, and then, abruptly, he vanished.

"Mrs. Willow's," Constance whispered. "Hurry!"

Solomon was already through the gate, loping along the muddy track as fast as he could without splashing in the puddles left by the evening's rain. The intruder hadn't latched the gate, and it too was so well oiled that he made so sound entering the garden. Nor did Constance or Ally behind him.

In the moonlight, the intruder was crouched down at the back door, unwrapping whatever it was he'd been carrying. He'd pulled off several flower heads in passing. Solomon could feel them thick beneath his feet, further silencing his steps. The man rose to his feet, leaving the wrapping—it must have been a towel or some other soft material, for it had made no rustling sound.

Only when the man hefted the unwrapped object mightily over his head did Solomon see that it was an axe.

He sprang forward without caring about noise any more, for the back door was opening to reveal a woman in a voluminous dressing gown. Solomon caught a glimpse of her face, wide-eyed and terrified before the descending axe.

Constance had rarely been as glad for Solomon's speedy reflexes. Her heart was in her mouth as he made a desperate leap for the axe. He seized it and the hand that held it, yanking them both back so hard that he fell, bringing man and axe down on top of himself.

But Ally was there, hauling the miscreant off Solomon by the arms, which he twisted up the man's back. Constance had swept past them to the terrified woman, who was gasping and weeping.

"Hush, hush, ma'am," she whispered, taking her by the hands. "He won't hurt you now. We have him safe—do you see?"

"I wasn't going to touch her, the silly old tart," whined the man in Ally's powerful hold. "What'd she want to go and open the door for?"

"Probably because she saw you creeping about in the garden," Constance said, but she barely noticed her own words, for looming up behind the first woman were another two, both fully dressed.

Mrs. Willow and Miss Morton. She recognized them well enough. Then who…?

"You're the housekeeper," Constance said. "Mrs. Robertson."

"Come in, come in!" exclaimed Miss Morton, plucking at Constance's shawl and Mrs. Robertson's arm. "Away from that awful man. Madam, gentlemen, how do we thank you? What is the world coming to?"

"Axe murderers!" wailed Mrs. Willow.

"Get off, missus," growled the captive, presumably encouraged by the fact that Ally and Solomon had not yet beaten him to a pulp. "If I'd wanted to kill you, you'd be dead."

"I hate to impose," Solomon said thoughtfully, "but would you mind very much if we continued this discussion inside?"

"Just to stop any gossip," Constance murmured, inspired.

"Of course, of course," Mrs. Willow said at once, retreating to make space, though she squeaked in alarm as Ally shoved his captive over the threshold too.

"Don't worry, ma'am, I've got him safe," Ally said cheerfully. "Stop wriggling, you, or I'll break your arm."

The housekeeper and the old ladies were all shaking like leaves, so Constance herded them to the table and sat them down with a gentle pat on each shoulder. "Let me make you some hot, sweet tea for your nerves. Brandy wouldn't go amiss, but—"

"Oh, we don't allow strong liquor in the house," Miss Morton said, shocked.

"Then we'll make do with the tea."

Shock seemed to have blinded all three women, for none of them seemed to recognize Constance. She pulled the kettle onto the stove and set about making tea while Solomon questioned their captive—a thin, malnourished individual with the kind of inhuman eyes she had seen all too often in the old days.

"So," Solomon said, "you didn't aim to hurt the ladies, just stick an axe in their back door?"

"That's it." The man sounded sullen now.

"What the devil for?"

The captive stretched his lips into a vicious grin. "Warning."

Mrs. Willow gasped. Her sister moaned.

Ally kicked his captive. "That'll do."

"Warning of what?" Solomon asked.

If the old ladies had been capable of speech, Constance saw by their anguished expressions and silently opening and closing mouths that they would have stopped him asking. And abruptly, she understood.

"*They* know," came the captive's contemptuous answer. "But I ain't saying. I ain't saying nothing, so there's no point even giving me to the rozzers. Won't say nothing to them neither."

"You don't need to," Solomon said. "I've seen you before—this very evening, in fact, in company with one Mr. Kenny of infamous repute. The ladies refused to pay his wife, and you were sent to persuade them with a little extra intimidation."

From the bully's chagrined expression, he might as well have admitted it in words. But he closed his lips and glowered.

The old ladies clung together, looking, if anything, even more horrified.

Constance poured the boiling water over the tea leaves and shut the lid of the teapot before carrying it calmly to the table and fetching the cups and saucers, sugar bowl, and cream jug.

"That was courageous of you," she said to her hostesses. "Blackmailers thrive on fear. You did the right thing."

"Oh no," gloated their tormentor. "Just wait to see what happens now—'specially if you breathe a word to the peelers."

Ally kicked him again, and he winced.

"They don't need to talk to the police," Solomon said. He sounded more amused than anything. "Neither do you. I shall do all the talking necessary. In fact…I am half inclined to let you go." His eyes met Constance's.

"Perhaps with a message," she agreed.

"My thoughts exactly. You tell Kenny and his dubious lady that they are rumbled, that they will get not one more penny from these ladies, nor from any other victim. I believe Madame Veronique's dress business is about to fail for lack of customers, even if she somehow escapes the law. But the police are most definitely coming for them. Just one question for you—which will decide your immediate fate. What else have you carried to back doors recently? Apart from the axe. A couple of bodies, perhaps? Horse droppings? Vulgar notes?"

"Wot?" The man was distracted, frowning at Solomon with a bafflement that looked genuine. "I never been here afore!"

At that moment, Constance saw the old ladies' eyes widening. Mrs. Robertson buried her face in her handkerchief. She had large, bony hands and broad shoulders for a woman. Constance glanced down at the woman's slippered feet, which were surely quite large enough to wear men's boots. Part of the puzzle fell into place.

"Not here," Solomon said. "Another house in the crescent, four doors down."

"But that's—" Miss Morton began.

"So it is," said her sister, and they both stared at Constance with their mouths hanging open. It seemed, belatedly, that recognition was dawning.

"I never!" the captive protested. "Wish I had, though!"

"All you're good for," Ally said with contempt. "What's it to be, ma'am? Guv? Want me to give him up to the peelers or send him back to his master's gutter?"

"Oh, I think his master's gutter," Solomon said affably. "The first of a few unpleasant surprises coming Kenny's way." He stood up. "Let's go."

While Solomon and Ally hauled the thug away, Constance smiled at the three women around the table. "Drink your tea, ladies. You've had a nasty shock. I suppose you find it strange that my husband and I were around at this time of night to see your intruder and his antics. We too have had a plague of nuisances: ugly notes pinned to the gate, manure left right on the doorstep, even a rotting corpse—forgive my indelicacy, ladies—on one occasion. So my household has been watching. When Ally saw your man, we followed him."

"And *he* saved us," Miss Morton said, sounding more dismayed than afraid. "He saved Mrs. Robertson. You gave us tea and made everything well…"

"Oh no," Constance said. "To be fair to that imbecile, he only meant to leave the axe in the door. And I only gave you your own tea, but I hope, between us, we have scared off your would-be blackmailers."

"What if they tell anyway?" Miss Morton whispered, her eyes suddenly swimming.

"They're in no position to," Constance said. "And even if they say vile things, who will believe extortionists and violent criminals? The worst that can happen is that you have to find a new dressmaker."

Mrs. Willow let out a sound halfway between a sob and a laugh. Constance smiled at her encouragingly.

"Are you really *her*?" Miss Morton blurted.

Constance smiled. "The chief Jezebel? The Whore of Babylon? I am Constance Grey, née Silver, and I am your neighbor four doors down. The friends who live there spent all their lives being as frightened as you were for less than five minutes this evening. Now they are safe. Some even find other work. They are good people. I hope we can agree that we have misjudged each other."

"How did you misjudge us?" Mrs. Willow asked, inclined to bridle at that.

Mrs. Robertson's gaze burned into the side of Constance's face. She turned her head slowly and found the woman's eyes desperate and pleading.

Constance considered. It was tempting.

She said, "I did not think you would have the courage to deny your blackmailers."

Mrs. Robertson sagged and blew her nose.

A knock at the door made all three older women jump and stare in renewed fright. Constance, who recognized the pattern of the knocks, smiled reassuringly.

"It's my husband," she said, and went to let him back in.

"He's bolted," Solomon reported. "Like a stone released from a catapult. Ally has taken the axe as evidence for the police, who may call upon you in the morning."

"The police have already asked us a lot of insolent questions," Mrs. Willow exclaimed. "I'm not sure I want to—"

"Veronique has my letter," Miss Morton interrupted, tragically. "They will soon know everything anyway, if they arrest her. It will come out at any trials."

"It need not," Solomon said. "In such sensitive cases, discretion can be exercised."

"You are a kind man," Mrs. Willow said abruptly. "We did not expect to find kindness coming from that house. We saw you at poor Mr. St. John's funeral, did we not? Please, sit down and have tea…"

While the old ladies cornered Solomon, Constance shifted her chair slightly closer to Mrs. Robertson, gazing at her until the housekeeper finally raised her head, her expression fearful.

"Why?" Constance asked.

Mrs. Robertson shook her head, then closed her eyes as if it would blot out Constance's presence.

"We never wronged you," Constance said mildly. "You could barely have noticed our presence, so careful and discreet as we are. And you spoke to Janey. You knew we were not monsters. And yet your…presents grew worse."

"I'm sorry. It's a habit—looking after *them*."

Constance was genuinely bewildered. "How does leaving a rotting corpse at my back door look after your mistresses?"

Mrs. Robertson flapped one hand as though it was impossible to explain, even to herself. "You're right. I didn't even know of your existence until a few months ago, when the ladies discovered it. They were outraged, of course, because this is a very good address, not some backstreet, or even too close to the gentlemen's clubs. They watched your household—to be fair, they watch everyone as far as they can, partly from curiosity, partly so they can keep sin at bay. Or so they imagine."

"And you helped?"

"Well, I made sure as best I could that none of our servants came in contact with any of your people. But the ladies wanted you gone. I look after them. I care for their comfort. So after the outrage of the dead bodies on your doorstep, I thought to hurry things along, to please them. I put the horse manure on your doorstep during the night. I nailed the notice to your back gate while the mews was quiet."

"And the corpse?"

Mrs. Robertson's bony face grew mottled. Impossible to tell if it was anger or shame.

"I'd met your girl—Janey—by then," she said. "I was angry because you didn't even seem to notice my efforts, much less be driven off by them. And because she had the nerve to speak to our servants as though they were equals." She swallowed. "I think I was angry too because they all liked her. *I* liked her. Until Mrs. Willow came down to the kitchen and recognized her… She told me off in no uncertain terms, for vigilance against sin.

"So I wondered what would be *really* bad for you, and re-membered the bodies already found on your doorstep. I thought another was bound to get you into trouble with the police, so I took the cart, and some old blankets and shawls we were saving for charity, and went to a paupers' grave I knew of in Holborn. The ladies give the odd donation to the workhouse there.

"You needn't say anything," she finished rapidly. "I heard the police inspector's lecture to the ladies. I got *them* into trouble, not you. I know the dangers of disease. To be honest, I was shocked by own behavior. And then *he* saved me. You all did. And the ladies. Despite what we'd said and done. It's almost as if…"

*As if we are better Christians?* Constance smiled wryly. "Don't go too far."

"No. But perhaps…*let he who is without sin cast the first stone.* I sinned. And I'm sorry."

Constance nodded, and they both regarded the old ladies, now well over their fright as they bombarded Solomon with questions.

"It seems neither are they," Mrs. Robertson said ruefully. "I wonder what on earth was in that letter…"

"Don't," Constance advised, and the housekeeper nodded fervently. She had had enough of secrets, her own and everyone else's.

Mrs. Willow was saying, "Of course my sister and I have always been members of the Anti-Slavery League. So was my husband."

Solomon looked weary. "I am pleased to hear it, though you should know I was never a slave."

"I think we should say goodnight, Solomon," Constance said firmly through the ladies' surprise, "and leave these good people to rest at last. Sleep well, ladies."

⟫⟩⟩✳⟨⟨⟪

"A FEW MYSTERIES solved," Constance said sleepily as the carriage finally took them home for a couple of hours' sleep. It was already dawn. "And a few bridges built." She was snuggled against Solomon, one arm across his chest. "After a bad start, we have had an unexpectedly successful day."

Solomon stirred, his arm tightening. "Yet we're no nearer solving the murder of Terrence St. John and, possibly, Gareth Neville."

Constance felt her stomach tighten with nerves and guilt.

"Or are we?" he said quietly.

He knew she was keeping something from him. Of course he did. They always knew such things. To keep anything from him felt ugly, and she knew it was a rot that might run out of control, threatening everything they had together. It was time—past time—to explain.

Only perhaps not when they were so tired that she might say the wrong thing, or not give him the support he needed. Not when he was so tired that he would make wrong judgments and equivalences.

"Tomorrow," she said, "I think we must know. There are still a few loose ends, to be sure—Jacintha St. John's maid at the time of her elopement, the arrest of Veronique and Kenny…"

He said nothing. Physically, they were just as close as the moment before. And yet the chasm opened between them, black, threatening, and terrifying.

"Solomon—"

"We're home."

Their marital home was in darkness, apart from the one lamp in the hall turned down low. Consideration kept them as silent as possible as they removed hats and coats and made their way upstairs to the bedchamber she had designed for them both.

They undressed in silence, put out the last light, and all but fell into bed. They lay side by side, without touching, until she took his hand. He did not pull away. His fingers even curled lightly around hers. Yet the hurt rolled off him in waves.

This was worse pain. The truth, as she believed it, would have to be now.

So she told him.

# CHAPTER SEVENTEEN

Jacintha St. John had not slept well since her husband's death. Which was foolish beyond belief. Infuriating, disappointing, and cold as he was, she had never expected to *miss* him.

She had been lying awake for hours as light slowly penetrated the curtains and proclaimed the new day. Terrence was buried. They had said goodbye for the last time, and now the children—whom he had loved despite everything—would have to face life without him.

Jacintha was afraid Bella was rushing into marriage with Han Cordell. It was a good match, and Han was a good man from an excellent family, though he had some odd ideas. Jacintha liked him, one of few people she and Terrence had agreed on. It was just that Bella was so young, as young as Jacintha had been when she met Jason Madly…

She shuddered. Jason had been wild, exciting, reckless, like no one she had ever met before or since. But love would never have saved her from the horror of marriage with him—turbulence, faithlessness, vile behavior, and viler friends she would no doubt have been expected to tolerate or even entertain. She had long ago accepted that would never have worked. Marriage with Jason Madly would have driven her to an early grave.

Twenty years as Terrence's wife. Almost a whole lifetime of lies and disgust that had in many ways passed her by. All those years of hurt and disappointment had never turned her inside out as Jason had.

*Just as well. I could not have survived it again.*

Now she was free. She spread her arms out like wings across the bed that Terrence had not shared with her for many years, free and still vaguely discontented. She had grown used to his presence in the house, in the thousand little things that made up marriage and family. No, she had never expected to miss him.

It was time to clear out the rest, burn the guilt.

She rose, washed, and dressed without summoning her maid, seized the reticule in which she kept the key, and went downstairs to Terrence's study. She delved into the reticule, but it was empty. The key was not there.

It must have fallen out in the bedroom. Brunton would have put it in a drawer. But before she went back to look, some impulse made her turn the handle of the door.

It opened at once, and Jacintha walked in.

Bella sat at her father's desk, his letters open in front of her. She had been weeping. She looked up and met her mother's gaze.

*Oh God, I should have burned everything when I had the chance…*

"He kept my letters," Bella whispered.

Jacintha's throat closed up. "Of course he did. You were the apple of his eye. You and Anthony. He loved you." *But he never loved me…*

She moved to put her arm around her daughter, and Bella clung to her. Horror and guilt swamped Jacintha. It was a secret she could never be free of, but her children could never know what she had done. Or why.

*The sins of the parents…*

THE SOUND OF her voice almost surprised Solomon.

He was so exhausted that, despite his misery and fear, he was nodding off to sleep when she said abruptly, "Men don't just fall in love with women. Nor women with men, come to that."

He opened his eyes and turned his head toward her in the dark. "I am not a complete innocent, Constance."

"Good," she said, "because I think St. John was one such man."

Solomon frowned, wishing he could see her face. "Because he played the violin and didn't have a string of mistresses?"

He felt the vibrations of her impatient head shake. "Of course not. Because of what Zenobia said to you. That his wife *knew* she was not St. John's mistress. Despite the smug belief of some married women, they *don't* always know. That made me think, look at him from a slightly different angle. She made a youthful escape and eloped with a dangerous man. Her reputation was on the edge of ruin, until St. John stepped in. It was the perfect solution. He protected her with his name. She protected him with marriage and children. So they were both safe."

"It's a consideration when his preferences are against the law," Solomon allowed. "But there is no evidence he was that way inclined."

"Because he didn't frequent the molly houses that cater to such tastes? Yes, I did inquire at a few. But I'm not talking about mere appetites, Solomon. I'm talking about *love*. Like yours and mine, like Dragan's, like Cordell's. Only he could never marry his love."

Understanding battered at him, dragging several pieces into place. "Nevvy. Gareth Neville was his love…" Impossible, tragic, devastating, and ultimately lethal love.

The whys and wherefores of that whipped through his mind before they drowned under the greater, much more personal mystery. Since he couldn't see her well enough, he loomed over her, taking her face between his hands.

"Why did you keep this from me? Do you really imagine I'm so precious that I didn't know of such things and would fly from the case at the mere mention of it?"

"No, of course not." Her voice was hoarse. Her fingertips found his face, gentle, caressing. "I was only afraid you would associate it with what happened to David. And we never talk about that."

"David," he said blankly. She was right. They didn't talk about it because he hated to even think about it. But it was there in the background always, that David had been taken at the age of ten by evil men who had sold him into a life of use and abuse that he had endured until he grew strong enough to escape it. Solomon had always concentrated on that strength of David's, in fighting, in finding his own way, through honest work at sea that enabled him heal to some degree. "But what happened to David was not *love*! It was the opposite—"

She reached up, pressing her cheek to his, and he felt the dampness of her tears. "I know. I know. I just wasn't sure *you* did. But you do understand. I should have known that you would."

He could not even be irritated, with her or with himself. The depth of her care of him, of her love, overwhelmed him, blotting out even the tragedy of St. John and Neville. Words eluded him. So he kissed her, and spoke with his body, and so did she. Even as the beauty of that carried them away, he hung on to his sense of blessedness, of his sheer luck in being able to be with her.

INEVITABLY THEY SLEPT late, leaving Janey and Hat to open the office. But it was rather lovely to enjoy a quiet breakfast in their own home, a moment of leisurely domestic peace at the start of what might well be a difficult day.

Constance, lethargic with relief after explaining her theory to Solomon, and blissful after the consequences of their understanding, drank her coffee, ate toast and poached eggs, and enjoyed a conversation without pitfalls.

"How was David last night? You said you went home with him to talk."

"Yes. He's restless, still. I think he feels wrong, doing nothing, as he sees it. But he didn't mention going away."

"Then nothing is troubling him that he needed your advice?"

"Oh, no, nothing like that." A rare look of bafflement crossed his unguarded face. "He wanted to know about *me*."

She smiled, nudging her forearm against his. "Darling, of course he does."

Solomon laughed, endearingly self-conscious, though he quickly turned the tables by swooping in and kissing her lips. He tasted of coffee and marmalade. *"Darling,"* he repeated huskily. "I like that."

Half an hour later, they departed together in the carriage for Scotland Yard, where Solomon placed the wrapped axe on Inspector Harris's desk.

He looked gratifyingly startled. "What the devil…?"

"A thug tried to bury it in a neighbor's back door last night," Constance said. "We believe he was sent by Veronique's husband, Kenny, as a warning and encouragement to pay up."

Harris cocked an eyebrow. "Another blackmail victim? Excellent. I'll add it to the rest. You'd better give Flynn your statement."

Solomon pounced. "The rest? Then you've found other victims of Veronique?"

"Two. After a lot of difficult conversations. Enough to arrest her first thing this morning. We missed her husband, though—he seems to have done a bunk. We know him, of course—Horatio Kenny, minor villain in the East End, recently came into some money that he likes to flash around his less-fortunate friends. We had nothing to link him to the blackmail before. But I think we'll bring in his associates too, shake the tree a bit harder and put the lot of them away till they're old."

"Sounds good to me," Solomon said.

"It's one of the cleverer schemes I've come across," Harris said without admiration. "She just wrote out extortionate invoices no one but the victim had cause to question. And the victim, or the victim's unwitting husband, simply paid up for items that were never bought, let alone received. The sums on Mrs. St. John's invoices match the amounts paid from St. John's bank account, so it all looks perfectly legitimate."

"These would be Veronique's special customers that her assistant wasn't allowed near," Constance said. "I wonder if she found me a likely mark for her next victim?"

"Did you find a hoard of blackmail material in her shop?" Solomon asked.

"In the flat above," Harris said.

"What will you do with it?" Constance asked uneasily.

"Go through it and return what we can with discretion. Blackmail is a despicable crime, and I'll rake up no more than I have to in order to jail the culprits."

"As a matter of interest to us," Solomon said, "since it involves nothing more than personal indiscretion, did you find anything related to Mrs. St. John? Perhaps under her maiden name?"

"Nothing, as it happens, though there was a letter written by your neighbor, Miss Morton. Which explains the axe." Harris hesitated then took a bound book from his desk. "We did find this. It's Veronique's, half journal, half list of her customers and their—er…weaknesses. The name Jacintha St. John is here, at the bottom of the page, underlined as a heading, and then…"

He flashed the open book at them, just long enough for them to see that the next page had been torn out.

"No, I didn't do it," Harris said dryly. "And Veronique says she didn't either. But I think she knows who did."

"Kenny," Solomon said grimly. "We need to find him. I don't want him trying to use this against Bella or Cordell."

Harris looked from one to the other. "You know what it says. We couldn't find a word against Mrs. St. John, and believe me, we tried. It's very often the wife, you know."

"Oh, we don't believe she murdered her husband or Neville," Constance said quickly. "Inspector, could we talk to Veronique?"

Harris considered, leaning his head to one side as he regarded them. "Not without my presence," he said at last. "But I suppose you might get her to talk where we didn't."

With one of his characteristically sudden flurries of movement, he sprang up, dispatched a constable to fetch his prisoner, issued a string of orders to his other underlings, and led Constance and Solomon on a quick march along dingy corridors to a small room with one rickety table and two hard chairs. After politely inviting Constance to sit, he vanished again and came back with two more chairs.

Veronique sailed in a moment later, dressed in her usual smart but modest dark dress, her head held high. A female warder followed her in and stood silently against the closed door. Veronique's turbulent gaze swept around the other occupants of the room. Surprise registered briefly and then she laughed.

She sat in the one remaining chair without invitation or command and met Constance's gaze with open mockery. "Shouldn't she be sitting in my place? Don't you know she's just a brothel-keeper?"

"Not *just,*" Constance said mildly. "At least I can afford your prices. Even when you inflate them, although, you know, I wouldn't have paid those."

Veronique looked her up and down with contempt. "They all say that. At first."

"And some of them pay at first and then object," Constance said. "Especially the oblivious husbands. When did Mr. St. John object to your prices? When the invoices came without dresses? About two or three weeks ago?"

A wary look entered Veronique's eyes, but the faintest twitch of her brow betrayed something more like puzzlement. And that made Constance uneasy.

"I don't know what you're talking about," Veronique said grandly.

"Where did you meet him?" Solomon asked. "At the shop? Was your husband there too?"

Veronique met his gaze and smirked. "She calls herself Mrs.

Grey, you know. Don't your rich nob friends laugh at you? Or don't you mind lending her out for cash?"

Constance's fingers itched to touch Solomon's, to stop the flow of his anger. But not for the first time, he surprised her. He didn't twitch a muscle, merely continued to regard Veronique as though she were a rather curious insect.

"Like Kenny lives off you?" he asked. "And swaggers about his old low-life drinking and gambling haunts in his gentleman's garb to impress his less-fortunate cronies? When did he meet St. John?"

"It's a mystery, isn't it?" Veronique retorted. "They didn't exactly use the same low-life haunts."

"I suppose that's where he is now," Constance said, "rubbing his hands together over the pages stolen from your book, ready to collect from all your hard work while you rot in prison. You picked a good man there, girl." She let her accent shift a little with the sarcasm and hint of contempt. "You haven't got the hang of this at all yet, have you? You want to see the light of day ever again, you blame it all on him, get him in here instead of you. That's what he's done, after all. We businesswomen can't afford to stand loyally by our treacherous men—that's always been women's weakness. You and I, we're not weak. Live to fight another day, girl. Tell us where he is and I know a clever lawyer will get you off."

Veronique stared at her, her eyes still hard and defiant.

Constance smiled. "Scary cove, is your Kenny, by all accounts. Weep to the judge, play the kind of woman you despise— and walk."

Was there a flicker there? Constance thought she had sown a seed, but it wasn't growing fast enough. They needed Kenny *now*. Yet Veronique continued to meet her gaze with contempt.

"You know your man's listening to this," she mocked.

"Her man is thinking exactly the same thing," Solomon said. "So is the inspector here, *and* the lady by the door. How many other poor fools do you imagine they've seen pass through here to the courts and the prisons and the scaffolds, loyal, stupid women who take the punishment for their faithless men? I suspect they pity you. I know I do."

Veronique looked as if she'd spit at him. She was not ready to give Kenny up, though she might in the end—by which time it could be too late. Kenny could have fled and begun again elsewhere, perhaps with Veronique's lists, perhaps just with her ideas. Either way, the trail of misery would go on.

And besides, they wanted Kenny for St. John's murder. She hoped…

A brief knock, and Sergeant Flynn stuck his head in the door. Harris rose and went to him, while Veronique leaned back in her chair and regarded Constance and Solomon with yet more undisguised contempt.

"You think I didn't know you," she said unexpectedly. "I did, the moment you entered my shop. I thought of throwing you out, actually—Kenny was in the back. But I make it my business to know things, and I know you hooked a rich man, a foreigner who doesn't know any better."

Constance laughed. "Like you? Madame, do yourself—and womankind—a favor. Give us your faithless coward of a husband."

Veronique started out of her chair, about to lunge across the table, but the warder's hand was already on her shoulder, pushing her back down, while Inspector Harris loomed over her, smiling genially.

"Dear, dear, Mrs. Kenny. What have we here?" He dangled a medicine bottle in front of her. It was only half empty, so the liquid sloshed up its sides. The label was perfectly clear.

Laudanum.

"My sergeant found it beneath the floorboards of your fancy water closet."

Now, at last, there was genuine fear in Veronique's eyes. And a flicker of confusion, quickly hidden. "Why shouldn't I have laudanum? I need it to help me sleep sometimes. The doctor recommended it."

"Then why on earth keep it under the floorboards?" Harris asked.

"Kenny does not like me to take it," Veronique said with dignity.

She was lying. Constance knew it with every instinct.

"Rubbish," she said. "He didn't care till he needed it himself. Half that bottle is more than enough to kill a man. Two men. And that's exactly what he did, isn't it? He met with St. John to discuss the halt in payments and found he would not budge. Probably St. John threatened to go to the police and end your entire operation. Somehow, Kenny managed to pour a lethal quantity of laudanum into his flask. And then he hid it under the floorboards, just in case. You couldn't find it, could you?"

"*Somehow?*" Veronique mocked, though she was rattled. She was twisting her fingers together, gripping hard, and her face had lost all color. She understood the significance of the find. "I don't see how. You'll have to explain that to the judge."

"It would be better coming from you," Solomon said.

"Either way, Mrs. Kenny," the inspector intervened, "your little blackmail venture is turning into very small beer beside a charge of murder. That's the scaffold."

"For you," Constance murmured. "Or for Kenny."

This time, Veronique did spit. Her fear emerged in a virulent stream of furious French and English obscenities, ending with, "Go to hell!" And after that, she refused to open her mouth.

"SHE *WILL* TALK," Constance said as the carriage carried them from Scotland Yard to Silver and Grey's offices. "I think she'll even give him up once she's adjusted to the fact that her great love isn't so great, just a squalid little partnership in crime. But we can't wait for that. We need to find Kenny."

"It's possible she doesn't even *know* where he is," Solomon said. "For more than ten years she's kept a façade of respectability and hard work. She probably never wanted to know when he skulked back to his old haunts. She certainly couldn't afford to be associated with them. Either way, you're right. We have to find him."

The police were looking, of course. They were not unfamiliar with Kenny and his regular haunts. Though he would be stupid to go near any of those.

"We need Janey and Lenny," Constance said. "Even my mother. I've been away too long to know where the desperate go to hide from the law. I want to warn Mrs. St. John too, though I don't see how…"

"I can warn her discreetly," Solomon said, "while mentioning no details. The same with Cordell."

"Then let's make plans."

A general council of war was held in the office. It helped that Lenny was present. Having completed his latest commission early, he had a free day before he needed to begin his next.

"You need to look out for each other and take no chances," Constance instructed them. "You know what I mean, Janey, and the sorts of places I mean."

Janey, who probably didn't want Lenny to see the sort of world she had once called home, had turned scarlet to the ears but was nodding gamely.

"If you come across him in person, don't confront him," Solomon warned. "Send a message to Inspector Harris and to Hat, then come and find us."

"Where will you be?" Lenny asked.

"First with the St. Johns," Solomon said, "and then at the docks."

"With my mother," Constance said, wrinkling her nose. "And then wherever she sends me. We'll keep in touch with Hat, too."

Lenny and Janey left with cheerful determination. Constance put her hat back on.

Solomon caught her at the door, drawing her quickly into his arms. "Don't be reckless, Constance. Don't go alone into dangerous places. Wait for me to come with you."

"I will," she said before giving him a quick, warm kiss on the lips. "If it comes to it, I'll take Gerry."

Gerry was her mother's longtime assistant who had known Constance since childhood. He was certainly street smart, though he didn't fill Solomon with confidence. As far as Constance was concerned, no protector could.

But dwelling on such issues only served as distraction. So he kissed her back, and they left the building together before going their separate ways.

SOLOMON WAS ADMITTED to the St. John residence immediately and was left alone only a few minutes before the footman conducted him to the lady of the house.

For once, Mrs. St. John was alone, standing in front of the empty fireplace to greet him.

"Mr. Grey," she said, not cold precisely, but not welcoming, either, which gave him an inkling that there had been some change.

He bowed. "Good morning, ma'am. I apologize if I am intruding."

She did not respond directly. "My soon-to-be son-in-law has told me of his…agreement with you. You should know that I do not altogether approve, either of your commission in particular or your profession in general."

"It is certainly not usual," he replied noncommittally, "but we have managed to help people in the past."

Her nostrils flared in disbelief, or perhaps just distaste. "And you have come to quiz me? Interrogate me in my own home? Like the *police?*" There was a wealth of disdain in the last word.

"No, ma'am," Solomon said, "although any information you might give me at this stage can only help. In fact, I come with news, which you might not yet have heard from the police. They have arrested a certain Veronique Kenny in connection with blackmail and, possibly, the murder of your husband."

She blinked, clearly startled. "Veronique?" she repeated, sinking onto the nearest fireside chair. She blinked rapidly as though clearing her head. "Murder, you say? But either it was an accident or the tramp was to blame!"

Solomon gazed down at her thoughtfully.

"And Veronique would not blackmail anyone!" Mrs. St. John declared as an incontrovertible fact.

"Seriously, ma'am? Have you never seen any of her accounts?"

"Why, no. They came straight to my husband." She grimaced. "Although I suppose it is one of the things I shall have to learn to do myself. At least while Anthony is away…"

There was no time for a gentle approach. Brutally, Solomon recited the items and the amounts on the bills he had seen.

"Nonsense," she scoffed. "Less than half of that for the most expensive of Bella's gowns!"

Solomon handed her the paid bills. Her mouth fell open. There was no doubting her astonishment.

"But why?" she blurted. "Why would he have paid such an exorbitant sum? Why did he not *ask* me?"

"Because he was being blackmailed," Solomon said patiently.

All color fled her face. "Nonsense," she said once more in a strangled voice. "You are ridiculous."

"I shan't explain how it was done, and believe me, the matter is being treated with sympathy and discretion. The blackmailers are the criminals here, and Veronique will pay. I came only to warn you to be wary of speaking to strangers. Veronique's husband, who was her partner in crime, has so far eluded the police. We know he has some information torn from Veronique's book, under your name, so make sure that until he is captured, your servants admit no strangers to the house."

Mrs. St. John held a handkerchief to her white lips. She seemed to try to speak and then closed her mouth again. The silence was so loud it seemed to drown out even the relentlessly ticking clock on the mantelpiece.

"I'm sure you are mistaken," she said at last. "But I will see no one until this man is apprehended."

She stood and rang the bell. The interview was at an end.

"Thank you," Solomon said, bowing again.

The same footman appeared to show him out, closing the door behind them.

"I don't suppose that Mr. Cordell is here?" Solomon murmured.

"He is escorting Miss Bella in a turn around the gardens," the footman said.

Solomon's neck prickled. He almost bolted across the square to the gardens, searching among all the strolling couples, the maids and nurses with their charges, the old men on the benches, and the dog walkers pretending not to see the vulgar actions of their canine companions. He was looking for Cordell and Bella, but also for Kenny. The police would never look for him here...

At first, he saw no one he recognized, not even Mrs. Willow or Miss Morton. He wondered distractedly how—or if—they would greet him in the bright light and safety of day.

At last, he saw Cordell and Bella, arm in arm and deep in conversation. Perhaps already wary, Cordell saw him coming and veered toward him with a murmur to his companion.

"Are you looking for us, sir?" Bella asked, with an unenviable mix of eagerness and apprehension. "Have you news?"

"Yes, but I shan't linger on details. Veronique has been arrested for blackmail, but her husband, who we think was her partner, is still loose and dangerous. We have reason to think he might approach Mrs. St. John, so I have suggested she admit no one but the closest of friends to her house. I would ask you the same thing. Cordell, will you stay with the family until this man is caught? Have a word with Anthony, too."

Cordell met his gaze and nodded. At the very least, he understood not to ask questions that Solomon did not want to answer in front of Bella. The last thing he wanted was to knock her mother off the parental pedestal. Mrs. St. John's secrets should remain just that.

"Did he kill my father?" Bella asked in a small, hard voice.

"I think perhaps he might have. It's one of the reasons the police need to question him. Try not to worry, but if you do see any strangers lurking, send word to Inspector Harris or to our office." Solomon all but shooed them toward the nearest gate and the St. John house. Only when he saw them at the front door did he turn away.

He wondered briefly if he should request David's company again, but in the end he decided against it. He had the feeling that he didn't have time, that urgency was of paramount importance. And besides, this was the life Solomon had chosen. David had not.

# CHAPTER EIGHTEEN

CONSTANCE, AFTER ARMING herself with a heavy stone inside a leather satchel, had obtained several ideas and a change of clothing from Juliet. Her mother had actually looked frightened when Constance agreed to take Gerry with her. But then, she had also looked disapproving when Constance hugged Marissa, the girl from her establishment whom Juliet had taken on only the day before yesterday.

It was a dangerous as well as frustrating search in some filthy places. Even the lie that she owed Kenny money and was anxious to pay it back was greeted with blank looks. The closest she got was a couple of people who had seen him last night but not since. A brief spark of hope was caused by Nevvy's vagrant friend Harry, who knew Kenny by sight.

"He don't live round here these days. Got a posh gaff in the West End and a rich wife, I heard."

"So did I," Constance said.

An hour later, she sent Gerry back to her mother and trailed back to the office to see if there was news from anyone else.

There wasn't.

She sat in her own office with her sore feet up, and Hat brought her a cup of tea.

"Maybe it's a job for your brain, ma'am," Hat said, "not your feet."

"Maybe you're right."

Where would the bully have gone? The axe-wielding character they had sent back to him last night—in retrospect, a mistake—must have warned him to bolt immediately. Kenny hadn't even had the decency to warn his wife, just torn the page out of her journal, no doubt taken what money he had found on the premises, and legged it alone. He could have been walking the streets ever since, dodging policemen and all the places he was known.

There were hundreds of hiding places in London, from cheap hostels to rookeries. Kenny could probably afford better, but unlike his performance last night, he would not want to stand out and be noticed.

So somewhere without people who might know him—an empty place—with little chance of encountering a policeman. Aside from the worst of the backstreets and slums—where he would stand out in his fine clothing, if he was wearing the same garb as Solomon had described last night—where could one avoid the police?

As a child, and a much younger woman, Constance had been quite adept at dodging local constables, a stolen apple or loaf of bread hidden about her person. One had to be inconspicuous and quick and know the terrain. And thinking quickly helped.

Unbidden, one such occasion flashed into her mind. She had still regarded the theft and evasion as a game of hide-and-seek in those days, but this time, the constable concerned had been young and spry and unafraid to follow her into the more dangerous alleys and closes. He had even enlisted the help of one of his fellows.

How had she shaken them off in the end? For they were annoyingly persistent. She had been about to hide her loot when the idea came to her. She had abandoned one of the apples in an alley, as if she had dropped it by accident, and then doubled back by circuitous routes to the scene of her original crime. There, she had walked openly among the costermongers' barrows and kiosks, mixed with the buyers who hadn't even noticed her theft the first time. The policemen had never imagined she would return there and hadn't come near her.

Slowly, she sat up straight. The police had been swarming all over Veronique's shop and the rooms above all morning. They had found all the evidence they could, from her books to the concealed bottle of laudanum. They had no reason to go back because they knew Kenny had gone into hiding, and *he* had no reason to go back.

Except that he would have keys.

Constance finished her tea, then changed into more respectable garb, told Hat where she was going, and sallied forth to Veronique's shop near New Bond Street.

It was worth a look, at least until she had a better idea.

Madame Veronique's still looked every inch the tasteful, fashionable modiste establishment. People milled up and down both sides of the street, some gazing at window displays, others entering or leaving shops. No one appeared to be skulking or paying undue attention to Veronique's.

Constance crossed the road. The window display had changed to a gorgeous dark-red gown and a pair of long ivory evening gloves. She paused in front of it, but there was no way to see into the shop beyond. She moved to the door, which was locked, as she expected. A sign proclaimed, *Closed*.

She moved back to the window, as though longing for the gown on display.

Two fashionable ladies stopped by the door, and one pushed it to get in. "Oh, drat the woman!" she exclaimed. "It's closed! And I have a fitting at four."

Her companion consulted her watch. "It's already ten minutes past. Perhaps she thought you weren't coming."

The first lady addressed Constance. "Your pardon, ma'am, but do you also have an appointment with Veronique?"

"No, but I had hoped to add to my order," Constance said. "There doesn't seem to be anyone there."

The lady knocked peremptorily on the glass door and shielded her eyes to peer inside. "Not even the girl!" she said disgustedly. "If one can't trust Veronique, whom can one trust? Come, Marcia."

Constance waited until they were out of sight and then began looking for the way to the back of the shop, from where deliveries must have been received and sent out. She also wondered about an outside entrance to the flat above.

The outside entrance was from an alley at the back leading onto a tiny backyard and a solid wood back door. No outside stairs. The upper windows were as blank as the ones at the front of the building. The lower ones gave nothing away either.

As though she had every right to be there, Constance marched into the yard. Immediately, the hairs on the back of her neck prickled.

*Someone is here...*

She flicked a careless gaze to right and left and saw no one. Only when she'd reached the door and knocked smartly did she whirl around, hefting her heavy bag like the weapon she had turned it into. Her heart thudded hard and seemed to stop.

The still, dark figure of a man stood against the yard wall, gazing at her with interest. He was badly dressed in clothes that might once have been fine. He wasn't young, though he still had a fine head of black curls and lively, hard, dark eyes. There was strength and unspoken menace in his very poise.

Worse, she recognized him.

"Good afternoon, Constance," drawled Jason Madly. "You always could surprise me."

When she could trust herself to speak, she said, "Mr. Madly. You do seem to keep turning up like the proverbial bad penny. Do you live here? Or are you just visiting?"

"Poking around, my dear," Madly said, coming closer. "Like you."

Madly had never offered her violence. But it had always been in him. She stood her ground, ready for him. "Visiting whom?"

"I always admired your superior grasp of grammar. So refreshing amongst the ignorance and the filth."

"I hope that doesn't also refer to me."

"My dear Constance, hardly." He looked her up and down, not quite insolently. "You are looking particularly well."

"Thank you. In all honesty, *you* are running a trifle to seed. But then, you'd have to be to associate with Mr. Kenny. Or is it Mrs. Kenny?"

"Hard to tell, but there's *someone* in the house. Upstairs."

Again, her heart thudded, and she only just stopped herself from glancing away from him to the windows. He looked, though.

"Who?" she asked.

"Just a shadow passing the window at the front when I first turned up. Faint sounds when I pressed my ear to the door."

Was he lying to her? Solomon had said Madly knew Kenny but hadn't seemed interested. What *was* his interest now?

"Why are you here?" she demanded.

"Oh, someone mentioned the name Veronique recently. I just came for a look. Why are *you* here? I can't believe the inestimable Kenny is a client of yours."

"Did you follow him here?" she asked bluntly.

"No. But he lives here, doesn't he? And no one has answered your knock. Yet."

He took another step forward, but to the side so that he stood beside her, slightly in front. Her heart in her mouth, she turned to face the back door and heard the distinct clunk of a key turning in the lock.

She could be trapped here, between Madly and Kenny. At best, if Madly proved to be on her side, she could be trapped in the middle of a vicious fight. She had no idea which of them would win, or what Madly's motive was for being here at all. Surely her best chance was flight.

And yet if she did flee, she might never know who was turning that handle. Kenny might slip away again. She had to know…

Poised for flight, her heavy bag again grasped like a weapon, she watched the door open.

Solomon stepped out, as elegant and suave as ever.

Her knees sagged with sheer relief, and yet somehow she closed the distance between them, as though protecting him from Madly's attack.

"Sol," she breathed, as his arm came around her waist, solid and soothing.

"Mr. Grey," Madly said, as though amused. "I should have known. Quite an ally, Constance."

"I see you have met my wife," Solomon said calmly, and she had the satisfaction of seeing surprise in Madly's jaded eyes.

"Oh, very well done," he said admiringly. "Quite the catch, Mrs. Grey. So you are the Silver part of the equation."

Constance had no interest in words. She was shaking Solomon by the lapel. "What were you *doing* in there?"

"Looking for Kenny," he said as though it were obvious—which, in retrospect, it was. He had had the same idea as she. "In vain, I might add."

"How did you get in?"

"The back door was unlocked. Sergeant Flynn was uncharacteristically careless." Solomon's gaze was locked to Madly's. "And you came to…?"

"Idle curiosity," Madly said, just a little too studied in his nonchalance. "You mentioned the name Veronique."

In connection with blackmail. In connection to Jacintha St. John, with whom he had once eloped.

"And the outside chance of seeing Mrs. St. John," Constance said. "But the shop was closed, so you skulked about, looking for a way in, and found Solomon was before you. And me."

"Not by much," Solomon said modestly. "I had only just got in when I saw Madly from the window. I wanted to see what he would do, only then you appeared too, and I thought it was time we conferred."

Or he thought it was time he gave Constance his physical protection.

"It's conceivable," he added, "that Fynn was *not* careless but left the door open on purpose to see who would take advantage. In which case, the police will be back, and we should probably not linger."

"Don't let me keep you," Madly said, even the politeness somehow insolent.

"There is no point in your staying, either," Solomon said. "I have warned Mrs. St. John to stay at home and not to speak to strangers."

Madly stared at him.

"God, I need a drink," he said unexpectedly. "Join me. Or don't you frequent such places now that you are so respectable, *Mrs. Grey?*"

"Just the same, Mr. Madly. I go where I choose and keep the company I choose."

"Then, for the first time ever, do pick mine."

It wasn't really a request, but Constance had no intention of refusing it. Neither had Solomon.

The three of them left together and found a respectable public house that had a parlor for mixed company. They were the only customers in that tiny room, so they took seats as far from the door as they could get and were soon served with ale and port for Constance. Madly's lips twitched at that.

"Is Kenny a danger to Mrs. St. John?" he asked abruptly.

"He has the same information that Veronique had," Constance said. "Do you have any idea where he could be found?"

"Probably no more than you or the police." He looked thoughtful. "Unless he plans to disappear for a long time. Go abroad, perhaps, to America or Australia."

"He would need papers," Solomon said impatiently.

"Forgers," Constance and Madly said together.

Constance had never been sorry before that she had moved so far away from the criminal world.

But Madly had not.

"Who?" Solomon asked him. "Do you know where he would go?"

"I might. But I have to live in these streets after you've gone back to your palaces."

"Actually, you don't," Solomon said. "You choose to. A man can change his mind."

"*This* man has limited options, but I shan't argue."

Constance met Solomon's gaze. "We could find Kenny through the forger. With the right story."

"And the right teller," Solomon said thoughtfully, transferring his gaze to Madly.

JANEY AND LENNY had spent an exhausting and frustrating day searching in some of the lowest and most dangerous places for any sign of Kenny. Besides discovering that his Christian name was, apparently, Horatio, they had learned nothing of any value.

As they trudged back toward the office, Janey couldn't understand why she wasn't more disheartened. She didn't like failing, and she didn't like letting Constance down. Nor Mr. Grey, who had become something of a hero to her. And yet, while she still worried at the problem of where Kenny could be hiding out, she was aware that her background sense of wellbeing had never really gone away. Which was odd in itself, considering where they had been.

"Maybe the others had more luck," she said. "Or even the peelers—they got to be useful for something."

"You always get more cynical when you're hungry," Lenny said. "My workshop's only in the next street. We can make a cup of tea and get some bread and cheese there, if you like."

"Why not?" she said, as though indifferent, though her heart suddenly beat faster.

She knew where his workshop was. She had dragged him out of it often enough to help with various investigations. But she had never even sat down there before, just stood by the door, waiting for him. His invitation was surely a gesture of trust. And certainly, she wouldn't mind resting her weary feet for a few minutes.

He was looking at her, a faint, friendly smile playing about his lips. "You're quite an asset to Silver and Grey, you know. They're lucky to have you."

"That's what I keep telling 'em. *You'd be nothing without me*, I say, and—"

"I'm serious," he interrupted. "You have an honest way of approaching people that makes them like you and tell you what we need to know."

She laughed. *"Honest? Me?"*

"Yes, you," he retorted. "I've seen you play brash and rollicking and respectable and seductive, but they're all you. Just different bits of you. So yes, you *are* honest, and still do your job."

Janey didn't know what to say, so she was glad they were approaching the workshop. On the other hand, while she liked his compliments, they'd turned her steady wellbeing into unease. The truths she didn't want him to know weighed her down, making each step heavier.

He unlocked the unassuming door with the wooden sign that said only, *Knox, Carpenter,* and stood aside to let her in.

She liked the smell of the workshop, all new wood and varnish. It wasn't a large room, containing only a workbench, a shelf for tools, a stove, and three stools.

"I'll get the tea," she said.

But he pushed her gently toward the stools. "Sit. I'll get it."

She shrugged and let him. And truly, it was sweet to take the weight off her poor feet. Sweeter yet to watch him light the stove beneath the kettle and set about spooning tea into the chipped pot and fetching two clean mugs from the shelf. He sliced some bread and cheese while waiting for the kettle to boil. His hands were quick and deft—strong, clever artisan's hands.

"Got no milk," he said apologetically.

"Don't need it," she said at once, watching him with a growing sense of desperation as he sliced bread and cheese and put it on a plate.

*Honest. He thinks I'm honest.* As long as he didn't know about her, he could be her friend. But not a close friend. Because she would always be waiting for him to find out, wouldn't she? And though it was novel and lovely to be admired, it wasn't real if he didn't know the truth. More than that, he *deserved* the truth.

"Honesty's not the reason I can talk to those people," she blurted. "The thieves and the pimps and the whores, the men who'd knife their own mothers for the price of a pint. I'm one of them, ain't I? That's where I come from. That's where Constance found me. They know me."

The kettle was boiling. He used a rag to lift it and pour the water into the teapot. He set the kettle down and put the lid on the pot, then picked up the plate of bread and cheese and came toward her.

"I know. Help yourself." He put the plate on one of the empty stools.

Her jaw must have dropped, for she had to close her mouth to swallow. "What do you think you know?" she demanded aggressively. "I ain't some poor bloody innocent rescued from noble starvation. I got sick on the streets selling myself to men, including the scum of the earth. I weren't fussy. That's where she found me."

He swirled the tea in the pot. Interestingly, he had a strainer, like the ones Constance used, to pour the tea into the mugs without the leaves. His poor, dead wife must have taught him that.

He brought both mugs, balanced them on the crowded stool, and sat on the other. "I'm sorry."

"Why?" she asked. "It ain't your fault."

He shrugged. "Not yours either, Janey. Everyone tries to survive. You and me, we're the lucky ones. I forgot that for a while."

He had been a mess when they first met, only half alive from shock and grief. Her reasonless anger vanished as quickly as it had sprung up.

"You helped me remember," he said unexpectedly. "Saved me, if you like."

She stared at him. "Mr. Grey did that."

Lenny nodded. "He gave me a chance. Him and Mrs. Grey. And Mrs. Juliet. You helped me take those chances. Because you took yours, and you saw *me*, not some pitiful wreck who'd lost everything." He gave a quick, awkward smile. "I learned from your strength."

She held his gaze with difficulty. "Don't you care what I did?" she blurted.

"No." He didn't even think about it. "Drink your tea."

Obediently, she lifted the cup to her mouth and drank, while her free hand reached for the bread and cheese. It seemed the sense of wellbeing had come back, for she smiled as she lowered the cup.

"Are you saying we're friends, Lenny Knox?"

"Yes. That's what I'm saying."

She munched in contented silence for a while. Then she sighed. "I hope someone's found a trace of that bastard Kenny."

JASON MADLY HAD much the same thought as he made his way up a creaking wooden staircase into the attic of a tall, dank building.

The attic door wasn't locked. It didn't need to be, for there were lookouts at the front and back of the building to warn of any approaching peelers. Anyone else who called was a prospective customer of someone in the building, if not the forger in the attic.

Madly stuck his head in and looked around. A balding, stoop-shouldered man in spectacles surrounded by paper, ink, and stamps sat at a large desk by the window. The room was remarkably bright after the gloomy stairwell, for the sun shone through a skylight as well as the window.

"Kenny not here?" Madly said in surprised tones. "He said he'd be here."

"Then he probably will be. Come in and tell me what you need."

"Can't tell you that till I've spoken to Kenny and seen what you can do."

"I am a professional," the forger said coldly.

"Of course you are. I'll wait for him."

It was not a large space in which to wait, and there was only one other chair, which Madly promptly sat in, letting his gaze linger on the forger's face and then travel slowly across the documents on his desk. There was little hope of privacy.

The forger put his pen carefully in the stand and glared at his visitor. "Really, sir, this is not a waiting room."

"If Kenny was here, I wouldn't have to wait, would I? Are his papers ready?"

The forger didn't answer.

Madly got up and set about being annoying. He stood under the skylight, gazing upward. He clomped about the room, whistling, and stood at the window, blocking the light. The forger tutted.

"When do you expect him?" Madly demanded.

The forger sighed. "When he gets here."

"With your money, I hope. What do you charge?"

"I'll tell you that when you tell me what you want."

"Damn Kenny's eyes! Where is the scoundrel?"

"Not here. It would please me if you could imitate him. Good day, sir!"

"He said he'd be here," Madly said firmly, and sat back down. He resumed whistling in a particularly tuneless manner. He struck his hat against the corner of the desk, causing papers to rustle and jump. "How long have you been in this business, then?" he asked. "Ever been caught?"

The forger set down his pen again. "*Will* you go away? Come back in an hour."

"An hour?" Madly said doubtfully.

"An hour."

Madly sighed. "Very well."

He left and clattered back down the attic stairs. But he paused at the foot and sat on the last step.

In the end, he only had to wait half an hour and scare off one other prospective customer before Kenny's heavy footsteps drifted upward and his large shape squeezed along the narrow passage toward him.

"Kenny," Madly said lovingly, rising to his feet. "Just the man I've been looking for."

Kenny had stopped dead at his first word, peering suspiciously into the gloom. "*Madly?*" he said in disbelief. "What d'you want me for?"

"Got a proposition for you."

"I ain't interested. Off to pastures new."

"Yes, I heard about your spot of bother. Thought this might help set you up—and give you a spot of revenge into the bargain."

"Revenge ain't my game," Kenny said virtuously.

"Really? But someone's stuck their nose into your business and set the peelers on you. I happen to know who. And I've got the information you need for one last job—help finance your travels, and you can do it at once. She'll pay up at once, being rich as Croesus. And off you go laughing into the sunset."

Kenny took a step nearer. "What's in it for you?"

"I'll take a quarter only, since it's to my satisfaction too. Fair?"

"Depends on your information."

"The woman who foiled and humiliated your man last night is Constance Silver, the madam of the Mayfair brothel. You must have heard it. Costs an arm and a leg just to get over the door— which is, I'm told, only four down from the scene of your man's, er, failure."

"What's she to me?" Kenny demanded.

Madly smiled with some malice. "Currently masquerading as Mrs. Grey, the wife of the shipping magnate. Society doesn't know who she is. I doubt *he* does, the doting fool. Either way, she'll pay not to have her name plastered all over the newspapers. So will he. All *you* have to do is turn up with me. I'll get you in and play the innocent while you do what you do best. You can be out of the country by morning."

Kenny thought about it. And he wasn't a fast thinker.

"Wait," he said at last, and brushed past Madly to go up to the attic.

Madly waited, his smile crooked. It was, he reflected, his only way into Constance Silver's establishment. And oh, the carnage he could cause once he was there…

Kenny emerged, his coat fatter with documents, and ran down the stairs. "Let's do it, then. You can get your quarter."

# CHAPTER NINETEEN

"**I** DON'T TRUST Madly," Constance said abruptly to Solomon during a quiet moment.

They were both in the upper salon of the establishment, entertaining guests. It was still the early part of the evening, though the daylight had faded.

"Neither would I, if the matter did not concern Jacintha."

"But if Kenny vanishes," Constance insisted, "so does any danger of her exposure. Madly will just warn him—if he does anything at all—and use our agreement to get into this house."

He caught her gaze, which was anxious behind her social smile. "It isn't like you not to allow someone the benefit of the doubt."

"I've met men like him all my life," Constance said. "Even before we heard about Jacintha, I knew what he was. Keeping his mouth shut about the past is not the same as making an effort or forgoing an imagined pleasure."

"He gets under your skin," Solomon observed. "Why?"

Constance sighed but didn't drop her gaze. "Because he tempted me once. On a personal level, when I was young and lonely. Not enough to overthrow my instincts, but enough to regret them occasionally. That always annoyed me."

It would annoy Solomon, filling him with rampaging jealousy, if he let it. But he wasn't a schoolboy, and he understood her past and her present.

He brushed his fingers against hers in a deliberate caress, felt their instant response. "Why?" he said gently. "You're only human. And there *is* something likeable about him, when he remembers."

"You trust him," she accused.

"Not entirely," Solomon admitted. "But if he can find Kenny, I think he'll do as we agreed."

"Maybe tonight is too soon," Constance fretted. "After all, four of us and the Metropolitan Police couldn't find him during the day."

"I don't think so." Solomon nodded toward the salon door. Max was making his way purposefully toward them through the chatting, flirting couples.

"Two gentlemen at the door, madam," he said to Constance. "They have no cards but say they're invited. One of them gave the name Madly."

"I'll come down," Constance said calmly.

Solomon followed her, his steps unhurried. He just hoped it was that Kenny that Madly had with him.

The lower hall was empty of all, save two footmen. Which was as it should be. Madly would have been put in the anteroom next to the closed doors of the main reception room. The anteroom door was open.

Solomon was right. He hadn't been as sure as he pretended that Madly would help. But he had indeed brought Veronique's equally large husband with him. Both men were standing. Kenny looked a trifle crushed compared with last night, and there was a small cut on his chin, as though Madly had made him shave to fit the part. Madly himself bowed with impeccable grace.

"Ma'am, your devoted servant," he said to Constance, while Solomon waited in the passage outside. "This is a friend of mine, one—er...Mr. Jones, whom I would like to recommend to your membership. He is, of course, happy to answer questions."

Constance looked Kenny up and down and flared her nostrils with distaste. "I will speak to him," she said with undisguised doubt. "Please, go upstairs, Mr. Madly. Mr. Jones, do sit down."

Solomon did not like the air of triumph with which Madly swaggered from the room. It faltered slightly at sight of Solomon, who spread his hand to show him the way.

Madly laughed. "Damn, but you're a complacent husband, Grey."

"Not in the least," Solomon said calmly. "No, this way," he added, getting in the way of the staircase and pointing to the open door opposite the main reception room. It was lit but empty.

Madly stopped outside it, but his eyes held more mockery than threat. "She said *up*stairs."

"That was for Kenny's benefit."

Madly elected to stroll into the small room. "I daresay I might make it upstairs when the kerfuffle begins. Although…would the kerfuffle be more interesting? A man likes a good fight."

"Not in this house he doesn't."

"Hmm. Aren't you afraid to leave her alone with that thug?"

In truth, he was. It was necessary, but every sense was on full alert, and Solomon stood by the open door, casting frequent glances down the passage.

"No," he said. "Constance has ways of taking care of herself. And she is surrounded by her own very capable people."

"You're not at all as I expected, you know," Madly said, sauntering toward the window and throwing him a curious look over his shoulder. "Yes, I did my own—er…investigation there. I thought you must be some poor sap the incomparable Constance was leading by the nose, tricked into marriage by a true professional."

"Somehow I didn't expect you to have quite such a common mind."

Madly blinked. Unexpected color seeped into his cheeks. "Oh, I left my aristocratic manners behind me decades ago. Constance always intrigued me, though I never got near her. Call me jealous. And impressed in my own common way. Are you going to guard me all night? Even through the kerfuffle?"

"One hopes for very little kerfuffling."

Something that was almost a smile flashed in Madly's hard eyes. "Just when I thought you were a serious man."

"I thought I was a poor sap tricked into marriage."

"You bear further study, but I can see why she likes you."

Solomon did not reply.

Madly mused, "She was like some exotic butterfly, fluttering through an ugly swamp. Beautiful, incomprehensible in such surroundings, and fascinating for that reason. And yet so insubstantial she could not be touched, let alone caught. I know because I tried."

Again, Solomon made no comment. He knew his Constance. She did not need a character reference from anyone, let alone from such a man as Jason Madly. And yet it struck him that Madly was giving her one, without request and without offense. His peculiar honor again? Or…

Solomon's blood ran cold. Was Madly making up for betrayal?

"SIT," CONSTANCE SAID regally to the unspeakable Horatio Kenny. "I shan't waste time interviewing you, *Mr. Jones*. We both know you would never obtain membership here. What do you want?"

"Two thousand pounds," Kenny said promptly. "And I'm out of your hair for good."

"You are not in my hair," Constance said. "And you don't strike me as a deserving case for charity. You should also be aware I have the means of removing you from my house."

"Bit hoity-toity for a whore, ain't you?" Kenny said, with the deliberate insult of the bully. "We knew you for who and what you are as soon as you walked into the shop. Lowering the tone of a respectable establishment, *Mrs. Silver*." He smiled, though it was more like a leer. "Or is that Mrs. Grey?"

Solomon—and Madly—were right. He really did think it was

a huge revelation, that word of Solomon Grey's very odd marriage had not begun to trickle out even before it happened. No doubt she had her powerful clients to thank for the discretion of newspapers. It had never even been blared across the worst scandal rags.

"That's my price," Kenny said. "Two thousand. Or I walk straight out of here into the office of a very good friend of mine. He works late at *Hush Magazine*."

Constance knew how to look frightened. "You can't go to the press. You have no proof."

"Don't need any. One paragraph's all it will take. And everyone knows. You'll have no punters 'cause the wives'll keep 'em at home. And no one'll do business with Mr. Solomon Grey no more. Pariahs," Kenny pronounced with relish. "That's what you'll be. Unless I get my two thousand pounds."

Constance swung away from him. She counted to ten, slowly, while the back of her neck prickled. She knew better than to turn her back on an enemy, but she had to convince him. Still, she didn't put it past him to hit her over the head or strangle her before he rummaged about the house looking for money and jewels. Her necklace alone was worth enough to get him abroad…

*Eight, nine, ten.* "I don't keep that kind of money in the house," she said. "I have nothing like it. If you wait until tomorrow—"

"Nope," Kenny interrupted. "It's all tonight. Payment—or *Hush Magazine*. Make up your mind. Unlike Mr. Madly, I ain't got all night."

Constance turned back to him at last. He hadn't moved. "What if I give you this necklace, and the few hundred in cash I have in my safe? Is that enough to stop you from giving this story to the magazine and ruining my husband and me?"

Kenny scowled. "How many hundred?"

"Four, maybe five."

"I ain't that cheap," he growled. He looked her up and down

with studied insolence. "Still, I'm a gent. Throw in the earrings and the ring on your finger, and I'll consider it."

Constance drew in her breath. "Very well… On one condition."

"No conditions."

"You blackmailed a friend of mine," Constance said, her voice shaky but determined. "Mrs. St. John. I've been looking into that for her, and I know it was Veronique. Give me the page you tore from your wife's book, the page with Mrs. St. John's name on it. And I'll give you the earrings, too. And one ring."

"Nope," said Kenny, smiling wolfishly as he sat back and folded his hands across his small paunch. "All three rings. Including the wedding band."

"No, please, not my wedding ring…"

"All of them. Or it's *Hush Magazine* and no hush for you!" He laughed at his own feeble joke, clearly settling into his familiar and comfortable role. His little piggy eyes gleamed.

Constance swallowed. "Then show me the paper. Or…or there is no deal."

Kenny laughed. He knew she was lying. But he did delve inside his coat for a paper that he let flutter to the floor at his feet. It was of no more use to him. He was fleeing. Constance went and picked it up. The St. John name leapt out at her, but she had no time for more at that moment.

She lifted her gaze slowly to his. "Did you kill Mr. St. John?"

There was no mistaking the startlement in his eyes. "Course I did," he boasted.

The trouble was, she knew he was lying.

He held out his hand. "Now hand over the jewels and fetch me my money."

Stuffing the page up her sleeve, she went to the cabinet and took out the small bundle of banknotes she had put there deliberately, along with the fat velvet bag beneath, which was full of cut-up newspaper.

"If I give you all this, you will keep my secret?"

"And if you don't, I'll shout it via all the papers I know."

She returned to him and handed over the bundle of notes. He snatched the bag and again held out his hand.

*Now. Come now.* Her heart was thudding. She unfastened her necklace and dropped it into his waiting palm. She took off her earrings and added them to the glittering heap. Something must have gone wrong. No one had heard. Were there enough of her own people in the hall to stop him?

*Solomon!*

Something had happened to Solomon. Madly had betrayed them after all, and was in league with Kenny…

In her urgent need to get to Solomon, she all but tore off her rings, shoving them into his hands before bolting for the door.

She was almost knocked over as it swung right open and Solomon threw himself inside, Madly, Jeremy, and Max at his heels. Kenny seemed almost not to notice, for, mouth open, he was staring at the wall on his right, which, it must have seemed to him, had suddenly collapsed under the weight of several men—Inspector Harris, Sergeant Flynn, and a constable, all in plain clothes.

In fact, it was only a small part of the wall that had opened, a secret door disguised on both sides. It was one of Constance's safety features, with a tiny spy-hole built in. From the place she had shown them in the main reception room, the policemen should have been able to see and hear everything.

The jewels fell from Kenny's nerveless hands, scattering across the floor. The money and the bag landed at his feet, even before Flynn seized him.

Solomon grabbed Constance, his grip so unusually firm that she knew he had been as scared as she.

"Well," Inspector Harris said genially, "I've never arrested you with so little trouble before. Horatio Kenny, you are under arrest for extortion, blackmail, and whatever else we can find to throw at you. Possibly murder."

Now, with Solomon safe and unharmed, Constance could think again. She retrieved the crumped paper from her sleeve.

Solomon read it over her shoulder.

Slowly, Constance lifted her gaze and met Solomon's. "We were wrong. Veronique knew nothing to Mrs. St. John's discredit."

It had always been about Terrence St. John. All of it.

And in that instant, the whole puzzle fell snugly into place.

CONSTANCE HAD NO idea if the whole family would accept their invitation, but they arranged enough chairs in Solomon's office to cater for Cordell, Mrs. St. John, and both her children.

In the end, they arrived together in the St. John crested carriage, all of them dressed in mourning black. Hat showed them in, but it took Janey's efforts as well to supply everyone with tea and offer biscuits.

Only when the pair had left did Solomon begin to speak of anything important.

"We appreciate you all coming at this difficult time," he began. "But we thought, in light of our own suspicions and those of the police, that you should know the results of all our inquiries. As I believe you know, Mrs. St. John, Mr. Cordell invited us to investigate matters surrounding your husband's untimely death in such unlikely circumstance, and I believe we can set your minds to rest on that score. The issue of blackmail has been dealt with by the police. Without involving your family, the court will have enough evidence to convict. There is nothing left that can sully the St. John name."

Mrs. St. John sat perfectly still. She might have been wearing a veil for all her face gave away. Cordell and Bella showed the most obvious relief.

Anthony was frowning and shaking his head. "I can't imagine what secrets worthy of blackmail any of my family has ever harbored!"

"Oh, none, I should think," Solomon said. "Blackmailers tend to work through fear, not truth. A mere half-truth in there, mixed up with lies and threats, and victims tend to pay up rather than risk their reputations. Your family was particularly vulnerable, with Miss Bella about to make such an advantageous marriage. I imagine your father wanted nothing to interfere with that. It was certainly nothing to do with where he was found. We are satisfied that he was entirely unknown in that house, even for purposes of the house's charities."

"Then why was he there?" Anthony demanded.

"Luck," Constance said. "Just luck. We think he had just discovered an old friend whom he had been seeking for many years. This friend, Neville, had fallen on hard—very hard—times, but word had finally reached him, by word of many mouths, that Mr. St. John wanted to see him. By this time, their paths were so diverged that there was nowhere appropriate for them to meet where one or the other would not be immediately noticed. I suspect they had arranged to meet in the gardens of Grosvenor Square, but they're not terribly safe or salubrious at that time of night. So they sought somewhere quieter to talk. They probably looked for lights to be sure they would not disturb sleeping occupants. So they chose that house where the lights were still lit. Probably. At any rate, it is not significant."

"And his death?" Cordell said. "Which is what this is all about."

Solomon spread his hands. "Pure accident. I suspect they were a little the worse for wear, as old friends often are at reunions. But Neville was dying of consumption and had opium for that purpose. We thought at first it could have been the laudanum found at Veronique's home, but in fact there was no way that could have got into Mr. St. John's flask. It seems likely that Neville had brought his own bottle of spirits, laced with enough opium to get him through the night—all he had, in fact. He may even have planned to die that night when he was not alone."

"The poor man," Bella whispered.

"At some point, they probably refilled the flask from Neville's bottle. St. John probably meant to stop drinking at that point. Either he forgot, or didn't know, and drank from it later, perhaps even to toast the sad passing of his old friend. A tragic accident, but an accident nonetheless."

"But the knife, the vagrant's knife," Cordell said, "that stabbed Mr. St. John after his death. How did that get there?"

"He had friends living on the street," Constance said. "I spoke to several. One in particular had known him for years and was fond of him. He, or some other acquaintance, must have followed Neville, worried for his health, no doubt. Finding him dead on the doorstep, they made the false assumption that St. John was responsible and stabbed him with Neville's knife. No doubt it seemed symbolic to them. It must have been this friend or friends who disturbed the bodies from their original position. But whatever the reasoning, the stabbing did not kill Mr. St. John, for he, poor man, was already dead."

"A tragic accident," Solomon repeated. "And accepted as such by both us and the police. We can't prove most of it, of course, but it is the only solution that makes sense with such evidence as we do have, including the characters of all concerned. The investigation is at an end."

There was silence as they all thought about it, and accepted it. Grief would fade more slowly, but at least now, they had peace.

"Thank you," Mrs. St. John said stiffly. "I did not approve of Han's actions in employing you, but you have been diligent, discreet, and efficient, and we are grateful."

Solomon rose. "Let me show you out."

"Might I have a brief, private word, Mrs. St. John?" Constance said as the widow began to rise.

A frown flickered on her brow, though she relaxed back into her chair.

"We'll wait in the carriage, Mama," Bella said.

The door clicked shut behind them, leaving Constance and

Jacintha alone.

Jacintha's gaze was haughty and just a little sardonic. "Woman to woman? If you mean to reassure me that my husband really was unknown in that house, there is no need. I never believed he was."

"I know," Constance said. "You never believed Zenobia Paul was his mistress either, did you?"

"No."

"Because he was a good, loyal man and a faithful husband—at least in body."

Jacintha's eyes grew wintry. "Are you trying to imply something by that remark?"

"Yes," Constance said frankly. "Look, the story we told stands up to scrutiny, satisfies the police and, more importantly, your family, but it isn't the truth, is it? Not the whole truth."

"My good woman—"

"I'm not a good woman," Constance interrupted. "Or, at least, you might not regard me as such. But I do know about love. I know we can't always choose it, or Solomon Grey would not have married me, nor I him. Nor did *you* choose, I suspect, to love Jason Madly, but I believe you did all the same. Your elopement was foiled by your family, and you were hurried into marriage with the first willing and suitable man.

"I suspect he knew you did not love him, and imagined that was all to the good, for he too loved someone he could never marry. He probably thought you could comfort each other. Or something equally idealistic and impossible."

A short, bitter laugh issued from between Mrs. St. John's lips, quickly suppressed. "Stop, please."

"Not yet. Let me tell you what I think happened. Stop me wherever you like and tell me the truth. I think Terrence had always loved Gareth Neville—a shocking, even illegal love that could never come into the open. So they separated, and Terrence decided to marry you. You, on the verge of scandal, were willing enough to marry him. Being the man he was, I suspect there was no further intimacy between him and Neville, but somehow you found out about their affair. Perhaps you saw an old letter, or some kind friend poured poison into your ears."

She said nothing, just sat rigid and white faced.

"He did his marital duty," Constance proceeded. "Gave you two wonderful children, whom you both loved deeply. But it grew to be all you shared. You had your life of social engagements, he his own of academia, bohemia, music, philanthropy. I think he made every effort except the one you needed to make you happy.

"It was hard on you," Constance allowed. "You married young and wanted his love. Who wants to waste their life, after all? But all you could do was keep him from his old affection. Neville had vanished for years. You hoped, perhaps, that he was forgotten, until you found out that Terrence was looking for him again.

"He did not appear to be successful, though, and then you were both distracted by Bella's engagement. And the blackmail began."

"I knew nothing about that," Jacintha whispered. "I never dreamed it. How did she know?"

"Veronique? I'm not sure. But from the note in her journal, she had seen him in the past with a man she called an *unnatural*."

Jacintha shuddered. "I knew he was worried about something. I had lived with the man for twenty years. That must have been when the blackmail started. And then his mood changed suddenly to wild happiness, and I knew, I *knew* he'd found Gareth Neville. I couldn't sleep for worry, for this could not come out, not now, with Anthony going to university and Bella to be married…"

"So when you heard him leave the house at midnight, you followed him," Constance suggested.

"I saw him go into the garden in the square. I wasn't foolish enough to follow him in there, but I walked around and around and never saw him come out. Somehow, I had missed him, so I walked further around the nearby streets, hoping for a glimpse of him, but never finding him. And then, as I gave up and was finally coming home via the crescent mews, I heard his voice..."

This, surely, was the moment of truth. Constance tried not to hold her breath.

"It came from one of the back gardens off the mews," Jacintha said, "and I only heard it for a moment. Then it stopped. I waited for him to come out, but again, he never did. I thought he must have gone into the house. I felt helpless. I could hardly wake the household and demand entrance. I didn't even know why I had followed him in the first place. I think I imagined my very presence would have shamed him, turned him away from his unnatural..."

Jacintha shuddered. "I don't know how long I waited there, huddled in the dark, waiting for him to come out. Somehow, I had to make him understand what he was doing to me, to our children. I could not allow him to disgrace us, for their sakes. And for mine. With Bella getting married, and Anthony beginning to make his own way in the world, the appearance of respectability was all I had. And he was risking it in such a *disgusting* way."

Constance opened her mouth, then closed it again. She had to allow Jacintha to tell her truth. It was what she had asked for.

"Finally, I realized it would be light soon, that servants would be stirring in the mews and in the kitchens. I wondered if I had been stupid. There may have been a way out of that garden, around the side of the house to the front. Or he could have gone through the house. Either way, I thought he was probably at home and in his own bed, while I skulked like some criminal in the dark and cold...

"When I went into that garden, I didn't really expect to see him. I was just removing the last possibility before I went home in defeat. But I had resolved to speak to him in private, to bring all this out between us and stop it. Dawn was just beginning, the light gray rather than black, so they were obvious..."

Her voice dropped to little more than a whisper. "They sat on the step below the kitchen door, side by side, touching. Even their heads leaned against each other." Involuntarily, it seemed, she clutched her heart, as though the image hurt in some way that was beyond disgust. "I didn't even realize they were dead at first. Until I pushed his shoulder and he slumped forward…"

Jacintha's gaze lifted, coming back into focus on Constance's face. "He smelled of laudanum. So did Neville."

"Then you recognized Neville?"

"Oh yes. He was still Gareth Neville beneath the filth and rags. And he held Terrence's flask in his hand, resting on his knee. It was laudanum. I knew what they had done. They had killed themselves together. You were right about that, only it wasn't an accident, as you said. I thought…I thought he had done it because Neville was so clearly dying and he could not bear life without him. Or perhaps he just could not bear life *with* me.

"I thought, *What is wrong with me that Jason would not fight for me, that my husband of twenty years preferred death to life with me?* And then I thought of the children. And so I did what I could, with shaking hands. I pulled them apart so that they were leaning away from each other instead of together, their heads at either side of the door. I took Terrence's notecase from his pocket and forced myself to shove it into Neville's. And while my hand was in there, I found Neville's knife. Terrence had given it to him, you know, when they were boys, and Neville had given the flask to Terrence." Her lips twisted. "Lovers' tokens. He had never used the flask since Neville left, not until that night. I shoved it under the potting shed."

She stopped talking, as though no longer capable of it. Constance continued for her, as gently as she could.

"And then you stuck Neville's knife into Terrence's back to make it look like robbery and murder. A scandal, but not such a terrible scandal as a lovers' suicide."

Jacintha gave a helpless little shrug. "I had no time to think. It was the best I could do. And then I fled back home, only just in time to avoid my own servants. It never entered my head that anyone could tell that the stabbing happened after death and was not the cause. I thought the smell of laudanum would dissipate, and no one would ever know."

Her voice stilled. Perhaps there was some kind of relief in confession.

"I didn't expect to care," Jacintha whispered. "Nor to miss him. I just didn't want the world to know that he was a suicide and a pervert. For the children's sake. Thank you for telling them it was an accident."

Constance said, "They call suicide a sin. I don't believe that. It is the ultimate despair and worthy of pity, not judgment. In your husband's case, it was not as much about Neville as about you and the children. He gave Neville his company into death and meant to die at home, breaking the blackmail cycle and saving you all from scandal. Only he misjudged the strength of the opium in the flask."

Jacintha's brow twitched. "Is that what you truly think?" she asked tragically.

"Yes." Constance leaned nearer and took the widow's hand. "There is no crime in love. It is not perversion, not disgusting nor dirty. It's what we all crave. The crime was in the blackmail that made Terrence consider suicide as the only solution, for everyone he loved. And perhaps in Society's self-righteous judgments."

Jacintha's face was serious, considering. Perhaps the view would help her, in time.

"You are kind," she said, almost in surprise.

"So was Terrence. He was a good man."

Jacintha swallowed, her eyes filling. "He was," she whispered. She stood abruptly. "I have kept you long enough. Goodbye."

She almost fled, looking neither right nor left. Constance followed more slowly, in time to see her open the door and walk briskly toward the waiting carriage. Also in time to see Jason Madly emerge from the open door of the waiting room and watch her go.

He looked smarter than before. He wore a cravat and a clean

coat, and he had shaved.

Constance closed the door. "You didn't fight for her, twenty years ago."

"It would have been a worse crime to marry her," Madly said bleakly. "I knew that even as we eloped. I wasn't bought off. I just stood aside."

"And went to the devil."

"Oh, I was already there."

"You don't have to stay there."

He looked down at her. "Does she hate me?"

"No. She thinks she was worth nothing to you because you let her go."

He was silent, then said, "If I did not know better, Constance Silver, I would think you a romantic."

And Constance laughed because, apparently, she was.

# CHAPTER TWENTY

"A ND THE FUNNY thing is," she told Solomon later, "I think he is, too."

"Romantic?" he said doubtfully.

They were at last spending time together in their new home, and Solomon had just hung their Venetian portrait above the drawing room fireplace. The artist Domenico Rossi had finally finished it and shipped it, and it had only been delivered that day. Constance seemed to need to talk about something else. The portrait was curiously…overwhelming.

She said, "I think Madly might try to make himself worthier and then contrive to be reintroduced to her."

"Will she allow it?" Solomon asked.

"I think so."

Solomon stepped back beside her and dropped his arm around her shoulder as they gazed up at the portrait. "You really are the romantic," he said, smiling.

She leaned against him. "I am. Do I really look like that?"

"Yes. I thought he would…beautify us, but he hasn't. He's caught a moment, several moments, perhaps, and combined them."

And yet the Constance standing in the frame against the background of the Cannaregio Canal *was* beautiful, fair and golden beside his darkness. Rossi seemed to have emphasized their physical differences, and yet he'd painted them leaning together, with Constance casting Solomon a glance that was at once humorous and adoring and completely her.

"It's me I don't recognize," he admitted.

"I do," Constance said.

Their new maid stuck her head in the door. "Mr. Grey to see you, sir, ma'am." She vanished again and David strolled into the room. He halted abruptly, staring at the portrait.

"That's by the same artist," he blurted. "The one who painted the picture you gave me. I should give up and go back to sea."

"No, you shouldn't," Constance said quickly, and to Solomon's surprise, David grinned.

"No, and I won't. I've decided to go abroad and learn what I can among the *struggling* artists, not the established ones. In Paris, maybe Rome. But I won't give up."

Solomon clapped him on the back, although his heart already ached for the loss of the brother so recently found.

David met his gaze. "I'll only be gone a month or so. I will come back. Home is family."

"It is," Solomon said. As he gazed at his twin, his mirror image, he realized something else. Just as Rossi had somehow made Constance and Solomon seem *more* by emphasizing their differences, so had his depiction of Solomon differentiated him from his brother. They were *not* the same, not by nearly a lifetime of experiences, and yet they were still together—all the more so for his sudden insight.

David *would* come home. And Solomon and Constance would be here.

# ABOUT THE AUTHOR

Mary Lancaster lives in Scotland with her husband, three mostly grown-up kids and a small, crazy dog.

Her first literary love was historical fiction, a genre which she relishes mixing up with romance and adventure in her own writing. Her most recent books are light, fun Regency romances written for Dragonblade Publishing: *The Imperial Season* series set at the Congress of Vienna; and the popular *Blackhaven Brides* series, which is set in a fashionable English spa town frequented by the great and the bad of Regency society.

Connect with Mary on-line – she loves to hear from readers:

Email Mary:
Mary@MaryLancaster.com

Website:
www.MaryLancaster.com

Newsletter sign-up:
http://eepurl.com/b4Xoif

Facebook:
facebook.com/mary.lancaster.1656

Facebook Author Page:
facebook.com/MaryLancasterNovelist

Twitter:
@MaryLancNovels